LIMERICK CITY LIBRARY

Issued subject to the Rules of the !
~~t~~ ~~urned~~ not later then th~
~~ed~~ below.

an ice cold grave

an ice cold grave

CHARLAINE HARRIS

Victor Gollancz

LONDON

Copyright © Charlaine Harris 2007
All rights reserved

The right of Charlaine Harris to be identified as the author of this
work has been asserted by her in accordance with the Copyright,
Designs and Patents Act 1988.

First published in Great Britain in 2008 by
Gollancz
An imprint of the Orion Publishing Group
Orion House, 5 Upper St Martin's Lane, London WC2H 9EA
An Hachette Livre UK Company

A CIP catalogue record for this book is available
from the British Library

ISBN 978 0 575 08397 4 (Cased)
ISBN 978 0 575 08398 1 (Export Trade Paperback)

1 3 5 7 9 10 8 6 4 2

Printed in Great Britain by Mackays of Chatham plc, Chatham, Kent

www.orionbooks.co.uk

The Orion publishing group's policy is to use papers that are natural,
renewable and recyclable products and made from wood grown in
sustainable forests. The logging and manufacturing processes are expected
to conform to the environmental regulations of the country of origin.

I'd like to dedicate this book to some people that always make me happy when I see them: Susan McBride, Julie Wray Herman, Dean James, Daniel Hale, Treva Miller, Steve Brewer, Dan Hale, and Elaine Viets. I have some more books to catch up to the ones I've missed!

ACKNOWLEDGMENTS

My heartfelt thanks go to Margaret Maron, who introduced me to Daniel E. Bailey, a chief deputy sheriff in North Carolina. He spent a lot of time answering my questions. I hope I haven't made any huge goof-ups. Molly Weston, a most mysterious woman, helped me with climate questions, and Dr. D. P. Lyle, once again, helped me with medical issues. My friend Toni L. P. Kelner gave me some great ideas about improving the book.

One

THE eastern seaboard is crammed with dead people. When work brings me to that part of America, the whole time I'm there it's like wings of a huge flock of birds are fluttering inside my brain, never coming to rest. That gets old pretty quick.

But I had some jobs in the East, so here I was, driving through South Carolina with my sort-of brother Tolliver in the passenger seat. He was sleeping now, and I glanced over at him, smiling because he couldn't see me and it was okay to smile at him. Tolliver has hair as dark as mine, and if we didn't run and spend quite a bit of time outdoors, we'd both be pale; and we're both on the thin side. Other than that, we're quite different. Tolliver's dad never took him to a skin doctor when Tolliver was a teen, and his cheeks are scarred from acne; his eyes are darker than my murky gray ones, and his cheekbones are high.

When my mother married his dad, it was a case of two yuppies joining together in the hurtling path down the drain. My mother was dead now, and Tolliver's father was somewhere, who knew where? He'd gotten out of jail the previous year. My dad was still in for embezzling and a few other white-collar crimes. We never talked about them.

If you have to be in South Carolina, it's beautiful in the late spring and the early summer. Unfortunately, we were nearly at the end of an especially nasty January. The ground was cold and gray and slushy from the melt of the previous snow, and there was more predicted in a few days. I was driving very carefully because traffic was heavy and the road was not clear. We'd come up from mild and sunny Charleston. A couple there had decided their house was uninhabitable due to ghost activity, and they'd called me in to find out if there were any bodies in the walls or flooring.

The answer was clear: no. But there were bodies in the narrow back yard. There were three of them, all babies. I didn't know what that meant. They'd died so soon after birth that they hadn't had much consciousness for me to tap into, so I hadn't been able to name the cause of death, which is usually quite clear. But the Charleston homeowners had been thrilled with the results, especially after an archaeologist dug up the meager remains of the tiny bodies. They would dine out on the dead babies for the next decade. They'd handed me a check without hesitation.

That's not always the case.

Tolliver said, "Where you want to stop to eat?"

I glanced over. He wasn't fully awake. He reached over to pat my shoulder. "You tired?" he asked.

"I'm okay. We're about thirty miles outside Spartanburg. Too far?"

"Sounds good. Cracker Barrel?"

"You must want some vegetables."

"Yeah. You know what I look forward to, if we really do buy that house we talk about? Cooking for ourselves."

"We do okay when we're at home," I agreed. We had bought a few cookbooks at secondhand bookstores. We picked very simple recipes.

Our apartment in St. Louis was hanging in the balance right now. We spent so much time on the road that it was very nearly a waste of money. But we needed a home base, somewhere to collect our mail, a place to call home when we weren't driving around the United States. We'd been saving up to buy a house, probably somewhere in the Dallas area so we'd be close to our aunt and her husband. They had custody of our two little sisters.

We spotted the restaurant sign we'd been looking for after about twenty miles, and I pulled off the interstate. Though it was about two o'clock in the afternoon, the parking lot was crowded. I tried not to grimace. Tolliver just loved Cracker Barrel. He didn't mind wading through all the kitsch in the store part of the building. So after we parked (about a half mile away) we slogged through the slush past the rocking chairs on the porch, stamping our feet on the mat so we wouldn't track the icy mess inside.

The restrooms were clean, and the place was warm. We were seated almost immediately, and the waitress, a very young woman with hair as straight as a horse's tail, was delighted to serve us. Well, Tolliver. Waitresses, barmaids,

maids in hotels: serving women love Tolliver. We ordered, and while I was simply enjoying not being in a moving vehicle, Tolliver was thinking about the next job.

"It's a law enforcement invitation," he warned me.

That meant less money but good buzz. We always wanted law enforcement professionals to give us a good recommendation. About half the referrals we got came from detectives, sheriffs, deputies, and so on. Though they might not believe in me, there'd be pressure on them from somewhere about a particular investigation, and they'd call me in, having heard about me through the law enforcement grapevine. Maybe there was someone influential they wanted to get off their back. Maybe they were stumped about finding someone, or they'd exhausted just about every venue in their search for a missing person. The law didn't pay well. But it paid off.

"What do they want me to do? Cemetery or the search?"

"Search."

That meant I'd have to go looking for the body. The jobs I got were about fifty-fifty. Since the lightning had snaked through the window of our trailer in Texarkana when I was fifteen, I'd been able to locate corpses. If the body was in its proper grave in the cemetery, the people who hired me wanted to know the cause of death. If the body was in an unknown location, I could track it, if the search was limited in scope. Luckily, the buzz given off by a corpse was less intense as the corpse aged, or I'da been batshit crazy by now. Think about it. Caveman corpses, Native American corpses, the early settlers, the more recently deceased—that's a lot of dead people, and they all let me know where their earthly remains were interred.

I wondered if it would be worthwhile sending my little brochure to archaeological digs, and how Tolliver would go about collecting the address information for such a mailing. Tolliver was much better with our laptop than I was, simply because he was more interested.

It wasn't like he was my servant or anything.

He was the first person I'd told about my strange ability, after I'd recovered from the physical effects of the lightning strike. Though at first he hadn't believed me, he'd been willing to humor me by testing what I could and couldn't do, and as we'd worked out the limits of my odd new power, he'd become a believer. By the time I'd graduated from high school, we had our plan all worked out, and we hit the road. At first, we'd just traveled on weekends; Tolliver had had to work a regular job, too, and I'd picked up money by working in fast-food places. But after two years, he'd been able to quit the day job. We'd been on the road together ever since.

At the moment, Tolliver was playing the peg game that's always on the table at Cracker Barrel. His face looked serious and calm. He didn't look like he was suffering—but then he never did. I knew Tolliver had been having a painful time since the discovery that a woman who'd been pursuing him had had an ulterior motive; even when you're not crazy about someone, even when in fact you're a little repelled by that person, that's got to sting. Tolliver hadn't talked about Memphis much, but it had left its mark on both of us. I watched his long white fingers moving, lost in my own sad place. Things hadn't been as easy between us in the past few weeks. It was my fault . . . all my fault.

The waitress came by to ask if we needed refills on our

drinks, managing to smile a little more brightly at Tolliver than at me.

"Where are you all going?" she asked brightly.

"Asheville area," Tolliver said, glancing up from the game.

"Oh, it's beautiful there," she said, doing her bit for the tourist board. He gave her an absent smile and bent back over the pegboard. She gave his downturned head a philosophical shrug and hustled off.

"You're staring a hole in me," Tolliver said, without looking up.

"You're just in my line of sight," I said. I leaned on my elbows. Where the hell was the food? I folded the paper band that had been around the napkin-rolled tableware.

"Your leg hurting?" he asked. I had a weak right leg.

"Yeah, a little."

"Want me to massage it tonight?"

"No!"

He looked up then. He raised his eyebrows.

Of course I wanted him to massage my leg. I just didn't know if that would work out. I might do something wrong—wrong for us.

"I think maybe I'll just put some heat on it tonight," I said. I excused myself and went to the ladies' room, which was filled with a mother and her three daughters, or maybe her daughter had some friends along. They were very young and very loud, and the minute I could get into a stall, I closed the door and pushed the bolt. I stood there for a moment, leaning my head against the wall. Shame and fear, in equal amounts, clogged my throat, and for a second I couldn't breathe. Then I gasped in a long, shuddering breath.

"Mama, I think that lady's crying," said a child's penetrating voice.

"Shhhh," said the mother. "Then we'll just leave her alone." And then there was blessed silence.

I actually did have to use the bathroom, and my leg actually was hurting. I eased down my jeans, rubbing the right leg after I'd sat down. There was a faint red spiderweb pattern above my right knee, extending to my upper thigh. I'd had my right side to the window when the lightning came in.

When I rejoined Tolliver, the food had come, and I was able to keep busy eating it. When we went out to the car, Tolliver slid into the driver's seat. It was his turn. I suggested a book on tape; at the last secondhand bookstore we'd visited, I'd gotten three. Unabridged, of course. I popped in a Dana Stabenow novel, leaned back, and walled my brother off. No, I wasn't walling him off; I was walling myself in.

Tolliver had booked one room in the motel in Doraville. At the desk, I could see that he was waiting for me to tell him to ask for another one, since I'd been acting so standoffish.

We'd often shared a room in the past few years of traveling together. At first, we hadn't had enough money for two rooms. Later, sometimes we wanted our privacy, and sometimes we didn't care. It had never been an issue. I wouldn't let it be an issue now, I decided recklessly. I didn't know how long we could trudge on down this dreary road without Tolliver blowing up and demanding an explanation I couldn't give him. So we'd room together, and I'd just have to be uncomfortable in silence. I was getting used to that.

We took in our bags. I always took the bed closest to the

bathroom; he got the one by the window. It was a variation on the same room we'd seen over and over again: slick polyester bedspreads, mass-produced chairs and table, television, beige bathroom. Tolliver got busy on his cell phone, while I stretched out on the bed and turned on CNN.

"She wants us to come by at eight tomorrow morning," he said, getting a pencil out of his bag and folding the morning's newspaper open to the crossword puzzle. Sooner or later, he'd break down and learn how to work sudoku, but he was sticking with his crossword pretty faithfully.

"Then I'd better run now," I said, and I noticed he didn't move for a few seconds, his pencil poised over the puzzle. We often ran together, though Tolliver usually took off toward the end of our exercise so he could go full-out. "It'll be too cold in the morning, even if I get up at five."

"You okay running alone?"

"Yeah, no problem." I got out my running gear and took off my jeans and sweater. I kept my back to him, but that was normal. While not having any modesty fetish, we tried to keep a boundary there. After all, we were brother and sister.

No, you're not, said my bad self. *He's really not related to you at all.*

I stuck a room key in my pocket and went outside into the cold wet air to run off my unhappiness.

Two

〜✦〜

"I'M the sheriff of Knott County," the lean woman said. She was leaning over the counter that divided the front of the station from the back, and she'd been chatting with the dispatcher when we entered. I've never understood how law enforcement people can stand to carry so much equipment around their hips, and this woman was bearing the full complement, too. I never like to stare long enough to identify all the items. I'd had a brief relationship with a deputy, and I should have taken a moment then to examine his cop equipment. I'd been more involved with his other equipment, I guess.

When the sheriff straightened, I saw she was a tall woman. She was in her fifties, with graying brown hair and a comfortable set of wrinkles at the corners of her eyes and

mouth. She didn't look like any true believer I'd ever encountered, yet she was the one who'd emailed us.

"I'm Harper Connelly," I said. "This is my brother, Tolliver Lang."

We weren't what she'd expected, either. She gave me a
scan up and down.

"You don't look like a dingbat," she said.

"You don't look like a prejudiced stereotype," I said.

The dispatcher sucked in her breath. Uh-oh.

Tolliver was right behind me, slightly to my left, and
I felt nothing but a calm waiting coming from him. He
always had my back.

"Come into my office. We'll talk," said the tall woman.
"My name is Sandra Rockwell, and I've been sheriff for one
year." Sheriffs are elected in North Carolina. I didn't know
how long her term was, but if she'd only been a sheriff a
year, she must have plenty to go. Politics might not be as
urgent a consideration for Sheriff Rockwell as they would be
during election year.

We were in her office by then. It wasn't very big, and it
was decorated with pictures of the governor, a state flag, a
U.S. flag, and some framed certificates. The only personal
thing on Sheriff Rockwell's desk was one of those clear cubes
you can fill with pictures. Her cube was full of shots of the
same two boys. They were both brown-haired like their
mother. One of them, grown, had a wife and child of his
own. Nice. The other one had a hunting dog.

"You-all want some coffee?" she asked as she slid into the
swivel chair behind the ugly metal desk.

I looked at Tolliver, and we both shook our heads.

"Well, then." She put her hands flat on the desk. "I heard about you from a detective in Memphis. Young, her name is."

I smiled.

"You remember her, then. She's partnered with a guy named Lacey?"

I nodded.

"She seemed like a sensible person. She was no flake. And her clearance rate and reputation are impressive. That's the only reason I'm talking to you, you understand?"

"Yes, I understand."

She looked a little embarrassed. "Well, I know I'm sounding rude, and that's not my intention. But you have to understand, this is not something I'd consider doing if you didn't have a track record. I'm not one of these people who listens to that John Edward—not the politician with an *s*, but the medium—and I'm not one of these who likes to have my palm read, or go to séances, or even read a horoscope."

"I fully understand," I said. Maybe my voice was even dryer.

Tolliver smiled. "We get that you have reservations," he said.

She smiled back gratefully. "That's it in a nutshell. I have reservations."

"So, you must be desperate," I said.

She gave me an unfriendly look. "Yes," she admitted, since she had to. "Yes, we're desperate."

"I'm not going to back out," I said baldly. "I just want to know what I'm up against."

She seemed to relax at my frankness. "Okay, then, cards on the table," she said. She took a deep breath. "For the past

11

five years, boys have been going missing in this county. It's up to six boys now. When I say 'boys,' I mean in the fourteen- to eighteen-year-old range. Now, kids that age are prone to run away, and they're prone to suicide, and they're prone to have fatal car accidents. And if we'd found them, or heard from the runaways, we'd be okay with that, as okay as you can be."

We nodded.

"But these particular boys, it's just—no one can believe they would run away. And in this time, surely some hunter or bird watcher or hiker would have found a body or two if they'd killed themselves or met with some accident in the woods."

"So you're thinking that they're buried somewhere."

"Yes, that's what I'm thinking. I'm sure they're still here, somewhere."

"Then let me ask you a few things," I said. Tolliver took out his pad and pencil. The sheriff looked surprised, as if the last thing she'd ever expected had been that I would ask her questions.

"Okay, shoot," Sandra Rockwell said after a brief pause.

"Are there bodies of water in the county?"

"Yes, there's Grunyan's Pond and Pine Landing Lake. And several streams."

"Have they been searched?"

"Yes. A couple of us dive, and we've searched as well as we can. Nothing's come to the surface, either. Both of those spots are well used, and anything that came up and a lot of things that went down would have been found, if they'd been there to find. And I'm sure the pond's clear. Still, it's possible that there's something in the deepest part of the lake."

The sheriff clearly believed that wasn't likely.

"What did the missing boys have in common?"

"Besides their age range? Not much, except they're gone."

"All white?"

"Oh. Yes."

"All go to the same school?"

"No. Four of them to the local high school, one of them to the junior high, one of them to the private academy, Randolph Prep."

"The past five years, you said? Do they vanish at the same time of year?"

She looked at a file on her desk, opened it. Flipped over a few pages. "No," she said. "Two in the fall, three in the spring, one in the summer."

None in the winter, when the conditions would be worst for an outdoor interment—so she was probably right. The boys were buried somewhere.

"You think the same person killed them all," I said. I was guessing, but it was a good guess.

"Yes," she said. "That's what I think."

It was my turn to take a deep breath. I'd never handled anything like this. I'd never tried to find so many people. "I don't know a lot about serial killers," I said, and the two dread words dropped into the room like unwelcome visitors. "But from what I've read and seen on television, I believe they tend to bury their victims in the same geographic conditions, if not in the exact same location. Like the Green River Killer dumping most of his victims in the river."

"That's true," she said. "Some of them prefer the same location. Then they can visit it over and over. To remember." She'd done her homework.

"How do you think I can help?"

"Tell me how you work. How do you find bodies?"

"My sister does two things," Tolliver said, launching into his familiar spiel. "She can find bodies, and she can determine the cause of death. If we have to search for a body, obviously that's going to take longer than someone taking her to the local cemetery, pointing to a grave, and wanting to know what killed the person in the grave."

The sheriff nodded. "It costs more."

"Yes," Tolliver said. There was no way to dress that up and make it prettier, so he didn't. Sheriff Rockwell didn't flinch or try to make us feel guilty about earning a living, as some people did. They acted like we were ambulance chasers. This was all I could do, my sole unique ability; and I was determined to bank as much money as I could while it was still operative. Someday, as quickly as it had been given to me, it might be taken away. I imagined I would be glad; but I would also be unemployed.

"How do you decide where to look?" the sheriff asked.

"We get as much information as we can. What did you find after the disappearances?" Tolliver asked. "Any physical clues?"

The sheriff very sensibly got out a map of the county. After she spread it out over her desk, we all three rose to peer at it. "Here we are," she said. "Here's Doraville. It's the county seat. This is a poor county, rural. We're in the foothills, as you see. There's some hilly land, and there's some steep land, and there's a valley or two with some level acres."

We nodded. Doraville itself was a town strewn about on many levels.

"Three of them had vehicles of their own," Sheriff Rockwell said. "We found Chester Caldwell's old pickup up here, in the parking lot at the head of the hiking trail."

"He was the first one?" I asked.

"Yes, he was the first one." Her face tightened all over. "I was a deputy then. We searched all along that trail for hours and hours. It goes through some steep terrain, and we looked for signs of a fall, or an animal attack. We found nothing. He'd gone missing after football practice, in the middle of September. This was when Abe Madden was sheriff." She shook her head, trying to shake the bad memories out of it. "We never found anything. He came from a tough home; mom drinks too much, divorced. His dad was gone and stayed gone."

She took a deep breath. "Next gone was Tyler Webb, who was sixteen. Went missing on a Saturday after swimming with friends at Grunyan's Pond, a summer afternoon. We found his car here, at the rest stop off the interstate." She pointed to the spot, which wasn't too far (as the crow flies) west of Doraville. About as far as the trailhead parking lot was from north Doraville. "Tyler's stuff was in the car: his driver's license, his towel, his T-shirt. But no one ever saw him again."

"No other fingerprints?"

"No. A few of Tyler's, a few of his friends', and that's all. None on the wheel or door handle. They were clean."

"Weren't you wondering by then?"

"I was," she said. "Sheriff Madden wasn't." She shrugged. "It was pretty easy to believe Chester had run off, though leaving his pickup behind? I didn't think so. But he had a tough time at home, he'd broken up with his girlfriend, and he wasn't doing well in school. So maybe he was a suicide and we simply hadn't found his body. We looked, God knows. Abe figured someone would come across his remains eventually. But Tyler was a whole different kettle of fish. He had a very close family, real devout boy, one of the solid kids. There just didn't seem to be any way he would run off or kill himself, or anything like that. But by then Abe wouldn't hear a word on the subject. He'd found out he had heart trouble by then, and he didn't want to upset himself."

There was a little moment of silence.

"Then?" I said.

"Then Dylan Lassiter. Dylan didn't have a car. He told his grandmother he was going to walk over three streets to see a friend, but he never got there. A ball cap that might have been his was found here." She pointed a finger to a spot on the map. "That's Shady Grove Cemetery," she said.

"Okay, a message," I said.

"Maybe, maybe the wind blew it there. Maybe it wasn't even his, though the hair looked like Dylan's. It was just a Tarheels cap. Eventually, we sent it to SBI, and the DNA was a match for Dylan's. But it didn't do us much good to know that. It just meant wherever he was, he didn't have his hat."

This was certainly the chronology of a botched investigation. I was no cop and would never be one, but I thought Abe Madden had something for which to answer.

16

"Hunter Fenwick, a month later," Rockwell said. "Hunter was the son of a friend of mine, and he's the reason I ran for sheriff. I respected Sheriff Madden—up to a point—but I knew he was wrong about these missing boys. Hunter . . . well, his car was parked the same place Chester's pickup was found. At the trailhead. And there was a little blood inside—not enough to be able to say for sure that he couldn't have survived losing it. And his wallet was found not a half mile out of town, in a ditch off this road." She pointed to a meandering county road that led northwest out of Doraville for about twenty miles before heading north and then northeast to the next town, up in the mountains.

"Who next?" Tolliver asked, because the sheriff was getting lost in her own dark thoughts.

"The youngest, Aaron Robertson. Junior high. Fourteen. Too young to drive alone. He stayed at the school to shoot some hoops one afternoon after basketball practice. He always walked home. But we'd had the time change the night before, and it was dark. He never made it to his house. His backpack was never found. No other trace of him." She pulled a sheet of opaque plastic back from a standing corkboard at one side of her desk. We looked at a row of young faces. Underneath each face was the date of the boy's disappearance. Hearing about it was hard, but seeing their faces was harder.

We all kept a moment of silence. Then Tolliver said, "The last one?"

"The last one was three months ago. Jeff McGraw. It was because of his grandmother that we called you in. Twyla didn't think we were getting anywhere, and she was right."

It galled the sheriff to say that, but she said it.

"Twyla Cotton donated a lot of money and raised some more from the families, the ones that could help. And she got some money from some people who just want this to stop, people not related to the missing boys in any way." Sandra Rockwell shook her head. "I've never seen anything like the time and energy she put into this. But Jeff was her oldest grandson. . . ." Her attention strayed from us to the cube of pictures on her desk. Rockwell was a grandmother, too. Her gaze shifted to the last photograph in the row of faces: a boy with freckles, reddish brown hair, a school sports jacket. Jeff McGraw had lettered in basketball and football. I was willing to bet he'd been a local hero in Doraville. I knew my southern towns.

"So you're like the frontman for this consortium of local people who've donated money to a fund to find the boys," Tolliver said. "Since the county, I'm guessing, didn't have the money."

"Yes," Sheriff Rockwell said. "We couldn't spend county money on you, or state money. Had to be private. But I wouldn't have you here unless they let me interview you. And I'm ambivalent about the whole thing."

Whoa, big words from the sheriff, in more ways than one. I'd never heard a law enforcement professional admit to being doubtful about a course of action involving me. Angry, disapproving, disgusted, yes; doubtful, no.

"I can see how you would be," I said cautiously. "I know you've done your best, and it must be, ah, galling to be asked to call in someone like me. I'm sorry about that. But I swear I'll give it my best shot, and I swear I'm not a fraud."

"You'd better not be," Sandra Rockwell said. "And now, I've arranged for you to meet with Twyla Cotton. It only seemed right. After that, we'll pick the place you start to search."

"Okay," I said, and that was that.

TWYLA Cotton was a very heavy woman. You read about fat people who walk very lightly; she wasn't one of them. She walked ponderously. She answered her door so quickly I figured she'd been standing right inside, since we'd called her to tell her we were on our way from the sheriff's department.

She was wearing jeans and a sweatshirt that read "Number One Grandma." Her face was bare of makeup, and her short dark hair had only a few threads of gray. I put her in her midfifties.

After shaking our hands, she led the way through the house. She didn't match the décor. Some designer had worked here, and the result was very pretty—lots of peaches and creams and beiges in the formal living room, dark blues and chocolate browns in the family room—but not very personal. The kitchen was Twyla's natural domain, and that was where she led us. It was full of exposed brick, stainless steel, and gleaming surfaces. It was warm and cozy after the chill gray of the morning. It was the homiest room in the house.

"I was Archie Cotton's cook," she said. She smiled at me as if she'd been reading my mind.

I'd had a white-collar upbringing for my first decade, but

after that my parents had descended pretty quickly through blue collar and down below, so you could say I was a medley. It had been a case of riches to rags. Twyla Cotton had gone the better way, the rags-to-riches way.

"And then he married you," I said.

"Yep, we got married. Have a seat, hon," she said to Tolliver, and she pointed at a chair for me. There was also a formal dining room, but this gleaming round table was positioned in a bay window at one end of the kitchen, and the chairs were wide, comfortable, rolling chairs. There was a newspaper and a few magazines, a little pile of bills, handy to the most convenient chair. Tolliver and I both knew not to pick that one. "Can I get you-all a cup of coffee? Some coffee cake?" our hostess asked.

"I'd like some coffee, if it's already made," Tolliver said.

"Me, too, please," I said. I sank into a chair and rolled up under the table.

In short order, we had mugs of coffee, spoons, napkins, and cream and sugar close to hand. It was very good coffee. The morning improved, just a bit.

"Archie had some children, already grown and gone," Twyla said. "They didn't come around as much after his wife died. He was lonely, and I'd been working for him for years. It just came natural."

"Any hard feelings from his children?" Tolliver asked.

"He gave 'em some money, quieted them down," Twyla said. "He laid it out to them about the will, and who would get what, in front of two lawyers. Got 'em to sign papers saying they wouldn't contest the will, if I survived him. So I got this house, and a good bit of cash, plus a lot of stock.

Archie Junior and Bitsy got their fair shake. They don't exactly love me, but they don't hate me, either."

"So why did you want us here, Mrs. Cotton?"

"I've got a friend you helped a couple of years ago. Linda Barnard, in Kentucky? Wanted to know what had happened to her little grandbaby, the one who was found a mile away from home, no marks on her?"

"I remember."

"So I thought about calling you in, and Sandra researched you-all. Talked to some policewoman in Memphis."

"Jeff, your grandson. Is he your son's son? He's sixteen?" Tolliver asked, trying to lead Twyla to the subject we'd come to discuss. Though almost everyone we looked for turned out to be dead, Tolliver and I had learned a long time ago to refer to the missing person in the present tense. It just sounded more respectful and more optimistic.

"He was sixteen. He was the older boy of my son Parker."

She'd had no hesitation in using the past tense. She read the question in our faces.

"I know he's dead," Twyla said, her round face rigid with grief. "He would never run away, like the police say. He would never go this long without letting us hear."

"He's been gone three months?" I asked. We already knew enough about Jeff McGraw, but I felt it would be indecent not to ask.

"Since October twentieth."

"No one's heard from him." I knew the answer, but I had to ask.

"No, and he had no reason to go. He was already playing varsity football; he had a little girlfriend; he and his mom and dad got along good. Parker—Parker McGraw, that was my last name before I married Archie—Parker loved that boy so much. He and Bethalynn have Carson, who's twelve. But you can't replace any child, much less your firstborn. They're all broken up."

"You understand," I began carefully, then paused to try to find some other way of saying what I needed to say. "You understand, I need some idea of where to search, or I might wander around this town forever without getting a location. The sheriff said she had an idea where we should start." America is so big. You never realize how big, until you're looking for something the size of a corpse.

"Tell me how you work," she said.

It was great to meet someone so matter-of-fact about it.

"If you have an area you think is more likely than any other, I just start walking around," I said. "It may take time. It may take a lot of time. I may never be successful."

She brushed that aside. "How will you know it's him?"

"Oh, I'll know. And I've seen his picture. The problem is, there are dead people everywhere. I have to sort through them."

She looked astonished. After a thoughtful moment, she nodded. Again, not the reaction I was used to.

"If he's in any of the areas you pick for me to search, I'll find him. If he isn't, I'm not going to lie to you—I may never find Jeff. What have you got, in terms of pinning his whereabouts down?"

"His cell phone. It was found on the Madison road. I can show you the exact spot." She showed me Jeff's picture anyway. It wasn't the same one I'd seen at the police station. It was a posed studio picture of Jeff and his whole family, plus his grandmother. My heart used to break when I saw the image of them alive, cradled in the arms of their nearest and dearest. Now, I just register the features, hoping I'll see them again, even if they're just scattered bones. Because that's how I make our living.

This particular gig in Doraville felt different. Time isn't much of a factor when you're dealing with the dead. They're not going to go anywhere. It's the living who are urgent. But in this case, time was important. If the sheriff was right, we were dealing with a serial killer who might snatch another boy at any moment. His pattern didn't include winter, but who's to say his pattern wouldn't change, that he wouldn't take advantage of this slushy time between snows; plan a final spree before a hard freeze.

I found myself hoping that if I were able to find the missing boys, then something about the way they were buried, something about the location or what was buried with them, would lead to the discovery of their killer. I know better than anyone that death comes to us all. I hate the murderers of the young, because they rob the world of a life that still held potential. This doesn't really make sense, I know; even a dissolute alcoholic seventy-five-year-old can push a woman out of the path of a speeding car, and change a bit of the world forever. But the death of children always carries its own particular horror.

Three

〜✦〜

TWYLA Cotton had a Cadillac, only a year or two old. "I like a big car," she said.

We nodded. We liked it, too. We were bundled up for the weather, and Twyla looked like a ball of fudge in her dark brown coat.

"Do your son and his wife know we're here and what we're doing?" I asked cautiously.

"Parker and Bethalynn do know, but they don't believe it will lead to anything. They think I'm wasting my money. But they know it's my money to waste, and if it makes me feel better . . ."

I hoped they were as philosophical about it as Twyla made it sound. Families can give us an awful lot of trouble—which I guess isn't too surprising, since they usually believe we're defrauding their grieving relative. Still, we've had a bellyful of trouble in our lives, and we don't want any that we can avoid. I exchanged a glance with Tolliver, who was in the back seat, and one glance said all this between us.

"Have you ever had a child, Harper?" Twyla asked.

"No, I've never been pregnant," I said. "But I know how you feel. My sister has been missing for eight years."

I didn't normally tell people that. Of course, some of them already knew it. It had made a big splash in the papers when it happened. But I was a high school student then, not a . . . whatever I was now.

"You have other family?"

I said, smiling brightly, "Well, I have Tolliver. I've got a half brother, Mark, and two half sisters, little ones, Mariella and Gracie. They live in Texas with our aunt and her husband." Mark wasn't my half brother any more than Tolliver was. He was simply Tolliver's older brother. But I wasn't in the mood to spell it out.

"Oh, I'm so sorry. Your parents already passed?"

"My mother has. My father is still living." In jail, but living. Tolliver's mother had died before his father met my mom, and Tolliver's father was out of jail and drifting . . . somewhere. Considering my mom and dad and Tolliver's father had all been attorneys, they'd had a long way to fall. They'd really thrown themselves into it.

Twyla looked a little shocked. "Well, how awful. I'm so sorry."

I shrugged. That was just the way it was. "Thanks," I said, but I knew I didn't sound sincere. Couldn't help it. When I heard that my mother had died, I was sorry, but not surprised, and not unrelieved.

We were quiet after that until we pulled up by the side of the road. Twyla glanced down at the list she'd taken down during a quick phone call with Sandra Rockwell. Sure enough, Sandra Rockwell had a prioritized list of places to check. This was place number one.

We were behind the high school at the football practice field, a stretch of barren level ground. One of those devices that the boys push around was still sitting by the side of the field, though football season was over. The field house was closed and locked until next year. Basketball would be the sport in play now.

"This is where his truck was," Twyla said. "We'd just gotten it for him. It was an old second-hand Dodge."

Sheriff Rockwell had said less about Jeff than about any of the other boys, perhaps because she'd known we'd be talking to his grandmother. Looking around now, I didn't see anyone. Not a soul. So an abduction at this point wasn't out of the question, though risky. At any moment, someone might come out of the school. But there weren't any houses nearby. The lane behind the practice field was just a bare strip of ground before a steep hill that had been sheared away to build the school.

Though it might be a fair spot for an abduction, I seriously doubted someone had killed the boy on the spot and buried him here, but I wanted to show I was willing. I stepped out, sent out that part of me that made me unique. There was no response. I was getting the tiniest tingle, which meant some incredibly old human remains were somewhere in the area. It was a feeling I'd learned to ignore in my search for modern bodies. Though the range would be almost the same, not enough to make a difference, I walked the length of the property and kept getting the same reading. I shook my head silently and climbed back into the Cadillac. We drove, Twyla pointing out this or that town landmark as we passed it. I didn't listen, concentrating instead on what I was picking up as we moved. The local cemetery provided a huge mass of static, but we had to stop there because that was where Tyler's hat had been found.

Of course there were tons of bodies here, and some of them were very fresh. It was way too cold to pull my shoes off, but I followed my instincts and went to the freshest graves. There was a heart attack, and there was a death by old age. Sometimes, you know, you just give out. Those were the most recent deaths. But Tyler Lassiter had been gone about two years, if I was remembering correctly, so I had to check out a lot more bodies. None of them turned out to be Tyler. They were all exactly who they were supposed to be according to their headstones. I was glad Doraville wasn't bigger, and glad some people were buried in the newer cemetery, which was south of Doraville.

We were now on the western edge of town, and Twyla once more pulled to the side of the road.

"The man that lives there was arrested for attacking a boy," she said, pointing to a dilapidated white frame house barely visible behind a tangle of vines and young trees. "He's been questioned over and over."

I wasn't getting anything from the car. I got out and took a couple of steps forward, closing my eyes. I picked up a buzz from my left, much farther back in the woods, but it was the faint buzz I associated with old cemeteries. I heard

Tolliver's window roll down. "Ask her if there's an old church back there with its own cemetery," I said.

"Yes," Twyla called to me. "Mount Ararat is back there."

I got back in the car and said, "Nope."

Twyla inhaled deeply, as if about to play her last card. She put the car in drive and we pulled out, heading even farther out of the small town of Doraville. We drove northwest, the readout on Twyla's car told me, and the ground began to climb. I looked up at the mountains and I thought that if Jeff's body were up there, I would never find it. I did not want to go hiking in those mountains, especially in this weather. I had a brief selfish thought: Why couldn't Twyla have called me in two months ago? A month, even? I shivered, and thought of the biting cold, the snow that lay in patches on the ground, the predictions of bad weather in a few days. We began to go up, though the pitch of the ground was not so steep here.

And then Twyla stopped again. I noticed how stiffly she sat in the driver's seat, how white she'd gotten.

"This is where the phone was," Twyla said. She jerked her thumb to the right. "I put that rock there, to mark where it was exactly, after the sheriff showed me."

There was a big rock with a blue cross on it, dug into the earth at the side of the road.

"You put it in pretty deep," Tolliver said.

"The mowers had to pass over it," she said. "That was three months ago."

Practical.

I got out of the Cadillac and looked around, pulling on my gloves as I did so. It was freaking cold up here, no doubt about it. The Madison road rose steeply ahead of us, cut out of the rising mountain to the left. On our side, there was a fairly level narrow strip, perhaps a half acre to an acre of land, before the rolling slope began its rise. In that half acre lay the site of an old home. The house had been abandoned years before. The plot wasn't in a neat rectangle because it followed the contours of the hill. It was long and thin in spots.

We were parked on the shoulder, and if I took a step I'd roll down the slope of a deep ditch. The driveway into the plot ran over a culvert so the flow of rainwater wouldn't be impeded. The remains of this driveway passed through the remains of a fence. Now, with all the leaves fallen, the stands of weeds were golden or brown with winter's death, and the occasional young pine looked startlingly green. The weeds and small trees appeared to be holding up the fence.

The house had been a humble one. The roof wasn't caved in, but there were holes in it, and the porch was sagging. There wasn't any glass in the windows. There was a listing two-car garage off to one side, with wide doors that hung ajar. Once it had been painted white, like the house. The whole thing was southern gothic picturesque decay personified.

The water in the drainage ditch was dark and would be very cold. There'd been a lot of rain the past couple of weeks. And I felt the raw chill of more rain coming.

I could tell from the inclination of Tolliver's head that he expected me to walk down the side of the road to where the hill leveled into the valley. He expected that someone had dumped the body on the more accessible ground and had tossed its accessories off while driving upward into the mountains. And under other circumstances, that's exactly what I would have done.

But there wasn't any need.

The minute my foot had touched the ground, I'd known I was going to have news for Twyla Cotton. The buzzing was intense, increasing as I stepped closer to the eroded driveway. This was not the signal from a single corpse. I began to have a bad feeling, an awful feeling, and I was scared to look at Tolliver. He took my hand, wrapped it around the crook of his elbow. He could tell I'd decided to go into the tangled area that had been the yard of the old house.

"The ground is rough in there. I wish we'd worn our high boots," he said. But I couldn't register what he was saying. I watched a blue pickup pass, slowing down for the curve, fading away from view. It was the only other vehicle we'd seen on this road.

After the sound of its motor died away, I could hear only the increasingly irrelevant registers of the two live people and the increasingly more compelling signals of the dead. I walked forward, pulling Tolliver with me. Maybe he tried to pull me back a little, but I kept on going, because this was my moment—my connection with the power, or ability, or electrical short, that made me unique.

"You better get the flags," I said, and he went back to get the lengths of wire topped with red plastic flags.

In the cold damp I stood in the middle of the former yard, between the fence and the ruined house. I turned in a circle, feeling the buzzing rising all around me, as they clamored to be found. That's all they want, you know. They want to be found.

I tried to speak, choked, gasped.

"What's wrong?" Tolliver asked distantly. "Harper?"

I stumbled to the left a couple of steps. "Here," I said.

"My grandson? Jeff's there?" Twyla had forged her way onto the property.

I moved six feet northwest. "Here, too," I said.

"He's in *pieces*?"

"There's more than one body," Tolliver told her.

I held my hands up to sharpen my focus. I turned again, more slowly, my eyes closed, my hands raised, counting. "Eight," I said.

"Oh, my Lord in heaven," Twyla said. She sat down heavily on an old stump. "I'm going to call the police."

She must have given Tolliver a glance of sudden misgiving, because he said, "You can bank on it. Harper's right." I heard the little beeps as she began punching in numbers.

"What happened to them?" he asked me quietly. He knew I was listening though my eyes were still closed.

I didn't say anything. It was time for me to find out, but I didn't want anyone else to watch while I did it. "Okay," I said, to steady myself. "Tolliver?" I wanted him to be ready.

"I'm here," he said. "I've got a hold." I could feel his grip on my arms.

I stepped directly onto the ground above the corpse, and I looked down through the soil and rocks, caught a glimpse of hell. That was the last thing I remember.

Four

"SHE ever gonna wake up?" The speaker was Sandra Rockwell. I remembered her voice, but she sounded strange and strained.

"Harper?" my brother said. "Harper?"

I didn't want to do this, but I had to.

"Okay," I said, and it came out as wobbly as I felt. "You found them yet?"

"Tell me what to do," Sheriff Rockwell said. She sounded as if she didn't want to be there.

I had to open my eyes, and I had to look at the anxious brown eyes under the hat. Sheriff Rockwell was in a padded coat that made her look twice as large.

"They're all there," I said. "If you can wait a minute, I can tell you who's where. And there are eight of them, not six."

"How do you know that?"

I was sitting in the back seat of Twyla's car, my head leaning against the cushion.

"Here, eat some sugar," Tolliver said anxiously, working a piece of candy out of his jeans pocket. He unwrapped it for me, and popped it in my mouth. I knew from experience that I would feel better in a few minutes, especially if I had a Coke.

"You were willing to believe me before I did anything," I said. "Have a little more faith. Dig for them."

"If you're lying, your ass will end up in jail," she said.

"And I would deserve it."

With a lot of effort, I turned my head to look out the car window. There were a couple of deputies standing on the site. Twyla was with them. The expression on her face would have made the most jaded con man weep—or maybe not. In our travels, in my line of work, we've met a few con men, and they almost all have no empathy. It's just not in their emotional repertoire.

"Come show me," Sheriff Rockwell said, and Tolliver helped me out of the car. Slowly we made our way to the place where I'd fainted, and though I was shaking all over because I would have to feel the death again, I stood on the spot where I'd sensed the most recent body.

"Here," I said, pointing straight down. I knew who it was, too. This was the body of Jeff, Twyla's grandson. Tolliver got out a spiral-bound notebook he had zipped in his jacket. He'd sketched a very rough outline of the site. "This is Jeff, Jeff McGraw," I told Tolliver. "He was strangled." Tolliver stuck a length of wire in the ground. The red flag flapped a little in the stiff breeze. He put his left arm around

me and took my right hand in his. I nodded in the direction we should go, a little uphill and to the north, and I centered myself above another corpse. Tears began rolling down my cheeks . . . I'd never encountered such suffering. "Here," I said. "Chester." Two yards farther, we had a boy Sheriff Rockwell hadn't mentioned. "This is someone named something like—Chad, Chad something that begins with a T." The sheriff was scribbling in her own notebook. The deputies were listening, too, but they were completely skeptical and not a little angry. I couldn't do anything about that. They'd learn soon enough.

I followed the next signal to the rear of the lot, right where the ground began to rise sharply. It was centered behind a clump of bushes. I wiped my face with a handkerchief, said, "Dylan," and staggered a bit south. Now I was behind the house. The sheriff and Twyla followed me, and the deputies, too. "Aaron," I said. "Wasn't there an Aaron?" And a few yards south again. This one was harder, for some reason. His horror and panic had short-circuited his brain while he was dying. "I think this is Tyler," I said. And then I went to the southernmost grave of all, and I knew it was the oldest, somehow. The vibrations it gave off were just a bit weaker. "This is the first one," I told the sheriff, who was keeping pace with us. That wasn't hard, because I was moving very slowly by now, and I was shaking all over. "His name was . . ." I shook my head slightly, tried to focus more intently. "His name was James something," I said. "James Ray, James Roy, James Robert. I'm not . . . I can't tell his last name. Oh, Tolliver, get me out of here." There was one more, a boy named Hunter. I could barely stand by the time

I had him pinpointed. He'd died of hypothermia. He must have been one of the November abductions.

"Can I take my sister back into town? She needs to lie down," Tolliver said.

"Nope," Sandra Rockwell, her jaw clicking shut with a snap. "Not until we check this out." If I was lying, Sandra Rockwell wanted me on hand when she discovered the lie. "You got any advice on which place to check first?" she asked.

I shook my head. "Any of the places we stuck a flag," I said.

Twyla had retreated to the Cadillac. I was glad I couldn't tell what live people were thinking, because imagining how she felt couldn't hold a candle to her actual misery. When Tolliver and I climbed in the back seat, she was kind enough to turn the car on so the heater would warm us. For what seemed like a long time, we just huddled there in the car. Not a word was spoken. My head seemed full of a white noise, and I couldn't think about anything. I'd seen horrors.

I didn't turn my head to watch what went on in the old homesite, but Twyla did. Finally, she said, "They've dug about two feet down, now. It sure is a sloppy day for it. I hope Dave and Harry don't catch a cold. Much less Sandra."

I thought, *I would have been glad to wait for better weather,* but I didn't say anything.

It was my first mass murder.

A little before eleven o'clock Dave and Harry, the two deputies, uncovered the first bones.

There was a pause, a palpable pause. The three law officers fell still around the hole that had finally gotten deep enough.

I'd been leaning back. I straightened. Tolliver's head rotated, and so did Twyla's.

"My grandson?" she asked. I'd been expecting the question.

"No," I said. "They picked the northernmost burial to start at. I'm so sorry. Your grandson is there, Twyla, at the first flag we put in. I wish I could make it better. I wish he wasn't out there." I didn't know how else to put it.

"You can't be sure." Her voice was hesitant. I hadn't known Twyla Cotton more than a couple of hours, but I knew that that wasn't her normal attitude.

"No, of course." I was sure, though. This strange skill is all I have, really. That, and Tolliver, and my two half sisters. So I'm careful of my skill, and I never say anything unless I'm sure. The boy I'd seen in the upslope grave was the same boy in the pictures at Twyla Cotton's house.

"How . . . how did these boys die?"

That was the question I'd been dreading.

"I really can't . . ." I couldn't finish the sentence. "I really can't," I said, making it declarative.

Tolliver winced and looked away at the ribbon of road traveling up and around the bend. It didn't take much imagination to know he wished he were traveling that road, getting away from this place. I wished I were, too. I was sick with horror. I had seen so much death I'd thought I was impervious to anything new, but I'd discovered today that was far from the truth.

"You can leave," Sandra Rockwell said, and I jumped in

my seat. She'd come over to the car and pulled open the door. "Go back to Twyla's, and wait for me there. I'm going to call in SBI, right now." The State Bureau of Investigation. They would be invaluable to a little force like this, but that's not to say they'd be real welcome. Sandra looked angry, she looked sick, and she looked scared.

Twyla started up the car, and we drove up the mountain a little ways until we got to a turnaround. She made a careful turn, and drove down, past the ruined house and its ghastly yard, down to Doraville. She parked in her garage, and got out of the car slowly, as though she'd added years to her bones while we were gone. Unlocking the house, she led the way ponderously into the kitchen, where we all three stood in awkward silence.

"I think she meant us to stay here, too," I said. "I'm sorry. I wish we could go back to the motel and get out of your way. You need some time off."

"I'll just go upstairs for a little," Twyla said. "You all help yourself to the drinks in the refrigerator, and call me if you need anything. If you get hungry, there's ham on the second shelf, and the bread is in the breadbox there." She pointed, and we nodded, and she went up the stairs slowly, her eyes on the steps in front of her and her face still with grief and unshed tears. After a minute, we heard her voice and realized she was making phone calls.

We sat at the table, not knowing what else to do. Even if we'd been in the mood, we wouldn't have turned on the television or the radio. We read the newspaper, and Tolliver got us each a Coke out of the refrigerator. Tolliver worked the crossword puzzle, and I found a *Reader's Digest* to read.

The kitchen door opened, and a man and woman came in, in a hurry. They stopped at the sight of us, but it was more so they could take a good look than because they were startled. He was very tall and had dark brown hair, and she was very curvy and blond by request.

"Where's my mother?" the man asked, and I said, "Upstairs."

Without wasting any more words, up the stairs the couple went. They were both wearing the Doraville winter uniform: heavy coats and jeans, flannel shirts and boots.

"Her son and his wife," Tolliver said. It seemed like a safe guess. "Parker and Bethalynn." He was much better at remembering names than I was.

The phone rang, and was answered upstairs.

To say this was an uncomfortable situation would be putting it mildly.

"We should leave," Tolliver said. "I don't care what the cop said. We don't need to be here."

"At least we could go sit out in our car. That would be better."

"We can do that."

We washed the coffee mugs we'd used earlier and put them in the dish drainer. We pulled on our outer gear. As quietly as though we were burglars, we stepped out of the kitchen door into the carport, and got in our car. A big pickup was parked behind Twyla's Cadillac, and I was relieved we weren't blocked in. Tolliver turned on the engine, and the temperature was barely tolerable after five minutes. It wasn't getting any warmer as the day wore on, and the sky was looking grayer and grayer.

After ten minutes, without us exchanging a word, Tolliver backed out of the driveway and we went back to the motel.

Our room was blessedly warm. I fixed us some hot chocolate, and we sat with our hands around the hot mugs, drinking the watery stuff. I got the book I was reading, and stretched out on my bed to try to get lost in it, but it was impossible to get away from the dead boys.

"Eight of them," Tolliver said. He was sitting in one of the chairs, his feet propped on his bed.

"Yeah," I said. "It was really, really awful."

"Do you want to tell me about it?"

"It's almost too bad to talk about, Tolliver. They were tortured with knives and beatings and all sorts of stuff. They were raped. They were killed slowly. It took a while. I got the impression that there was more than one person there."

Tolliver looked sick.

"I'm sorry for Twyla, then," he said. "This will be worse than just finding him as a skeleton with a broken leg at the bottom of a steep slope."

"It's going to get even worse before it gets better." We'd found plenty of accidental deaths—particularly in the mountains. Most people didn't understand that the terrain could kill you, or perhaps they became complacent in a familiar environment. Hunters, especially, grew so used to carrying guns outdoors that they grew lax about the basic safety rules. They carried their rifles carelessly. They let their cell phone batteries die out. They didn't tell anyone where they were going to hunt. They didn't carry any first aid equipment. They didn't have a hunting buddy. They forgot to wear orange.

But these deaths were far from accidental.

"Yes, it'll be a lot worse," I said again. "And there'll be someone to blame. Someone around here did this."

Tolliver stared at me for a minute. "Right," he said finally. "No one but someone local would bury the bodies there. All together."

"Yeah, no one from out of town would make a trip back to that site to bury a body eight times." That seemed like a reasonable assumption to me.

"Were they killed there? Do you know?"

"I didn't read all of them," I said. "The first one, the first grave—yeah, he died in the old house, or in the shed. Without looking inside, I can't be sure which."

"He took them in there, did everything?"

I puzzled through the rush of impressions I'd gotten. "Yeah, I think so," I said doubtfully. There was something about the feeling of the deaths, something a little off.

"Definitely someone local," my brother said.

"In a small community like this, how is that possible?" I asked.

"You mean, how could a man conceal from other people the fact that he wanted to torture and kill boys?"

I nodded. "And how come the people around here haven't been up in arms about the fact that so many boys are missing?"

"I guess, if no bodies are found, it's a little easier to explain away," Tolliver said.

And then we sat, thinking dark but separate thoughts,

pretending from time to time to read, until the early darkness fell. Then Sheriff Rockwell knocked on our door. Tolliver ushered her in. Her dark green uniform pants were covered with stains, and her heavy jacket was smudged, too. "Me and the SBI guys, we've been digging," she said. "You were right. All our boys are there, and even a couple extra."

Five

～～

SHE sat in one of the two chairs. Tolliver and I sat on the side of his bed facing her. She was already holding a cup of steaming coffee from McDonald's, so I didn't offer her hot chocolate. She didn't bring up our departure from Twyla's. She looked exhausted but wired up.

She said, "We're going to get a lot of attention in the next few days. The TV stations are already calling the office. They'll be sending crews. The State Bureau of Investigation has taken charge, but they're letting me stay in it. They want me to liaise with you two, since I brought you in. The supervising agent, Pell Klavin, and Special Agent Max Stuart will want to talk to you.

"You know what I wish?" she said, when we didn't speak. "I wish I could write you your check, and you could just leave town. This thing is going to focus attention on

Doraville. . . . Well, I guess you-all know what it's like. Not only are we going to look like we were so uncaring we let some maniac kill eight boys before we noticed, but we're going to look credulous in the extreme."

If the shoe fits, I thought.

"We'd leave now if we could," Tolliver said, and I nodded. "We don't want to be around for the circus." Some media attention was good for my business; a lot of media attention was not.

Sheriff Rockwell sat back in the motel chair, a sudden motion that made us look at her. She was giving us a strange look.

"What?" Tolliver asked.

"I'd never have believed you two'd pass at the chance for free publicity," she said. "I think the better of you for it. Are you really ready to go? Maybe I can ask the SBI boys to drive to the next town to talk to you, if you want to switch motels tonight."

"We'll leave Doraville tonight," I said. I felt like a huge weight had been shifted off my shoulders. I'd been sure the sheriff would insist we stay. I hate police cases. I like the cemetery bookings. Get to the town, drive out to the cemetery, meet the survivors, stand on the grave, tell the survivors what you saw. Cash the check and leave the town. Sheriff Rockwell was at least allowing us to get out of the immediate vicinity.

"Let's wait until morning," Tolliver said. "You're still pretty shaky."

"I can rest in the car," I said. I felt like a rabbit one jump ahead of the greyhounds.

"Okay," Tolliver said. He looked at me doubtfully. But

he was picking up on my almost frantic anxiety to leave Doraville.

"Good," said the sheriff. She still sounded faintly surprised at our agreement. "I'm sure Twyla will want to give you a check and talk to you again."

"We'll talk to her before we leave the area for good. How's the work at the scene going?" he asked as the sheriff pulled herself wearily from the chair and walked to the door.

She had mentally shoved us aside, so she turned back with reluctance. "We've dug just enough at all the spots to confirm that there are remains there," she said. "Tomorrow morning, when the light is good, the forensic guys will be here to supervise the digging. I'm guessing my deputies will do most of the preliminary heavy work. Klavin and Stuart are supposed to keep me in the loop." She seemed pretty dubious about that.

"That's a good thing, right?" I said, almost babbling in my rush of relief. "Having the forensic guys in? They'll know how to dig the bodies up without losing any evidence that's there to be found."

"Yeah, we don't like admitting we need help, but we do." Sandra Rockwell looked down at her hands for a minute, as if making sure they were her own. "I've personally gotten phone calls from CNN and two other networks. So you should leave really early in the morning, or take off right now. And call me when you check into another motel. Don't leave the state or anything. Don't forget that you'll have to talk to the SBI guys."

"We'll do that," Tolliver said.

She left without further advice, and I grabbed my suitcase. It would take me less than ten minutes to be out of there.

Tolliver got up, too, and began sticking his razor and shaving cream into his valet kit. "Why are you so anxious to go?" he asked. "I think you need to sleep."

"It was so bad, what I saw," I said. I paused in my packing, a folded sweater in my hands. "The last thing in the world I want to do is get sucked into this investigation. I'll get the atlas. We better decide which way we want to go."

Though I was still a little unsteady on my feet, I grabbed our keys off the top of the TV. While Tolliver checked the stock in our ice chest, I stepped out into the dark to open the car. I shut the door behind me. The night was cold and silent. There were lots of lights on in Doraville, including the one right above my head, but that still didn't amount to much. I pulled on my heavy jacket while I looked up at the sky. Though the night was cloudy, I could see the distant glitter of a scattering of stars. I like to look at them, especially when my job gets me down. They're vast and cold and far away; my problems are insignificant compared to their brilliance.

Sometime soon, it would snow. I could almost smell it coming in the air.

I shook off the spell of the night sky, and thought about my more immediate concerns. I clicked the car's keyless entry pad and stepped off the little sidewalk that ran outside our door. Something moved in my peripheral vision and I began to turn my head.

A crushing blow struck my arm just below my elbow. The pain was immediate and intense. I shouted, wordless with alarm, and pressed the panic button on the keypad. The horn began to blare, though in the next instant the keys fell from my numb fingers. I tried to turn to face the danger, trying to throw my hands up to protect myself. The left arm would not obey. I could only make out a man clad in black with a knit hood over his head, and a second blow was already arcing toward the side of my head. Though I launched myself sideways to avoid the full force of the impact, I thought my head would fly off my shoulders when the shovel grazed my skull. I started down to the sidewalk. The last thing I remember is trying to throw my hands out to break my fall, but only one of them answered my command.

"SHE'LL be okay, right?" I heard Tolliver's voice, but it was louder and sharper than usual. "Harper, Harper, talk to me!"

"She's going to come around in a minute," said a calm voice. Older man.

"It's cold out here," Tolliver shouted. "Get her into the ambulance."

Oh, shit, we couldn't afford that. Or at least, we shouldn't spend our money this way. "No," I said, but it didn't come out coherently.

"*Yes,*" he said. He'd understood me; God bless Tolliver. What if I were by myself in this world? What if he decided . . . Oh, Jesus, my head hurt. Was that blood on my hand?

"Who hit me?" I asked, and Tolliver said, "Someone hit you? I thought you fainted! Someone hit her! Call the police."

"Okay, buddy, they'll meet us at the hospital," said the calm voice again.

My arm hurt worse than anything I'd ever felt. But then,

just about every part of my body hurt. I wanted someone to knock me out. This was awful.

"Ready?" asked a new voice.

"One, two, three," said the calm one, and I was on a gurney and choking on a shriek at the pain of being moved.

"That shouldn't have hurt so much," New Voice said. New Voice was a woman. "Does she have another injury? Besides the head?"

"Arm," I tried to say.

"Maybe you shouldn't move her," my brother said.

"We've already moved her," Calm Voice pointed out.

"Is she all right?" asked still another voice. That was a really stupid question, in my opinion.

Then they rolled me to the ambulance; I opened my eyes again, just a crack, to see the flashing red lights. I had another pang of dismay about the money this was going to cost; but then when they slid me in, I had no pangs about anything for a while.

I fluttered up to awareness in the hospital. I saw a man leaning over me, a man with clipped gray hair and gleaming wire-rimmed glasses. His face looked serious but benevolent. Exactly the way a doctor ought to look. I hoped he was a doctor.

"Do you understand me?" he said. "Can you count my fingers?"

That was two questions. I tried to nod to show I could understand him. That was a big mistake. What fingers?

The next thing I knew, I was in a dim warm room, and I had the impression I was wrapped in swaddling clothes. No room at the inn? I opened my eyes. I appeared to be in a bed, and very snugly wrapped in white cotton blankets. There was a light on over my bed, but it was on low, and there was a hush that told me the night was in its small hours, its weak hours . . . probably about three a.m. There was an orange recliner by the bed, and it was as stretched out as it could get. Tolliver was asleep on it, wrapped in another hospital blanket. There was blood on his shirt. Mine?

I was very thirsty.

A nurse padded in, took my pulse, checked my temperature. She smiled when she saw I was awake and looking at her, but she didn't speak until her tasks were complete.

"Can I get you anything?" she asked in a low voice.

"Water," I said, hopefully.

She held a straw to my lips and I took a tug or two on the cup of water. I hadn't realized how dry my mouth was until it filled with the refreshing coldness. I was on an IV. I needed to pee.

"I need to go to the bathroom," I whispered.

"Okay. You can get up, if I help you. We'll take it real slow," she said.

She let down the side of the bed, and I began to swing upright. That was a real bad idea, and I held still as my head swam. She put an arm around me. Very slowly, I finished straightening. While her arm continued to support me, she spared a hand to lower the bed. I slid off slowly and carefully until my bare feet touched the chilly linoleum, and we shuffled over to the bathroom, rolling the IV along. Getting down on the toilet was tricky, but the relief that followed made the trip worthwhile.

The nurse was right outside the partially open door, and

I heard her talking to Tolliver. I was sorry he'd been wakened, but when I was on my journey back to the bed, I couldn't help but feel glad I was looking into his face.

I thanked the nurse, who was the reddish brown of an old penny. "You push the button if you need me," she said.

After she left, Tolliver got up to stand by my bedside. He hugged me with as much care as though I were stamped "Fragile." He kissed my cheek.

"I thought you'd fallen," he said. "I had no idea anyone had hit you. I didn't hear a thing. I thought you'd had—like maybe a flashback, from the crime scene. Or your leg had given way, or something else from the lightning."

Being struck by lightning is definitely an event that keeps on giving. The year before, out of the blue, I'd had an episode of tinnitus that had finally cleared up; and the only thing I'd ever been able to attribute it to was the lightning strike when I was fifteen. So it wasn't surprising that Tolliver had blamed my old catastrophe when he'd found me on the ground.

"Did you see him?" he asked, and there was guilt in his voice, which was absurd.

"Yes," I said, and I wasn't happy with the weakness of my voice. "But not clearly. He was wearing dark clothes and one of those knitted hoods. He came up out of the darkness. He hit me on the shoulder first. And before I could get out of the way, he hit me in the head." I knew it was lucky I'd been dodging. The blow hadn't landed squarely.

"You have a hairline fracture in your ulna," Tolliver said. "You know, one of the bones in your lower arm. And you have a concussion. Not a severe concussion. They had to take some stitches in your scalp, so they had to shave a little of your hair. I swear it doesn't show much," he said when he saw the look on my face.

I tried not to get upset about a couple of square inches of hair that would grow back. "I haven't had a broken bone in ten years," I said. "And then it was just a toe." I'd been trying to cook supper for the kids, and my mom had lurched into me when I was taking a nine-by-thirteen glass dish from the oven, which incidentally had been full of baked chicken. My toe had not only been broken, but burned. I was awake enough to realize that the pain I'd experienced then was nothing compared to the pain I'd be feeling now if I weren't heavily drugged.

I wasn't looking forward to those drugs wearing off.

Tolliver was holding my right hand; luckily for me, the broken arm was my left. He was staring off into space. Thinking. Something I was way too foggy to attempt.

"So, it must have been the killer," he said.

I shuddered. As slow as my brain processes were at the moment, the thought that that person—the one who'd done those unthinkable things to the boys in the ground—had been so close to me, had touched me, had looked at me through the eyes that had enjoyed the sight of so much suffering, was absolutely revolting.

"Can we leave tomorrow?" I asked. I couldn't even draw enough breath for the words to come out in a strong voice.

"No," he said. "You're not doing any traveling for a couple of days. You have to get better."

"But I don't want to stay here," I said. "Leaving was a good idea."

"Yeah, but now we're pinned here for a little while," he said, trying to sound gentle, but the undertone of anger was clear and strong. "He took care of that. The doctor said you were lucky to have a concussion; at first he thought it would be a lot worse."

"I wonder why he didn't go on and kill me?"

"Because you hit the panic button and I got to the door pretty quick," Tolliver said. He got up and began pacing. It made my head hurt worse. He was very angry, and very worried. "No, I didn't see a soul in that parking lot, before you even ask. But I wasn't looking. I thought you'd fallen. He might have just been a yard away when I came through that door. And I was moving pretty fast."

I almost smiled, would have managed the real thing if my head hadn't been hurting so badly. "I'll bet," I whispered.

"You need to sleep," he said, and I thought it might be a good idea if I closed my eyes for a minute, sure enough.

The next thing I knew, the sun was coming through the curtains, and there was a sense of activity all around me; the hospital was awake. There were voices and footsteps in the hall, and carts rumbling. Nurses came in and did things to me. My breakfast tray came, laden with coffee and green Jell-O. I discovered I was hungry when I put a spoonful of the Jell-O in my mouth, surprising even myself. When I found I'd swallowed the jiggly green stuff with actual pleasure, I realized I couldn't remember the last time I'd eaten. Jell-O was better than nothing.

"You should eat some breakfast yourself, and go to the hotel and get a shower," I said. Tolliver was watching me eat with horrified fascination.

"I'm staying till I talk to the doctor," he said. "He'll be by soon, the nurse says."

The gray-haired man I remembered from the night before turned out to be Dr. Thomason. He was still up. "Busy night last night, for Doraville," he said. "I'm on call for the ER three nights a week. I've never worked as hard."

"Thanks for taking care of me," I said politely, though of course it was his job.

"You're welcome. In case you don't remember, I told you and your brother last night that you have a hairline fracture of the ulna. It's cracked, not completely broken through. The soft cast will protect it. You need to keep it on as close to 24-7 as you can manage. The cast'll have to stay on for a few weeks. When you check out of the hospital, you'll have directions on when to get the arm checked. It's going to hurt for a couple of days. Combined with the head injury, you'll need some pain meds. After that, I think Tylenol will do you."

"Can I get out of bed and walk a little?"

"If you feel up to it, and if you have someone with you at all times, you can stroll down the hall and back a time or two. Of course if you experience any dizziness, nausea, that kind of thing, it's time to get back in the bed."

"She's already talking about checking out of the hospital," Tolliver said. He was trying for a neutral tone, but he fell far short.

The doctor said, "You know that's not a good idea." He looked from me to him. I may have looked a little sullen. "You need to let your brother get some rest, too," the doctor said. "He's going to have to take care of you for a few days, young lady. Give him a break. You really need to be here. We need to observe that head of yours. And you've got at least a bit of insurance, I think?"

Of course there was no way I could insist on being released after he'd said that. Only a bad person would refuse
to give her brother a break. And I hoped I wasn't such a bad
person. Dr. Thomason was counting on that. Tolliver was
counting on that.

I debated making myself so unpleasant the hospital
would be glad to be rid of me. But that would only make
Tolliver unhappy. I looked at him, really looked at him, and
I saw the circles under his eyes, the slump in his shoulders.
He looked older than twenty-eight. "Tolliver," I said, regret
and self-reproach in my voice. He stepped over and took my
good hand. I put his knuckles against my cheek, and the
sun came in the window and made a pool of warmth against
my face. I loved him more than anything, and he should
never know that.

With a sudden briskness, Dr. Thomason said, "Then I'll
see you tomorrow morning, at least. You can have a regular
diet the rest of the day, I'll tell them at the desk. You take it
easy today, and get well." He was out of the room before
I could say anything else, and I let go of Tolliver's hand,
guiltily aware I'd held on to him far too long. And I didn't
mean holding his hand against my cheek, which was comforting for us both.

He leaned over to kiss my cheek. "I'm gonna go shower
and have breakfast and a nap," he said. "Please, don't try to
get out of bed by yourself while I'm gone. Promise you'll
ring for a nurse."

"I promise," I said, wondering why everyone seemed to
think I would break the rules as soon as their back was
turned. The only odd thing about me was that I'd been struck

53

by lightning. I didn't think of myself as a rebel, a hell-raiser, a rabble-rouser, or anything else exciting or upsetting.

After he left, I found myself at a loss. I didn't have a book; Tolliver had promised to bring me one when he returned. I had doubts about whether my head could tolerate reading anyway. Maybe I'd ask him to bring an audiobook and my little CD player with its headphones.

After ten minutes' boredom, I carefully scrutinized the controls on the side of my hospital bed. I succeeded in turning on the television. The channel that came on was a hospital channel, and I watched people come in and out of the lobby. Even though my boredom threshold was quite high, that palled after ten minutes. I switched to a news channel. As soon as I did, I was sorry.

The quiet, derelict home in its picturesque setting looked a great deal different now from how it looked a day before. I remembered how lonely the site had felt, how isolated. And after all, there'd been enough privacy there to bury eight young men with no one the wiser. Now you couldn't sneeze up there without four people rushing at you with microphones.

I was assuming the film I was seeing was very recent, maybe even live, because the sun looked about in the same position as the sun I could see outside my window. By the way, it was nice to see the sun; I only wished I could be out in it, though from the bundled look of the people I could see on the screen it was still pretty damn cold.

I ignored the commentary and stared instead at the figures behind the newscaster. Some of them were wearing law enforcement uniforms but others were wearing coveralls. Those must be the tech guys from SBI. The two men in suits, they would be Klavin and Stuart. I was proud of myself for remembering their names.

I wondered how long it would be before someone came to see me. I hoped no one from the media would try to call me in the hospital or come in to see me. Maybe I could be released tomorrow and we could follow our plan of getting out of town to keep a little distance between us and the crimes.

I'd been rambling on in my head about this for a few minutes when inevitability knocked at the door.

Two men in suits and ties; exactly what I didn't want to see.

"I'm Pell Klavin, this is Max Stuart," the shorter man said. He was about forty-five, and he was trim and well dressed. His hair was beginning to show a little gray, and his shoes were gleaming. He wore wire-rimmed glasses. "We're from the State Bureau of Investigation." Agent Stuart was a little younger and his hair was a lot lighter, so if he had gray he wasn't showing it. He was just as shipshape as Agent Klavin.

I nodded, and I was immediately sorry. I gingerly touched my bandaged head. Though that head felt like it was going to fall off (and that would be an improvement over how it felt now), the bandage still felt dry and secure. My left arm ached.

"Ms. Connelly, we hear you got attacked last night," Agent Stuart said.

"Yes," I said. I was angry with myself for sending Tolliver away, and irrationally angry with him for taking me at my word and going.

"We're mighty sorry about that," Klavin said, exuding so much down-home charm I thought I might throw up. "Can you tell us why you were attacked?"

"No," I said. "I can't. Probably something to do with the graves, though."

"I'm glad you brought that up," Stuart said. "Can you describe how you found those graves? What prior knowledge you had?"

"No prior knowledge," I said. It seemed they weren't interested in the attack on me anymore, and frankly, I could understand why. I'd lived. Eight other people hadn't.

"And how did you know they were there?" Klavin asked. His eyebrows shot up in a questioning arch. "Did you know one of the victims?"

"No," I said. "I've never been here before."

I lay back wearily, able to predict the whole conversation. It was so unnecessary. They weren't going to believe, they would try to discover some reason I'd be lying about how I found the bodies, they'd waste time and taxpayer money trying to establish a connection between me and one of the victims, or me and the killer. That connection didn't exist, and no amount of searching would uncover one.

I clutched the covers with my hands, as if they were patience.

"I don't know any of the boys buried in the graves," I said. "I don't know who killed them, either. I expect there's a file on me somewhere that you can read, that'll give you the background on me. Can we just assume this conversation is already over?"

"Ah, no, I don't think we can assume that," Klavin said.

I groaned. "Oh, come on, guys, give me some rest," I said. "I feel terrible, I need to sleep, and I have nothing to do with your investigation. I just find 'em. From now on, it's your job."

"You're telling us," Stuart said, sounding as skeptical as a man can sound, "that you just find corpses at random."

"Of course it's not at random," I said. "That would be nuts." Then I hated myself for responding. They just wanted to keep me talking, in the hope that I'd finally reveal how I'd found the bodies. They would never accept that I was telling them the truth.

"That would be nuts?" Stuart said. "You think *that* sounds nuts?"

"And you gentlemen are . . . who?" asked a young man from the doorway.

I could scarcely believe my eyes. "Manfred?" I said, completely confused. The fluorescent light glinted off Manfred Bernardo's pierced eyebrow (the right), nostril (the left), and ears (both). Manfred had shaved his goatee, I noticed distantly, but his hair was still short, spiky, and platinum.

"Yes, darling, I came as soon as I could," he said, and if my head hadn't felt so fragile, I would have gaped at him.

He moved to my bedside with the lithe grace of a gymnast and took my free hand, the one without the IV line. He raised it to his lips and kissed it, and I felt the stud in his tongue graze my fingers. Then he held my hand in both his own. "How are you feeling?" he asked, as if there were no one else in the room. He was looking right into my eyes, and I got the message.

"Not too well," I said weakly. Unfortunately, I was almost as weak as I sounded. "I guess Tolliver told you about the concussion? And the broken arm?"

"And these gentlemen are here to talk to you when you're so ill?"

"They don't believe anything I say," I told him pitifully. Manfred turned to them and raised his pierced eyebrow.

Stuart and Klavin were regarding my new visitor with a dash of astonishment and a large dollop of distaste. Klavin pushed his glasses up on his nose as if that would make Manfred look better, and Stuart's lips pursed like he'd just bitten a lemon.

"And you would be . . . ?" Stuart said.

"I would be Manfred Bernardo, Harper's dear friend," he said, and I held my expression with an effort. Resisting the impulse to yank my hand from Manfred's, I squeezed his bottom hand as hard as I could.

"Where are you from, Mr. Bernardo?" Klavin asked.

"I'm from Tennessee," he said. "I came as soon as I could." Manfred bent to drop a kiss on my cheek. When he straightened, he said, "I'm sure Harper is feeling too poorly to be questioned by you gentlemen." He looked from one of them to the other with an absolutely straight face.

"She seems all right to me," Stuart said. But he and Klavin glanced at each other.

"I think not," Manfred said. He was over twenty years younger than Klavin, and smaller than Stuart—Manfred was maybe five foot nine, and slender—but somewhere under all that tattooed and pierced skin was an air of authority and a rigid backbone.

I closed my eyes. I really was exhausted, and I was also not too awfully far from laughing out loud.

"We'll leave you two to catch up," Klavin said, not sounding happy at all. "But we're coming back to talk to Ms. Connelly again."

"We'll see you then," Manfred said courteously.

Feet shuffling . . . the door opening to admit hospital hall noises . . . then the muffling of those noises as the SBI agents carefully pulled the door shut behind them.

I opened my eyes. Manfred was regarding me from maybe five inches away. He was thinking about kissing me. His eyes were bright and blue and hot.

"Nuh-uh, buddy, not so fast," I said. He withdrew to a safer distance. "How'd you come to be here? Is your grandmother okay?"

Xylda Bernardo was an old fraud of a psychic who nonetheless had a streak of actual talent. The last time I'd seen her had been in Memphis; she'd been frail enough then, mentally and physically, to necessitate Manfred driving her to Memphis and keeping tabs on her while she talked to us.

"She's at the motel," Manfred said. "She insisted on coming with me. We drove in last night. I think we got the last motel room left in Doraville, and maybe the last one in a fifteen-mile radius. One reporter checked out because he got a more comfortable room at a bed and breakfast, and Grandmother had told me to drive to that motel fast and go into the office in a hurry. Every now and then, she comes through in a helpful way." His face grew somber. "She doesn't have long."

"I'm sorry," I said. I wanted to ask what was wrong, but that was a stupid question. Did it really make a difference? I knew death quite well, and I'd seen it stamped on Xylda's face.

"She doesn't want to be in a hospital," Manfred said. "She doesn't want to spend the money, and she hates the ambience."

I nodded. I could understand that. I wasn't happy about being in one, myself, and I had every prospect of walking out of this one in one piece.

"She's napping now," Manfred said. "So I thought I'd drive over to check out how you were doing, and I found the Dynamic Duo asking you questions. I thought they'd listen to me if I said I was your boyfriend. Gives me a little more authority."

I decided to let that issue ride for the moment. "What are you-all doing here in the first place?"

"Grandmother said you needed us." Manfred shrugged, but he believed in her, all right.

"Wouldn't she be more comfortable at home?" It made me feel very guilty to think about the aging and ill Xylda Bernardo dragging herself and her grandson to this little town in the mountains because she thought I needed her.

"Yes, but then she'd be thinking about dying. She said to come—we came."

"And you knew where we were?"

"I wish I could say Grandmother had seen it in a vision, but there's a website that tracks you."

"What?" I probably looked as dumbfounded as I felt.

"You've got a website devoted to you and your doings. People email in to report sightings of you."

I didn't feel any smarter. "Why?"

"You're one of those people who attracts a following," Manfred said. "They want to know where you are and what you've found."

"That's just weird." I simply didn't get it.

He shrugged. "What we do is weird, too."

"So it's on the Internet? That I'm in Doraville, North Carolina?" I wondered if Tolliver knew about my fan following, too. I wondered why he hadn't told me.

Manfred nodded. "There are a couple of pictures of you taken here in Doraville, probably with a cell phone," he said, and I was floored all over again.

"I can hardly believe that," I said, and shook my head. Ouch.

"Do you want to talk about it?" Manfred asked. "What happened here?"

"If I'm talking to you and not a website," I said, and the look on his face made me instantly contrite. "I'm sorry," I said. "I'm just freaked out about the idea that people are following my whereabouts and watching me, and I didn't have a clue about it. I don't think you'd ever do that."

"Tell me how you came to get hurt," he said, accepting my apology. Manfred settled into the chair by my bed, the one Tolliver had been snoozing in.

I told Manfred about the graves, about Twyla Cotton and the sheriff, about the dead boys in the cold soil.

"Someone here's been vanishing guys for years, and no one noticed?" Manfred said. "This is like an Appalachian Gacy, huh?"

"I know it's hard to believe. But when the sheriff explained why there hadn't been a public outcry about the disappearances, it seemed almost reasonable. The boys were all at that runaway age." There was a silence. I wanted to ask Manfred how old he was.

"Twenty-one," he said, and I gave a jerk of surprise.

"I have a little talent," he said, trying for modesty.

"Xylda can be such a fake," I said, too tired to be tactful. "But she's the real deal underneath."

He laughed. "She can be an old fraud, but when she's on her game, she's outstanding."

"I can't figure you out," I said.

"I talk good for a tattooed freak, don't I?"

I smiled. "You talk good for anybody. And I'm three years older than you."

"You've lived three years longer, but I guarantee my soul is older than yours."

It was a distinction too fine for me just at the moment.

"I need to take a nap," I said and shut my eyes.

I hadn't anticipated that sleep would drag me down before I'd even had a chance to thank Manfred for coming to see me.

Bodies have to have rest to heal, and my body seemed to need more than most. I don't know if that had to do with the lightning that passed through my system or not. A lot of lightning strike victims have trouble sleeping, but that has seldom been my problem. Other survivors I've talked to on the Web have a grab bag of symptoms: convulsions, loss of hearing, speech problems, blurry vision, uncontrollable rages, weakness of the limbs, ADD. Obviously, any or all of these can lead to further consequences, none of them good. Jobs can be lost, marriages wrecked, money squandered in an attempt to find a cure or at least a palliative.

Maybe I would be in a sheltered workshop somewhere if I hadn't had two huge pieces of luck. The first was that the lightning not only took things away from me, but left me with something I hadn't had before: my strange ability to find bodies. And the second piece of luck was that I had Tolliver, who started my heart beating on the spot; Tolliver, who believed in me and helped me develop a way to make a living from this newfound and unpleasant ability.

I could only have been asleep for thirty minutes or less, but when I woke up, Manfred was gone, Tolliver was back, and the sun had vanished behind clouds. It was nearly eleven thirty, by the big clock on the wall, and I could hear the sound of the lunch cart in the hall.

"Tolliver," I said, "do you remember that time we went out to get a Christmas tree?"

"Yeah, that was the year we all moved in together. Your mom was pregnant."

The trailer had been a tight fit: my older sister, Cameron, and me in one room, Tolliver and his brother, Mark, in another, Tolliver's dad and my pregnant mom in the third. Plus, there was a never-ending flow of the low-life friends of our parents coming in and out. But we kids had decided we had to have a tree, and since our parents simply didn't care, we set out to get one. In the fringe of woods around the trailer park, we'd found a little pine and cut it down. We'd gotten a discarded tree stand from the Dumpster, and Mark had mended it so it would work.

"That was fun," I said. Mark and Tolliver and Cameron and I had come together during that little expedition, and instead of being kids who lived under the same roof, we became united together against our parents. We became our own support group. We covered for each other, and we lied to keep our family intact, especially after Mariella and Gracie were born.

"They wouldn't have lived if it wasn't for us," I said.

Tolliver looked blank for a minute, until he caught up with my train of thought. "No, our parents couldn't take care of them," he said. "But that was the best Christmas I'd had. They remembered to go out and get us some presents, remember? Mark and I would rather have died than say it out loud but we were so glad to have you two, and your mom. She wasn't so bad then. She was trying to be healthy for the baby, when she remembered. And that church group brought by the turkey."

"We followed the directions. It turned out okay."

There'd been a cookbook in the house, and Cameron had figured we could read directions as well as anyone. After all, our parents had been lawyers before they fell in love with the lifestyle and vices of the people they defended. We had smart genes in our makeup. Luckily, the cookbook was a thorough one that assumed you were totally ignorant, and the turkey had really been good. The dressing was strictly Stove Top Stuffing, and the cranberry sauce came out of a can. We'd bought a frozen pumpkin pie and opened a can of green beans.

"It turned out better than okay," he said.

And he was right. It had been wonderful.

Cameron had been so determined that day. My older sister was pretty and smart. We didn't look anything alike. From time to time, I wondered if we really were full sisters, given the way our mom's character had crumbled. You don't suddenly lose all your morals, right? It happens over time. I caught myself wondering if my mother's had started to erode a few years before she and my dad parted. But maybe

I'm wrong about that. I sure hope so. When Cameron went missing, it felt like my own life had been cut in half. There was before Cameron, when things were very bad but tolerable, and after Cameron, when everything disintegrated: I went to foster care, my stepfather and my mother went to jail, and Tolliver went to live with Mark. Mariella and Gracie went to Aunt Iona and her husband.

Cameron's backpack, left by the side of the road the day she'd vanished on her way home from school, was still in our trunk. The police had returned it to us after a few years. We took it with us everywhere.

I took a sip of water from my green hospital cup. There wasn't any point in thinking about my sister. I'd resigned myself long since to the fact that she was dead and gone. Someday I'd find her.

Every now and then, I'd glimpse some short girl with long blond hair, some girl with a graceful walk and a straight little nose, and I'd almost call out to her. Of course, if Cameron were alive, she wouldn't be a girl any longer. She'd been gone now—let's see, she'd been taken in the spring of her senior year in high school, when she was eighteen—God, she'd be almost twenty-six. Eight years gone. It seemed impossible to believe.

"I called Mark," Tolliver said.

"Good. How was he?" Tolliver didn't call Mark as often as he ought to; I didn't know if it was a guy thing, or if there'd been some disagreement.

"He said to tell you to get well soon," Tolliver said. That didn't really answer my question.

"How's his job going?"

Mark had gotten promoted at work several times. He'd been a busboy, a waiter, a cook, and a manager at a family-style chain restaurant in Dallas. Now he'd been there at least five years. For someone who'd only managed three or four college semesters, he was doing well. He worked long hours.

"He's nearly thirty," Tolliver said. "He ought to be settling down."

I pressed my lips together so I wouldn't say anything. Tolliver was only a couple of years younger, plus a few months.

"Is he dating someone special?" I asked. I was pretty sure I knew the answer.

"If he is, he hasn't said anything." After a pause, Tolliver said, "Speaking of dating, I ran into Manfred at the motel."

I almost asked why that reminded him of dating, but I thought the better of it. "Yeah, he came by," I said. "He told me Xylda had had a vision or something and decided she better come here, too. He told me that Xylda is dying, and I guess he's indulging her as much as he can. He's sure a good grandson."

Tolliver looked at me skeptically. His eyebrows had risen so far that they looked like part of his hairline. "Right. And Xylda just happens to have a vision telling her that a woman he wants—he thinks you're hot, don't pretend you don't know that—needs her help. You don't think he had something to do with that?"

Actually, I felt a little shocked. "No," I said. "I think he came because Xylda said to."

Tolliver practically sneered. I felt a strong dislike for him, just for that moment. He shot to his feet and walked around the little hospital room.

"Probably he can't wait until his grandmother dies. Then he can stop carting her around, and be your agent instead."

"Tolliver!"

He stopped speaking. Finally.

"That's an awful thing to say," I said. We'd seen the flawed side of human nature over and over, no doubt about it. But I liked to think we weren't wholly cynical.

"You can't see it," he said, his voice quiet.

"You're seeing something that isn't there," I said. "I'm not an idiot. I know Manfred likes me. I also know he loves his grandmother, and he wouldn't have hauled her out into this cold weather with her failing, unless she told him he had to."

Tolliver kept his head down, his eyes to himself. I felt I was trembling on the edge of saying something that would push our little barrel over the waterfall, something I'd never be able to take back. And Tolliver was suffering under some burden of his own. I could read the secrets of the dead, but I couldn't tell what my brother was thinking at that moment. I wasn't completely sure I wanted to.

"This past Christmas, just us alone, that was a pretty good Christmas," he said.

And then the nurse came in to take my temperature and my blood pressure, and the second was gone forever. Tolliver straightened out my blanket, and I lay back on my pillows.

"Raining again," the nurse remarked, casting a glance out at the gray sky. "I don't think it'll ever stop."

Neither of us had anything to say about that.

The sheriff came by that afternoon. She was wearing heavy outdoor clothes and her boots were coated with mud. Not for the first time I reflected that there were worse places to be than this hospital. One of those places was digging through nearly freezing dirt for clues, breathing in the reek of bodies that were in different stages of decay, telling the bad news to families who'd been waiting to hear about their missing boys for weeks, months, years. Yes, indeed. A concussion and a broken arm in the Doraville hospital were far preferable to that.

The sheriff may have been thinking the same thing. She started off angry. "I'll thank you to keep your media-seeking friends away from here," she said, biting the words out as if they were sour lemons.

"I'm sorry?"

"Your psychic friend, whatever her name is."

"Xylda Bernardo," Tolliver said.

"Yes, she's been down at the station making a scene."

"What kind of scene?" I asked.

"Telling anyone who'd listen how she'd predicted you'd find these bodies, how she'd sent you up here, how she knew you were going to be hurt."

"None of that is true," Tolliver said.

"I didn't think it was. But she's clouding the issue. You know—you show up, of course we're all skeptical, we all think the worst. But then you came through for us somehow. You did find the boys, and we know you couldn't have had prior knowledge of their burial place. Or at least if you did we haven't figured out how."

I sighed, tried to make it unobtrusive.

"But then she showed up with that weird grandson of hers. She acts out, he just smiles."

There was nothing else he could do, of course.

"Plus, she looks like she's gonna drop dead any minute. At least you-all are adding to our hospital revenue," the sheriff added more cheerfully.

There was a cursory knock at the door and it drifted open to show a big man, his fist still raised.

"Hey, Sheriff," he said, sounding surprised.

"Barney, hey," she said.

"Am I interrupting?"

"No, come on in, I was just leaving," Sheriff Rockwell said. "Back out into the cold and wet." She stood and began pulling her gloves on. I wondered why she had come by. Complaining about Xylda just didn't seem like a meaningful reason. After all, what could we do about her? "Have you come by to throw Ms. Connelly out?"

"Ha-ha. Nope, this is my courtesy visit. I go around to every patient's room after they've been here a day, make sure things are going okay, listen to complaints—and every now and then maybe even a compliment." He gave us a big smile. "Barney Simpson, hospital administrator, so I'm at *your* service. You're Ms. Connelly, I take it." He shook my hand very gently, since I was the sick person. "And you're . . . ?" He held out his hand to Tolliver.

"I'm her manager, Tolliver Lang."

I tried not to look as surprised as I felt. I'd never heard my brother introduce himself that way.

"I really shouldn't ask if you two are enjoying your stay in our lovely little town," Simpson said. He looked as sad as it was in his nature to look. He was a tall man, and thick-bodied, with thick brushy black hair and a big smile that seemed to be his natural expression. "Our whole community is grieving now, but what a relief and a blessing that these young men have been found."

There was another knock on the door, and yet another man entered. "Oh, I'm sorry!" he said. "I'll come back another time."

"No, Pastor, come on in, I just dropped by to see if these folks had any questions they wanted to ask about the hospital and the service it's given them, the usual thing," Barney Simpson said briskly.

I noticed we hadn't had a chance to do any of those usual things.

"I've got to get back out to the site," Sheriff Rockwell said. There was no need for her to specify which site. In Doraville, there was only one.

"Well, then . . ." The new visitor was as tentative as Simpson was self-assured. He was a small man, about five foot eight, pale and thin, with clear skin and the smile of a happy baby. He shook hands with our two outgoing visitors before he gave his attention to us.

"I'm Pastor Doak Garland," he said, and we went through the handshaking ritual again. I was getting tired just from greeting people. "I serve Mount Ida Baptist Church, over on Route 114. I'm on chaplain duty here at the hospital this week. The local ministers take it in turn, and you folks were unlucky enough to get me." He smiled angelically.

"I'm Tolliver Lang, and I accompany this lady, Harper Connelly. She finds bodies."

Doak Garland cast a quick glance down at his feet, as if to conceal his reaction to this unusual introduction. What the hell was going on with Tolliver?

"Yes, sir, I heard of you-all," the preacher said. "I'm Twyla Cotton's pastor, and she especially asked me to come by. We're going to have a special prayer service tomorrow night, and if you should happen to be out of the hospital by then, we hope you'll attend. This is a special invitation, from our hearts. We are so glad to know what's happened to young Jeff. There comes a point when knowing, whether good or bad, is more important than not knowing."

I agreed with this completely. I nodded.

"Since you-all were instrumental in finding poor Jeff, we were hoping you would come, if you're well enough. I won't lie and say we don't *wonder* about this special talent you have, and it seems to pass our understanding, but you've used it for the greater glory of God and to comfort our sister Twyla, and Parker, Bethalynn, and little Carson. We want to say thank you."

On behalf of God? I tried not to smile openly because he was so sincere and seemed so vulnerable. "I appreciate your taking the time to come by the hospital to invite me," I said, filling in time while I thought of a way to refuse the invitation.

Tolliver said, "If the doctor says Harper can leave the hospital tomorrow, you can count on us coming."

Well, an alien had possessed him. That was the only conclusion I could draw.

Doak Garland seemed a bit surprised, but he said gamely, "That's just what I wanted to hear. We'll see you at seven o'clock tomorrow night. If you need directions, just give me a call." He whipped a card out of his pocket in a surprisingly professional way and handed it to Tolliver.

"Thank you," said Tolliver, and I could only say "Thanks" myself.

By the time my room cleared out, I was tired again. But I needed to walk, so I got Tolliver to help me out of bed, and hold on to me while I and my IV walked down the hall. No one who passed us paid us any attention, which was a relief. Visitors and patients had their own preoccupations and worries, and one more young woman in a terrible hospital gown wasn't going to rouse them out of their tunnel vision.

"I don't know what to say to you," I told Tolliver when we reached the end of the hall and paused before we started the journey back to the room. "Is something wrong? Because you're acting really strange."

I glanced at him, the quickest sideways look so he wouldn't catch me checking, and I decided Tolliver himself looked like he didn't know what to say.

"I know we need to leave," he said.

"Then why'd you accept the minister's invitation?"

"Because I don't think the police will let us drive away at this point, and I want us to be around other people anytime we can be. Someone's already tried to kill you once, the police are so wrapped up in the murder investigation that they don't seem to be sparing anyone to try to find out who attacked you, and the best guess I have is that the attacker was the one who killed the boys. Otherwise, why the rage, why take the chance? You ended his fun and games, and he got mad and came by to take a swipe at you if he could. He got his chance. He almost killed you. I don't know if you've considered how lucky you are that you got away with a concussion and a cracked arm."

This was a long speech for Tolliver, and he delivered it in a low voice in bits and pieces to avoid the attention of the other people. We'd reached my room by the end of it, but I waved my hand down the corridor opposite and we trudged on. I didn't say anything. I was angry, but I didn't know who to aim it at. I believed Tolliver was absolutely right.

We looked out the window at the end of this wing. The rain had turned into a nasty mix of sleet and snow. It rattled when it hit the glass. Oh, joy. The poor searchers. Maybe they would give it up and retreat into the warmth of their vehicles.

I was going very slowly by the time we crossed in front of the nurses' station and neared my room. I still hadn't thought of anything smart to say.

"I think you're right," I said. "But . . ." I wanted to say: *that dodges the issue of your hostility to Manfred and his grandmother. Why does his interest in me make you so angry? Why Manfred more than anyone else who's given me a second look?* I didn't say any of these things. And he didn't ask me to finish my thought.

I was glad to see the bed, and I leaned against it heavily as Tolliver arranged the IV stand and line. He helped me sit on the side, pulled off my slippers, and eased me back onto the pillows. We got the covers pulled up and straight.

He'd brought a book for himself and one for me, too, in case my head was feeling better. For an hour or so we read in peace, the snick of the ice against the window the only noise in the room. The whole hospital seemed to be in a lull. I looked up at the wall clock. Soon people would be getting off work, coming by to visit relatives and friends, and for a while the traffic in the hall would pick up. Then the big cart with the supper trays would come around, and the nurse with the medication, and after that a spurt of early evening visitors. Then there would be another lull as everyone who didn't have to stay at the hospital left for the night, and the only ones remaining would be the staff, the patients, and a few dedicated souls who slept in the reclining chairs by their patients' beds.

Tolliver asked me if I wanted him to stay. I was obviously better, and I thought it was touching that he would think of staying in that chair a second night in a row. I was oddly tempted. Maybe I was just better enough to have the energy to spare for fear. I was afraid.

In the end, I couldn't be selfish enough to condemn him to a night in the chair because I was a scaredy-cat. "You go on back to the motel," I said. "There's no reason why you shouldn't be comfortable tonight. I can always ring for the nurse." Who might come in thirty minutes. This little hospital, like so many others, seemed to be understaffed. Even the cleaners moved briskly because they had so much to do.

"Are you sure?" he asked. "The motel's so full of reporters that it's quieter here."

He hadn't mentioned that before. "Yes, I guess it is," I said. "I'm probably lucky I'm here."

"No doubt about it. As it is, I have to pretend I'm not in the room. One woman knocked for twenty minutes this morning."

He'd been going through his own problems and I hadn't even asked. I felt guilty. "I'm sorry," I said. "I didn't think about the press."

"Not your fault," he said. "You're getting a lot of publicity out of this, you know. That's another reason . . ." But then his face closed down on the thought. He'd been thinking about Manfred and Xylda again, sure that Xylda was in town to jump on the free ride of publicity the multiple murders would engender. No, I'm not a mind reader. I just know Tolliver very well.

"I'm not above thinking Xylda would cash in under ordinary circumstances," I said. I was trying to be practical and honest. "But she's so frail, and Manfred was so reluctant to bring her."

"He said," Tolliver pointed out.

"Well, yeah, he said. And you seem to think that Manfred's capable of dragging a sick woman somewhere she doesn't need to be just to satisfy his lust for me, but I don't think that's true." I gave Tolliver a very level look. After a second, he looked just a bit abashed.

"Okay, I'll agree he really loves the old bat," he said. "And he does take her wherever she wants to go, as far as I know."

That was as much of a concession as I was going to get, but at least it was something. I hated the idea of Tolliver and Manfred meeting up and getting into it with each other.

"Are they at our motel?"

"Yeah. There aren't any rooms anywhere else, I can tell you. The road up the mountain is nearly blocked off to traffic because there are so many news trucks and law enforcement vehicles. There's one lane open with guys with walkie-talkies at either end of the bottleneck."

Again, I felt a twinge of guilt, as if I were somehow

responsible for the disruption of so many peoples' lives. The responsibility, of course, was the murderer's, but I doubt he was staying up worrying about it.

I wondered what he *was* thinking about. He'd vented his rage with me. "He'll lie low now," I said. Tolliver didn't have to ask me who I was talking about.

"He'll be cautious," Tolliver agreed. "That turning out to try to get you, that was just rage that his games were ended. He'll have cooled off now. He'll be worried about the cops."

"No time to spare for me."

"I think not. But this guy has to be a loony, Harper. And you never know what they're thinking. I hope you get out of the hospital tomorrow. Maybe the cops'll be through with questions and we can leave this place. If you feel well enough."

"I hope so," I said. I was better, but it would be stretching a point to say I felt good enough to travel.

Tolliver gave me a hug before he left. He would pick up something to eat on his way back to the motel, he said, and stay in the rest of the evening to dodge the reporters. "Not that there's anywhere to go," he said. "Why don't we get more work in cities?"

"I've asked myself that," I said. "We had that job in Memphis, and that other one in Nashville." I didn't want to talk about Tabitha Morgenstern again. "And before that, we were in St. Paul. And that cemetery job in Miami."

"But most of our calls are from small places."

"I don't know why. Have we ever done New York?"

"Sure. Remember? But it was really really hard for you, because it was right after 9/11."

"I guess I was trying to forget," I said. That had been one

of the worst experiences I'd ever had as a professional . . . whatever I was. "We'll never do that again," I said.

"Yeah, New York is out." We looked at each other for a long moment. "Okay then," he said. "I'm gone. Try to eat your supper, and get some sleep. Since you're better, maybe they won't come in so much tonight."

He fussed around for a minute or two, making sure the rolling table was positioned correctly, clearing it for the supper tray, drawing my attention to the remote control built into the bed rail, moving the phone closer to the edge of the bedside table so I could reach it easily. He put my cell phone in the little drawer beneath the rolling table. "Call me if you need me," he said, and then he left.

I dozed off for a little while, until the supper tray came. Tonight I got something more substantial. I'm embarrassed to say that I ate most of the food on my tray. It wasn't awful. And I was really hungry. I hadn't exactly been packing in the calories the last two days.

After that, by way of excitement, a different doctor dropped in to tell me I was making progress and he thought I'd be able to go home in the morning. He didn't appear to care anything about who I was or where home was. He was as overworked as everyone else I'd encountered there at Knott County Memorial Hospital. He wasn't from around these parts, either, judging from his accent. I wondered what had brought him to Doraville. I figured he worked for the same emergency-room-stocking service that employed Dr. Thomason.

Barney Simpson's assistant, a very young woman named Heather Sutcliff, came in soon after the doctor's visit.

"Mr. Simpson just wanted me to stop by and check with you. Lots of reporters want to see you, but for the peace and privacy of the other patients we've been denying them visiting privileges. And we've screened the calls to your room . . . that was your brother's idea."

No wonder I'd been able to recover in peace. "Thanks," I said. "That's really a big help."

"Good. Because it really wouldn't be fair to the other people in this wing, to have all kinds of strangers tromping through." She gave me a serious look to show she took my reporter problem as a bad thing. And then she slipped out the door, closing it gently behind her.

The most interesting thing that happened after her departure was the tray guy removing my emptied tray. After that surge of excitement, I tried to watch television for a while; but the laugh tracks made my head ache. I read for maybe half an hour. I gradually grew so sleepy that I left the book where it fell on my stomach and just moved my hand enough to switch out the light I could control from my bed rail.

I was awakened by a brilliant flash and the sense of sound and movement very close to me. I cried out, and flailed my good arm to drive the attacker away. In a moment of sense, I punched the button that turned on the light and the one that called the nurse. I was stunned to see there were two men in the room. They were bundled up in coats and they were yelling at me. I couldn't understand a word they said. I punched the nurse's button over and over, and I yelled louder, and in about thirty seconds there were more people in my room than it was designed to hold.

The evening nurse was a starchy woman of considerable width. She was tall, too, and she scorned makeup, but she'd met a bottle of red hair dye she was real fond of in the past week or so. I admired her more by the second. She went for those reporters with both guns. Actually, if she'd had guns, the two men would've been dead without a doubt. Hospital Security was there (a man older than my doctor and not nearly as fit), an orderly was there (satisfyingly tall and muscular), and another nurse who added her opinion to that of my big nurse, as I thought of her.

Of course this was a silly episode, and one I should have been able to throw off; and once I considered it, one I should have anticipated. Right at the moment, I couldn't recognize any of those points. I'd been scared very badly, and my heart was thumping like a rabbit's, and my head was hurting as if someone had hit me again, and my arm ached where I'd bumped it when I'd lurched sideways against the railings in my panic.

When it all got sorted out the nurses had given the reporters a first-rate tongue-lashing, the security guard and the orderly were escorting the intruders out, and the two men were trying to hide their smiles.

And I was a mess: frightened, hurting, and lonely.

Six

TOLLIVER was livid when he came in the room the next morning. The nurses had been full of the night's excitement, and they'd been quivering to fill him in on the big event. They'd pounced on him with avidity. The result was that Tolliver was all but breathing fire when he flung open my door.

"I can't believe it," he said. "Those bastards! To sneak into a hospital in the night and actually into your room! Jeez, you must have . . . were you asleep? Did they really scare you?" He went from rage to concern in two seconds flat.

I was too tired to put a good face on for him. I'd come awake with a jolt at least three times during the night, sure there was someone else in the room with me.

Tolliver said, "How'd they even get in here, anyway? The doors are supposed to be locked after nine o'clock. Then you

80

have to punch a big button outside the emergency room door to get in. At least that's what the sign says."

"So either a door was left open by accident or someone let them in. Might not have known who they were, of course." I was trying to be fair. I'd really gotten good treatment at this little hospital, and I didn't want to believe any of the staff had been bribed or were malicious enough to simply let reporters in for the hell of it.

Tolliver even sounded off to the doctor about it.

Dr. Thomason was back on duty. He seemed both angry and embarrassed, but he also looked as though he'd heard enough about the incident.

I gave Tolliver a look, and he was smart enough to back off.

"You're still going to let me go, right?" I said, trying to smile at the doctor.

"Yeah, I think we'll toss you out. You're recovering well from your injuries. Traveling isn't going to be easy on you, but if you're determined, you can leave. No driving, of course, not until your arm is well." The doctor hesitated. "I'm afraid you'll leave our town with a bad impression."

A serial killer, an attack out of the blue, and a rude awakening . . . why would I get a negative picture of Doraville? But I had manners and sense enough to say, "Everyone here has been very kind to me, and I couldn't have gotten better treatment in any hospital I've seen." It was easy to see the relief pass across Dr. Thomason's face. Maybe he'd been concerned that I was the kind of person who slapped a lawsuit on anyone who looked at me cross-eyed.

I'd been thinking of the good people I'd met here, and the fact that Manfred and Xylda had come here expressly to see us. That had made me wonder if we shouldn't spend the rest of the day here in town to wind up our loose ends. But after the scare the night before, I was twitching with my desire to get out of this place.

Of course, there was the usual long wait while the paperwork made its way around the hospital, but finally, about eleven o'clock, a nurse came in with the mandated wheelchair, while Tolliver bundled up and went out to pull our car around to the entrance to pick me up. There was another wheelchair waiting just inside the front door. A very young woman, maybe twenty, was perched in it, her arms full of a swaddled bundle. An older woman who had to be her mother was with her. The mother was herding a cart loaded down with pink flower arrangements, a pile of cards that were also predominantly pink, and some gift boxes. There was a pile of pamphlets, too. The top one was titled "So You're Taking Your Baby Home."

The new grandmother beamed at me, and she and my nurse began chatting. The young woman in the wheelchair looked over at me. "Look what I got," she said happily. "Man, the last time I was in the hospital I left my appendix. Now I get to leave with a baby."

"You're lucky," I said. "Congratulations. What have you named her?"

"We named her Sparkle," she said. "Isn't that cute? No one will ever forget her."

That was the absolute truth. "It's unforgettable," I agreed.

"There's Josh," the grandmother said and wheeled her daughter and granddaughter through the automatic door.

"Wasn't that the cutest little old girl?" my nurse asked.

"The first grandbaby in that family." Since the grandmother had been in her late thirties, at the most, I was relieved to hear it.

I wondered if my lightning-fried body could produce a child.

Then it was my turn to be wheeled to the cut-down curb, and Tolliver leaped from the car to hurry around to help me. After I'd carefully eased into the car, he bent over to fasten my seat belt and then rounded the car again to get in the driver's seat.

The nurse leaned down to make sure I was sitting straight with all my bits in so she could close the door. "Good luck," she said, smiling. "Hope we don't see you back here anytime soon."

I smiled back. I was sure the other departing patient had felt sorry for me, but I felt much better now that I was in our familiar car and Tolliver was with me. I had prescriptions and doctor's instructions, and I was free to leave. That was a great feeling.

We turned right out of the hospital parking lot, and I didn't see any traffic out of the ordinary. No reporters. "Back to the motel, or can we leave?" I asked.

"We're getting your prescriptions filled and then we're leaving town," Tolliver said. "What more could they want from us?"

We stopped at the first pharmacy we saw. It was a couple of blocks from the hospital, and it was a locally owned business. Inside it was a cheerful mixture of smells: candy, medicine, scented candles, potpourri, nickel gum machines. You could get stationery, a picture frame, a Whitman's Sampler, a heating pad, a magazine, paper party plates, or an alarm clock. And at a high counter in the very back, you could actually get your prescriptions filled. There were two plastic chairs arranged in front of that counter, and the young man behind it was moving with such a languid air that I was sure Tolliver and I would have time to find out how comfortable they were.

My only exertion had been getting out of the car and walking into the pharmacy, so it was unpleasant to find how relieved I was to see those plastic chairs. I sat in one while Tolliver surrendered the prescription slips to the young man, whose white coat looked as if it had been bleached and starched—or maybe it was the first one he'd ever worn. I tried to read the date on the framed certificate displayed on the wall behind him, but I couldn't quite manage the small print at that distance.

The young pharmacist was certainly conscientious. "Ma'am, you understand you have to take these with food," he said, holding up a brown plastic pill container. "And these have to be taken twice a day. If you have any of these symptoms listed here on this sheet, you need to call a doctor." After we'd discussed that for a moment, Tolliver asked where we paid, and the pharmacist pointed to the register at the front of the store. I had to get up to follow Tolliver, and when we got to the checkout clerk, we had to wait for another customer to get her change and have her chat. Then we had to reveal to the clerk that our insurance didn't cover a pharmacy bill and that we were paying cash for the entire amount. She seemed surprised but pleased.

We'd actually stepped outside the store to get back in the

car when the sheriff found us. We got so close to being out of Doraville.

"I'm sorry," she said. "We need you again."

It wasn't snowing at the moment, but it was still gray everywhere. I looked up into Tolliver's face, which seemed as pale as the snow.

"What do you need?" I asked, which was probably stupid.

"It's possible there are more," she said.

WE had to renegotiate. The consortium hadn't written me a check for the first successful episode, and I didn't work for free. And the reporters were everywhere. I don't work in front of cameras, not if I can help it.

Since the parking lot at the back of the police station was protected by a high fence topped with razor wire, we got in the back door of the police station without anyone the wiser—anyone among the media, that is. Everyone on duty that wasn't out at the burial site made an opportunity to walk past Sheriff Rockwell's office to have a peek at me. With my arm in a cast and a little bandage on my head, I was something to look at, all right. Tolliver sat at my good side so he could hold my right hand.

"You need to be in bed," he said. "I don't know what we're going to do about housing if we stay. I gave up our motel room, and I'm sure it's gone by now."

I shook my head silently. I was trying to decide if I was up to any more bodies or not. There was always the fact that it was the way I made our living; but there was also the fact that I felt like hell.

"Who do you think the bodies are?" I asked the sheriff. "I found all the locals that were missing."

"We went over the missing persons reports for the past five years," Rockwell said. "We found two more, somewhat over the age range of the boys in the Davey homesite."

"The what?"

"That house and garage and yard used to belong to Don Davey and his family. Don was a widower in his eighties. I barely remember him. He died about twelve years ago, and the house has been empty since. The relative who inherited lives in Oregon. She's never come back over here to look at the property. She hasn't made any move at all to dispose of it. She's about eighty herself and very indifferent to the idea of doing anything at all with the land."

"Did anyone offer to buy it before?"

Rockwell looked surprised. "No, she didn't mention anything like that."

"So where is this other place?"

"Inside an old barn. Dirt floor. Hasn't been used in ten years or more, but the owners just left it to fall down."

"Why do you think there might be more bodies there, specifically?"

"It's actually on the property of a mental health counselor named Tom Almand, who never comes this far back on the property. With all the to-do at the Davey place, the next-door neighbor, a deputy named Rob Tidmarsh, thought he'd check it out because it meets the same criteria as the Davey place: secluded, not in use, easy to dig. The barn floor's mostly dirt. Lo and behold, Rob found some disturbed spots on the floor."

"Have you checked it out yourself?"

"Not yet. We thought you could point us in the right direction."

"I don't think so. If the spots are that easy to make out, just sink a rod in and see if smell comes up. Or go for broke and dig a little. The bones won't be that deep, if the surface disturbance is so easy to see. It'll be a lot cheaper, and I can get out of Doraville."

"They want you. Twyla Cotton said they had money left, since you found the boys in one day." Sheriff Rockwell gave me a look I couldn't read. "You don't want the publicity? The press is all over this, as you found last night."

"I don't want any more to do with this."

"That's not my call," she said, with some apparently genuine regret.

I looked down at my lap. I was so sleepy, I was worried I'd drift off while I sat there in the sheriff's office. "No," I said. "I won't do it."

Tolliver rose right along with me, his face expressionless. The sheriff was staring at us as if she couldn't believe what she was hearing. "You have to," she said.

"Why?"

"Because we're telling you to. It's what you can do."

"I've given you alternatives. I want to leave."

"Then I'll arrest you."

"On what grounds?"

"Obstructing an investigation. Something. It won't be hard."

"So you're trying to blackmail me into staying? What kind of law enforcement officer are you?"

"One who wants these murders solved."

"Then arrest me," I said recklessly. "I won't do it."

"You're not strong enough to go into jail," Tolliver said, his voice quiet. I leaned against him, fighting a feeling of terrible weariness. His arms went around me, and I rested my head against his chest. I had a few seconds' peace before I made my brain begin working again.

He was right. With a cracked arm and a head that hadn't healed, I wouldn't have a good time even in a small-town jail like the one in Doraville. And if the town shared a jail with other nearby towns, as was probably the case, I might fare even worse. So I'd have to do what "they" wanted me to, and I might as well bite the bullet and get it done. But who were "they"? Did Sheriff Rockwell mean the state police?

I had to pull myself away from Tolliver. I was accepting his support under false pretenses, and sooner or later I'd have to admit it.

"You need to eat," he said, and I thudded back down to reality.

"Yes," I said. I did need something to eat, and it would help if we had a place to stay afterwards. I'd need to rest, whether or not the result was a fresh crop of bodies.

"All right then," I said. "I'm going to go eat something, and then we'll meet you."

"Don't think you can get out of town without us seeing you," she said.

"I really don't like you," I said.

She looked down. I don't know what expression she wanted to hide. Maybe at the moment she wasn't too fond of herself.

We stole out of the back of the station and finally found a fast-food chain place that looked pretty anonymous. It was too cold to eat in the car. We had to go in. Fortunately, no one in there seemed to read the papers, or else they were simply too polite to accost me. Which meant there weren't any reporters. Either way, I got to eat the food in peace. At least with food this simple, there was nothing Tolliver had to cut up for me. All the aid he had to supply was ripping open the ketchup packets and putting the straw in the drink. I ate slowly because after we finished I'd have to go to the damn barn, and I didn't want to.

"I think this sucks," I said after I'd eaten half the hamburger. "Not the food, but the situation."

"I do, too," he said. "But I don't see how we can get out of it without more fuss than doing it will be."

I started to snap at him, to remind him that it was me that would be doing the unpleasant task; that he would be standing by, as always. Fortunately, I shut my mouth before those awful words came out. I was horrified at how I could have ripped up our relationship based on a moment's peevishness. How many times a week did I thank God that I had Tolliver with me? How many times did I feel grateful that he was there to act as a buffer between me and the world?

"Harper?"

"What?"

"You're looking at me weird. What's the matter?"

"I was just thinking."

"You must have been thinking some bad thoughts."

"Yeah."

"Are you mad at me for some reason? You think I should have argued more with the sheriff?"

"I don't think that would've done any good."

"Me, either. So why the mad face?"

"I was mad at myself."

"That's not good. You haven't done anything wrong."

I tried not to heave a sigh. "I do wrong things all the time," I said, and if my voice was morose, well, I just couldn't help it. I knew I wanted more from Tolliver than he could or should give me, and I had to hide that knowledge from everyone, especially from him.

I was definitely on a "my life sucks" kick, and the sooner I got off of it, the better life would be.

We called Sheriff Rockwell on our way back to the station so she could meet us outside. We parked our car and climbed into hers. "He doesn't need to come," she said, nodding her head at Tolliver.

"He comes," I said. "That's not a negotiation point. I'd rather talk to the reporters for an hour than go somewhere without him."

She gave me a very sharp look. Then she shrugged. "All right," she said. "He comes along."

As she turned out of the parking lot, she turned yet again so she wouldn't drive past the front of the station. I'd wondered if she might be a glory hound, yet she was avoiding the media. I couldn't figure her out at all.

Even though I'd had some food and some time out, by the time we reached our destination at the very edge of town I was realizing my body was far from healed. There were some pain pills in the pharmacy bag back in our car. I wished I'd brought them with us, but I had to admit to my-self that I wouldn't have taken one before I worked. I didn't know what would happen if I fiddled with the procedure. For a moment, I entertained myself with a few possibilities, but the fun of that palled pretty quickly. By the time Sher-iff Rockwell pulled to a stop, I was leaning my head against the cold glass of the window.

"Are you feeling well enough to do this?" she asked re-luctantly.

"Let's get it over with."

Tolliver helped me out of the car and we walked toward the cluster of men standing at the entrance to a barn that had formerly been red. It wasn't in as bad shape as the garage of the house in the foothills, but there were gaps between the boards, the paint was only clinging to the boards in streaks, and the tin roof seemed to be all that was holding the struc-ture together. I looked around: there was a house a distance away at the front of the property, a house that seemed in much better condition than the barn. So, someone hadn't wanted to farm or keep livestock; they'd just wanted the house and maybe some space around them.

The little knot of men unraveled to show two people standing huddled at its center. One was a man about forty, wearing a heavy coat that he hadn't buttoned. He was a small man, no larger than Doak Garland. The coat engulfed him. I could see a dress shirt and tie underneath. He had his arm around a boy who was possibly twelve. The boy was short, thickset, with long blond hair, and he had a huskier build than his father. At the moment he looked over-whelmed with shock and a kind of anticipatory excitement.

Whatever was in the barn, the boy knew about it.

The sheriff didn't pause as we passed the two, and I let my eyes linger on the boy. *I know you,* I thought, and I knew he could see my recognition. He looked a little frightened.

My connection is with the dead, but every now and then I come in contact with someone who has his or her own preoccupation with the departed. Sometimes these people are quite harmless. Sometimes such a person will decide to work in the funeral industry, or become a morgue worker. This boy was one of those people. I'm sure a lot of times I don't pick up on it—but since the boy didn't have all the mental guards and trip wires of the average adult, I could see it in him. I just didn't know what form this preoccupation had taken.

The barn had an overhead bulb that left more in darkness than it illuminated. It was a fairly large structure, quite open except for three stalls in the back full of moldy hay. They looked like they hadn't been touched in years. There were old tools hanging on the walls, and there was the detritus of a household: an old wheelbarrow, a lawn mower, a few bags of lawn fertilizer, old paint cans stacked in a corner.

The air was very cold, very thick, very unpleasant. Tolliver seemed to be trying to hold his breath. That wasn't going to work.

This was more a job for Xylda Bernardo than me, I could tell already.

I told the sheriff so.

"What, that crazy old woman with the dyed red hair?"

"She looks crazy," I agreed. "But she's a true psychic. And what we've got here isn't dead people."

"Not corpses?" It was hard to say if Rockwell was disappointed or relieved.

"Oh, I think we've got corpses. They're just not human. There's death, but I can't find it. If you don't mind, I'll call her. If she can tell you what's here, you can give her my fee."

Rockwell stared at me. The cold had bleached the color out of her face. Even her eyes looked paler. "Done," she said. "And if she makes a fool out of you, it's your own fault."

Xylda and Manfred got there pretty quickly, all things considered. Xylda came into the barn wearing her ratty plaid coat, her long dyed bright red hair wild and tangled around her head. She was a big woman in all ways, and her round face was lavishly decorated with powder and lipstick. She was wearing heavy support hose and loafers. Manfred was a loving grandson; most young men his age would run screaming before they'd appear in public with someone as crazy-looking as Xylda.

Xylda, who was carrying a cane, didn't greet us, or even acknowledge we were there. I couldn't remember if she'd needed one a couple of months ago or not. It gave her a rakish air. I noticed that Manfred kept his hands lightly on her waist, as if she might topple over all of a sudden.

She pointed with the cane to one of the slightly mounded areas in the dirt floor. Then she stood absolutely still. The men who'd come in with her—everyone who'd been outside, with the addition of the boy and the man I was sure was his father—had been eyeing her with derision, and a few of them had made comments not quite softly enough. But now they were silent, and when Xylda closed her eyes and appeared to be listening to something no one else could hear, the level of tension rose almost palpably.

"Tortured animals," she said crisply. She spun with as much agility as you can expect from a rather old and hefty woman. She pointed the cane at the boy. "You're torturing animals, you little son of a bitch."

You couldn't accuse Xylda of mincing words.

"They cry out against you," she said, her voice falling to an eerie monotone. "Your future is written in blood."

The boy looked as if he wanted to break and run when those old eyes fixed on him. I didn't blame him.

"Son," said the little man with the big coat. He looked at the boy with a heartbreaking doubt in his face. "Is what she says true? Could you have done something like that?"

"Dad," the boy said pleadingly, as if his father could stop what would happen next. "Don't make me go through this."

Tolliver's arm tightened around my waist.

The man gave the boy a little shake. "You have to tell them," he said.

"It was already hurt," the boy said, his voice exhausted and dead. "I just watched it till it died."

"Liar," Xylda said, her voice dripping with disgust.

After that, things really went downhill.

THE deputies did their digging and found the aforementioned cat, a dog, some rabbits—baby rabbits—and a bird or two. They kicked around the stalls, making dust from the stale hay rise up in thick clouds. All they discovered was the stalls had bare-board flooring, so there couldn't be any animal corpses underneath. The father, Tom Almand, seemed absolutely stunned. Since he was a counselor at the mental health center, he would know as well as anyone there that one of the early signs of a developing serial killer was the torture of animals. I wondered how many kids who tortured animals *didn't* grow up to be murderers, but I assumed that would be impossible to document. Was it possible to do something so vile and yet become a well-adjusted adult with healthy relationships? Maybe. I hadn't studied the phenomenon, and I sure didn't plan to do any research on it. I saw enough in my day-to-day work life to convince me that people were capable of dreadful things . . . and wonderful things, too. Somehow as I looked at the tear-wet face of Chuck Almand, age thirteen, budding sadist, I couldn't feel optimistic.

I was sure that Sheriff Rockwell would be pleased. We'd kept the locals from making a foolish mistake, we'd uncovered a genuinely disturbed source of future trouble, and I wasn't going to charge a penny on my own behalf for the distress I'd been put through. They did owe Xylda some cash, though, and I wanted to be sure they'd pay it.

The sheriff was not looking sunny, though. In fact, she looked tired, discouraged, and disheartened.

"Why so glum?" I asked her. Tolliver was making conversation with Manfred; he'd forced himself to do the polite thing. Xylda had hold of the arm of one of the officers, and she was giving him an earful of talk. He looked dazed.

"I hoped we'd wrap it up," she said. She seemed too down to disguise her thoughts and emotions. "I hoped this would be it. We'd find more bodies here. We'd find evidence—maybe trophies—tying someone, maybe Tom, to all the murders. It would all be over. We would have solved the case ourselves, instead of having to turn it over to the state boys or the FBI."

Sandra Rockwell was not the clear pool she'd seemed at first.

"There aren't any human corpses here. I'm sorry we can't wave a magic wand and make that come true for you," I said. And I was sincere. Like most other people, I wanted the bad guys caught, I wanted justice to prevail, and I wanted punishment of the wicked. But so often you didn't get all three at the same time, or in the same degree. "Can we leave now?" I asked.

The sheriff closed her eyes, just for a second. I had a creepy-crawly feeling in my belly. She said, "The SBI has asked that you remain on site for another day. They want to question you some more."

The creepy-crawly feeling resolved into a knot of anxiety. "I thought we'd get to leave after we did this." My voice must have gone up, because a lot of people turned to look at us. Even the boy at the heart of this brouhaha turned to look. I stared right into Chuck Almand's face, and for the first time I consciously looked into another human being.

"You might as well shoot him now," I said. It was an awful feeling. I wondered if this was how Xylda saw things, if this was what had made her so peculiar. I wondered if Manfred would go the same way. It wasn't like free choice had been taken away from the boy, that he was doomed from the beginning by his nature. It was more like I could see what choices he would make. And they were almost all on the side of becoming one of those people who end up as the subject of a documentary on A&E.

Was what I was seeing the truth? Was it inevitable? I hoped not. And I hoped I never experienced it again. Maybe I was able to see inside Chuck Almand only because I was close to two genuine psychics, and their proximity sparked a touch of it in myself. Maybe it was the rumble of thunder far away. That sound always triggered the lightning feelings in me—a jittery combination of fear and agitation. Maybe I had the completely wrong perspective.

"Tolliver," I said, "we have to find a place to stay. They're not going to let us leave after all." We should have taken off from the pharmacy, taken off and never looked back.

My brother was beside me instantly. He looked at Sheriff Rockwell for a long, long moment. "Then you have to find us a place to stay," he said. "We gave up our motel room."

With unexpected lucidity, Xylda said, "You can stay with us. It'll be cramped, but it's better than staying in the jail."

I thought of squeezing in a bed with Xylda while Tolliver and Manfred slept two feet away. I thought of other possible sleeping arrangements. I thought the jail might be better. "Thanks so much," I said, "but I'm sure the sheriff can help us find something."

"I'm not your travel agent," Rockwell said. She seemed to be glad to find something to be mad about. "But I realize you had planned on leaving, and I'll try to think of something. It's your fault the town's this crowded."

There was a long moment of silence in the barn, as everyone within hearing range stared at her.

"Not exactly your fault," she said.

"I think not," I said.

"Everyone in town has rented out every room they've got," a deputy said. His uniform said he was Tidmarsh— Rob Tidmarsh, the neighbor, then. "The only place I can think of is Twyla Cotton's lake house."

The sheriff brightened. "Give her a call, Rob." She turned back to us. "Thanks for coming here, and we'll figure out what to do with the juvenile delinquent here."

"He won't go to jail?"

"Tom," the sheriff said, raising her voice, "you and Chuck come here."

The two looked relieved that someone was finally talking to them. I didn't want Chuck anywhere close to me, and I took a couple of steps back. I knew he was only thirteen. I knew he wasn't going to hurt me there and then. And I knew that his life was still full of choices and possibilities, and he could change himself if he saw the need to.

Sheriff Rockwell said, "Tom, we're not going to take Chuck away from you."

Tom Almand's narrow shoulders slumped in relief. He was such a pleasant-looking man, the kind of guy who'd be glad to accept your UPS package from the carrier or to feed your cat while you were out of town. "So what will we need to do?" His voice caught on the words as though his mouth were dry.

"There'll be a hearing with the judge. We'll work it all out. What would help is you getting Chuck into some counseling—that should be easy, huh?—even before the hearing. And you gotta keep a watch on your kid."

Sheriff Rockwell looked down at the boy, so I did, too. For God's sake, he had freckles. There'd never been an *Andy Griffith* episode called "Opie Skins a Cat."

Chuck was looking at me with almost equal fascination. I don't know why most young men are so interested in me. I don't mean guys my own age, I mean younger. I sure don't intend to attract them. And I don't look like anybody's mom.

"Chuck, you look at *me*," the sheriff said.

The boy did look toward Rockwell, with eyes as blue and clear as a mountain lake. "Yes'm."

"Chuck, you've been having bad thoughts and doing bad things."

He looked down hastily.

"Did any of your friends help you, or was this all your doing?"

There was a long pause while Chuck Almand tried to work out which answer would give him some advantage.

"It was just me, Sheriff," Chuck said. "I just felt so bad after my mom . . ."

He paused artistically, as if he could not speak the word.

Tolliver and I knew lying when we heard it. We had lied convincingly to everyone in the school system in Texarkana to keep our family together as our parents circled the drain. We knew this boy was not telling the truth. I was ashamed of him hiding behind his mother's death. At least she'd died of something honorable. She hadn't wanted to leave her family.

The boy made the mistake of glancing back at me. He probably thought he could pull any adult female under with that little hitch in his voice. When my eyes met his, he twitched—not quite a flinch, but close.

"Maybe the psychic could tell us more," Sheriff Rockwell suggested. "Such as whether he's telling the truth about working alone or not." I don't think she meant it; I think she was looking for a reaction from the boy that would tell her what she wanted to know. But of course, the psychic in question took her quite seriously.

Xylda said from behind me, "I'm not going within a yard of the little bastard," and Tom Almand said desperately, "This is my *son*. My child." He put his arm around the boy, who made a visible effort not to throw it off.

I turned to look at the old psychic. Xylda and I exchanged a long gaze. Manfred looked down at his grandmother and shook his head. "You don't have to, Grandmother," he said. "They wouldn't believe you anyway. Not the law."

"I know." She looked sadder and older in that moment.

"Lady," said Chuck Almand. His voice was very young and very urgent, and I found he was talking to me. "It's true that you can find bodies?"

"Yes."

"They have to be dead?"

"Yes."

He nodded, as if confirming a suspicion. "Thanks for telling me," he said, and then his father drew him away to talk to a few more people.

After that, the day was out of our hands. After a lot of chatter right out of our range of hearing, Sheriff Rockwell told us that Twyla had said we could use her lake house.

"It's at Pine Landing Lake," Sandra Rockwell said. "Parker, Twyla's son, is coming to lead you there."

It was a huge relief to have a place to stay, though if no one had supplied a bed, they would simply have had to let us leave town. I was definitely feeling just like a person who'd been released from the hospital that morning; not seriously ill, but tired and a little shaky. The police were digging for the animal corpses, I suppose to make sure there weren't any human remains mixed in. We were shunted over to the side of the barn where the earth was clearly undisturbed. Tolliver and I, Manfred, and Xylda stood in a silent row. Every now and then someone in uniform would dart a curious glance in our direction.

By the time Parker McGraw got there to take us to his mother's lake house, the media had discovered the police were at the old barn and were swarming around like flies on a carcass, though they were kept at a distance by the town cops. They were yelling my name from time to time.

After a handshake with Tolliver, Manfred led Xylda out to draw them off us. "Grandmother loves the photographers," he said. "Just watch." We did. Xylda, her flaming red hair outlining her creased round face like a scarf, strode off across the empty meadow with Manfred in colorful attendance. She paused by her car, with a reluctance so fake it was almost funny, to give the eager reporters a few well-chosen words. "She's ready for her close-up, Mr. DeMille," Manfred said. He leaned over to kiss my cheek and followed her.

While Xylda was enjoying her moment, Tolliver and I did an end run around the mob to reach Parker's truck.

Though I had only a faint recollection of what the truck looked like, Tolliver had admired it when we'd seen it in Twyla's driveway and he led me right to it.

Twyla's son was big and burly, dressed in the usual jeans and flannel shirt and down vest. His boots were huge and streaked with dirt. His mom hadn't had enough money when he was young to take him to the orthodontist.

He shook Tolliver's hand heartily. He was a little more tentative about shaking mine, as if women in his milieu didn't often offer to shake.

"Let's get out of here while the getting's good," he said, and we slid into his truck as quickly as we could. Tolliver had to give me a boost. We were really jammed in, since Parker had brought his son Carson. He introduced us, and even under the circumstances, Parker's pride in the boy shone through.

Carson was a dark boy, with a husky build. He was short; he hadn't gotten his growth yet. He had a broad face like his grandmother, and his eyes were clear and brown. He was subdued and silent, which I guess was no wonder, since the body of his brother had been discovered.

"Our car's at the back of the police station," Tolliver said, and Parker nodded. He seemed friendly enough, but he was a man of few words.

However, once we were clear of the media traffic Parker said, "I didn't get a chance to thank you the other day. We didn't show you any hospitality, either, but I guess you can understand why."

"Yes," I said, and Tolliver nodded. "Don't think twice about it. We did the job we came here to do."

"Yes, you did it. You didn't take my mama's money and run for the hills with it. She's a woman who's always done what she thought was right, and she thought calling you two in was right. I don't mind telling you, I disagreed with her real strong, and I told her so. But she knew her own mind, and she was right. Them other two . . ." He shook his head. "We didn't know how lucky we was with you-all until we saw those two."

He meant Manfred and Xylda. I glanced to my side to see how Carson was taking all this. He was certainly listening, but he didn't seem upset.

"I'm glad you have a high opinion of us," I said, struggling to find a way to express myself tactfully. "But you really can't judge a book by its cover, at least in Xylda Bernardo's case. She's the real deal. I do realize that the way she looks and acts does put some people off." I hoped I'd been conciliatory enough to coax him into listening to me.

"That was real Christian of you," Parker McGraw said after he'd thought over my words for a few minutes. Just when I was beginning to think the subject was closed he added, "But I guess we'll be coming to you for all our supernatural needs." He had a sense of humor after all. But it went back behind the cloud of his grief as soon as I'd glimpsed it. "It don't seem right, enjoying anything, when our son is gone from this earth." In a gesture that just about broke my heart, Carson laid his head on his dad's shoulder just for a second.

"I'm so sorry," I said. "I wish I could tell you who did it."

"Oh, we're going to find out who done it," he said, without a shadow of a doubt in his voice. "Me and Bethalynn, we got to. We got Carson here, he deserves to grow up without being afraid."

Carson's eyes met mine. He didn't seem afraid right now, but he had his dad beside him. The boy's calm eyes told me that Carson had been brought up in the expectation that adults would protect him from harm. Nothing had happened to shake that expectation. Even though his brother had been taken, Carson was sure he would not be. I hoped he was right.

Parker seemed to think that Doraville would be safe if he discovered and eliminated the man who'd killed his son. He seemed to think it would be easy to do this. For a moment, I jeered at him in my head; but then I reminded myself of what this man had gone through. He had a right to any fantasy he chose if it would help him get through this life.

We all have our fantasies.

Seven

THE cabin at the lake had been used by the Cotton family for forty years or more. In recent years, the McGraw family had enjoyed it. Parker said that at first they'd felt like intruders, but the surviving children of Archie Cotton were well into their sixties and had no children of their own living in Doraville any longer. They seemed content to let the children of their dad's wife enjoy the old place.

"Jeff loved it out there," Parker said. "Me and Carson, we'll stay out there and go fishing in the spring, won't we, Carson?"

"Sure," Carson said. "We'll catch some fish for Mom to clean. She loves to clean fish *so much.*" That startled a smile out of his dad.

The deputy on duty had buzzed us into the fenced parking lot behind the police station. Tolliver and I scrambled out of the truck and got in our car. We followed Parker out of the parking lot.

Pine Landing Lake was about ten miles out of Doraville in a northeastern direction, and those ten miles were up a twisting, narrow two-lane road. We had met light traffic along the way. The lake seemed to be close to a community much smaller than Doraville, a dot on the map called Harmony. We didn't drive all the way around the lake, but at some points I could see its farther shore quite clearly. There were dwellings scattered around the lake, ranging from homes that looked year-round habitable to structures that were little more than open-air pavilions.

"This would be beautiful in summer," I said, and Tolliver nodded.

We followed Parker's truck at a respectful distance, and when he turned into a narrow driveway we followed, going sharply downhill for a few yards until we could park beside the truck at a broad flat spot by the shore.

The Cotton property was on one of the larger lots. It was a two-story building of very modest size, and you could tell it had been there a lot longer than some of the others because of the huge trees around it. Maybe it had just been built with more landscaping care than the others. Appropriately rustic, with cedar shingles on the roof and cedar siding, it blended into its surroundings better than most of the others we could see.

The bottom level appeared to be a storage area for the boats and other recreational miscellany. There was a heavy padlocked set of doors on this ground-level entrance, facing the lake. Stairs went up the south side of the building to a landing outside the main door. The outer door was screen, of course, the inner a heavy wooden door. Parker unlocked this door and gestured us in.

"Lots of the cabins out here don't have heating or cooling," he said, "but this one does. Mr. Archie did things right. Now, if the electricity goes off, which it does out here with some regularity, you've got your fireplace there, should be in working order. We had the guy clean it out last month."

I looked around. The interior was pretty much one big room. There were two double beds set up with their heads against the west wall, and there were several folding beds rolled up against the wall by them, covered with plastic cases. The air in the cabin felt musty, but not unpleasant. The smell of old cedar was strong. The fireplace was in the east wall, and it was faced with natural rock. The walls were unpainted cedar boards, adding to the feel that we were really roughing it. There was a small stove, an ancient refrigerator, and a couple of cabinets by the door where we'd entered, and a walled-off west corner indicated a tiny bathroom. Besides the fireplace, the east wall facing the lake was almost all glass, and through the glass we could see a screened-in porch inhabited by a few heavy wooden rocking chairs.

"Now, the bedding should be in here," Parker said, opening the cabinet below the sink. "Yep, right where Bethalynn said it would be." He pulled out a zippered plastic bag, plopped it on one of the beds. "Should be enough blankets in there. Sometimes we're out here in the spring and the nights are pretty cold. If you need to start a fire up, the wood is downstairs. You can go directly down to the boat room, now you're inside." He pointed to a trapdoor in the floor. "We used to keep the wood outside, but people just aren't as honest as they used to be. They'll take anything we don't lock up, and even then we get broken into every two, three years."

We all shook our heads over this evidence of modern slack morals.

Parker sighed from the toes of his boots, a gusty sound that was supposed to mask the grief that crossed his face. Carson silently patted his father's shoulder. "I'll see you two later at the church hall," he said. "Mom's got your cell phone number." And he was gone before we could see him cry. I guess it just got to him every now and then, and I wasn't surprised that was so. I wondered when they would get to bury what was left of their oldest son.

Tolliver opened the trapdoor and descended. "No windows down here!" he called. I heard a click and the rectangle in the floor illuminated. "I'm bringing up some firewood," he said, his voice muffled. While I slung my suitcase on the bed closest to the bathroom, I heard a series of thunks and thuds, and then Tolliver's head appeared, the rest of him following along, his arms loaded with split oak.

I hadn't had much truck with fireplaces. While Tolliver dumped the wood on the hearth, I crouched down and looked up to see if the flue was open. Nope. I found a handle that looked promising and twisted it awkwardly with my good hand. Voila! With a great creak the flue opened and I could see the gray sky. There was a basket of pinecones on the hearth that I'd assumed were for rustic decoration, but Tolliver said he thought they were to help start the fire.

Since they were absolutely ordinary pinecones and there were a million more where they came from, I let him put some in the hearth like the former Boy Scout he was. Since neither of us had matches or a lighter, we were relieved to find matches in a Ziploc bag on the mantel, and we were even more relieved when the first one Tolliver struck flared with a tiny flame.

The pinecones caught with gratifying speed, and Tolliver carefully put a few of the logs in the fireplace, crisscrossing them to allow the passage of air, I assumed.

Fire tending seemed to make him feel manly, so I left him to it. I had some granola bars in my suitcase, luckily, and I ate one while he brought up the ice chest, still fairly full of sodas and bottled water.

"We better get some groceries when we go into town tonight," I said.

"Do you really want to go to the meeting at the church?"

"No, of course not, but if we're going to be here we might as well. I don't want the people here taking against us." I glanced at my watch. "We have at least three hours. I'm going to lie down. I'm worn out."

"You shouldn't have carried that bag upstairs."

"It was on my good shoulder. No problem." But I'd taken a pain pill while he was out rummaging in the car, and it was taking effect.

There was a knock on the door, and I jumped a mile. Tolliver jerked in surprise himself, which made me feel a little better. We glanced at each other. We hadn't noticed anyone following us out here, and we'd hoped to dodge the reporters altogether.

"Yes?" Tolliver asked. I moved to stand behind him, peering out from behind his shoulder. Our caller sure didn't look like any reporter I'd ever seen. He was a wizened old man wearing battered cold-weather gear and carrying a casserole dish.

"I'm Ted Hamilton from next door," the old man said, smiling. "Me and my wife saw Parker pull up with you-all, and she could hardly wait to send you something. You friends of the family?"

"Please come in," Tolliver said, because he had to. "I'm Tolliver Lang; this is my sister Harper."

"Ms. Lang," Ted Hamilton said, bobbing his head at me. "Let me just put this down on the counter here." He set down the dish he'd been carrying.

"Actually, I'm Ms. Connelly, but please call me Harper," I said. "You and your wife live out here year-round?"

"Yep, since I retired, that's what we do," he said. The Hamiltons must live in the small white house next door, to the north. I'd seen the Hamiltons' house out the window and noted it was inhabited. Ordinarily the Hamiltons and the McGraws wouldn't really have to see each other a lot, since the McGraw parking was on the south side of the cabin. The Hamiltons' white frame house was a very ordinary little place that just happened to have been put down at the lakeside, with no concession made to setting or locale. It did boast a very nice pier, I'd noted.

"We're just going to be here a couple of days," I said, pretending to be rueful. "This was awful nice of Mrs. Hamilton."

"I guess you know Twyla, then?"

He was obviously dying to get the scoop on us, and I was

just as determined not to spell it out for him. "Yes, we know her," I said. "A very nice woman."

"Just for a couple of days? Maybe we can persuade you to stay longer," Mr. Hamilton said. "Though with the bad weather coming in, you may want to rethink staying out here. You'd be better off with a room in town. It takes them a while to get out here when the electricity goes out."

"And you think that's gonna happen?"

"Oh, always does when we get a lot of ice and snow like they're predicting for tomorrow night," Ted Hamilton said. "Me and the wife have been getting ready for it all day. Went to town, got our groceries, stocked up on water and got oil for our lanterns, and so on. Checked the first aid kit to make sure we can patch up cuts and so on."

You could tell the oncoming bad weather was a big event for the Hamiltons, and I got the distinct impression they'd enjoyed themselves to the hilt preparing for it.

"We may be on our way tomorrow, with any luck," I said. "Please tell your wife we appreciate her fixing us something. We'll get the dish back to you, of course." We said all this a few more times, and then Ted Hamilton went back down the outside stairs and around our cabin to get back to his. Now that I was listening for it, I could hear his cabin door open and I thought I heard a snatch of his wife's voice raised in eager query.

I took the aluminum foil off the dish to reveal a chicken and rice casserole. I sniffed. Cheese and sour cream, a little onion. "Gosh," I said, feeling respect for someone who could whip up a dish like that in the forty-five minutes Tolliver and I had been in residence in the cabin.

"If you had some leftover chicken," Tolliver said, "it would only take twenty minutes for the rice to cook."

"I'm still shocked," I said. My stomach growled, demanding some of the casserole.

We found plastic forks and spoons and some paper plates, and we ate half the dish on the spot. It wasn't restaurant food. It smelled of home . . . a home, any home. After we'd put the aluminum foil back on and put the remainders in the old refrigerator, I lay down to take a nap, and Tolliver went out exploring. The fire was crackling in a very soothing way, and I wrapped myself in a blanket. We'd made the beds, working together, my rhythm all thrown off by my bad arm. There hadn't been any pillows here—presumably the family brought their own each time they camped out here—but Tolliver and I each had a small pillow in the car, and once I was swaddled in the blanket and warm and full, I drifted off to sleep feeling better than I had in days.

I didn't wake up until almost four o'clock. Tolliver was reading, lying stretched out on his bed. The fire was still going, and he'd brought more wood up. He'd positioned two wooden chairs close to the fire.

There wasn't a sound to be heard: no traffic, no birds, no people. Through the window above my head, I could see the bare branches of an oak tree motionless in the still air. I put my hand to the glass. It was warmer. That wasn't good. The ice would come, I was sure.

"Did you go fish?" I asked Tolliver, after moving around a little to let him know I was awake.

"I don't know if you're supposed to go fishing in the winter," he said. He hadn't had a bubba upbringing; no hunting and fishing for Tolliver. His dad had been more interested in helping hard men dodge the law, and then in getting high with the same men, than in taking his sons out in the woods for some bonding time. Tolliver and his brother, Mark, had had to learn other skills to prove themselves at school.

"Good, because I have no idea how to clean 'em," I said.

He rolled off his bed and sat on the edge of mine. "How's the arm?"

"Pretty good." I moved it a little. "And my head feels a lot better." I moved over to give him room and he stretched out beside me.

He said, "While you were asleep, I checked our messages on the phone at the apartment."

"Mm-hm."

"We had a few. Including one about a job in eastern Pennsylvania."

"How long a drive from here?"

"I haven't worked it out yet, but I would guess about seven hours."

"Not too bad. What's the job?"

"A cemetery reading. Parents want to be sure their daughter wasn't murdered. The coroner said the death was an accident. He said the girl slipped down some steps and fell. The parents heard from some friends that, instead, her boyfriend hit her on the head with a beer bottle. The friends are all too scared of the young man to tell the cops."

"Stupid," I said. But we encountered stupid people all the time, people who just could not seem to see that elaborate plots almost never worked, that honesty usually was the best policy, and that most people who supposedly died by accident actually *had* died by accident. If the boyfriend was so frightening that a group of young people were too scared to talk about him, there might be a good chance that this girl's "fall" was an exception.

"Maybe we'll get away from here in time to take it up," I said. "They mention any time constraints?"

"The boy's about to leave town—he's joined the army," Tolliver said. "They want to know if he's guilty before he goes to basic."

"They understand, right? That I can't tell them that. I can tell if the girl was hit on the head, but I won't know who did it."

"I spoke to the parents briefly. They feel that if she was hit on the head, they'll know it was the suspect who did it. And they don't want him to leave before they have a chance to interrogate him again. I said we'd let them know something definite in the next forty-eight hours."

I hated not being able to tell people yes or no right away, but you have to keep the law happy until their demands become unreasonable. My testimony is no good in court, right? So it's very irksome when the law stops me from leaving town. They don't even believe in me, but they can't seem to let me go.

"Damned if you do, damned if you don't," I muttered. I remembered my mother's mother saying that: it was one of the few memories I had of her. I remembered her with a child's affection, though she hadn't been one of those sweet cuddly grandmas you see in TV ads. She'd never baked a cookie or knitted a sweater, and as far as dispensing wisdom, the aforementioned saying was about as profound as she'd gotten. She'd vanished as thoroughly as she could when my mother became a predator because of her drug habit. Of course, dodging her needy and dishonest daughter meant she also lost contact with us; but maybe it hadn't been an easy choice.

"You ever hear from your grandmother?" I asked Tolliver. He didn't follow my line of thinking, but he didn't look startled.

"Yeah, every now and then she calls," he said. "I try to talk to her once a month."

"Your dad's mother, right?"

"Yeah, my mother's parents are both gone. She was their youngest, so they were pretty old when she died. It just took the life out of them, my dad said. They both passed away about five years after my mother."

"We don't have a lot of relatives." The McGraw-Cotton family seemed pretty united. Parker loved his mom, though she'd remarried. She'd stayed loyal to him instead of going all country club with her accession to money. Twyla had said Archie Cotton's adult children were okay with the marriage.

"Nope." Tolliver didn't seem concerned. "We have enough."

I reached up with my good hand to pat him on the shoulder. "Damn straight," I said, with an overly hearty cheer, and he laughed a little.

"Listen, we need to go into town a little early."

"Why?"

"Well, the computer was down at the hospital this morning, and they wanted to check your bill again."

"You mean they let me out without you paying the total?"

"I paid it, but they wanted to be sure there weren't any later charges on it. So they asked me to drop by."

"Okay."

"You due any medicine?"

We checked, and I took a pill. I decided to take the pain medicine with me in my purse. I was able to use the bathroom by myself, but Tolliver had to help me readjust my clothes; and I let him take a swipe at brushing my hair, too. It was very awkward to attempt that one-handed. We managed to camouflage the bandage a little.

Tolliver went down the steps first, and I came down carefully after him. The gust of relatively warm air that blew in my face was a startling change. It was getting dark fast.

"And there's cold air coming down from the north?" I asked.

"Yeah, late tomorrow," he said. "And it'll be this warm here through part of tomorrow. We need to listen to the news on our way into town."

We did, and the weather prediction was discouraging. Temperatures would remain in the upper forties through tomorrow, and by the evening the hot and the cold air would collide with the strong chance of a resultant ice storm. That sounded terrible. I'd only seen such a thing one other time, in my childhood, but I still remembered the trees down across the road in our trailer park, the bitter cold, and the lack of electricity. It had been a long thirty hours before our power came back on then. I wondered if we could drive out of the area likely to be affected before the storm hit.

The hospital lobby was almost deserted, and the girl on duty at the business window was busy closing out her paperwork. She wasn't too happy to see us, though she was polite. She glanced at a yellow Post-it Note stuck to my file and picked up her telephone. Punching in some numbers, she said, "Mr. Simpson? They're here." After hanging up, she said, "Mr. Simpson, the administrator, asked to be notified when you came by. He'll be here in just a minute."

We sat in the padded chairs with the metal legs and stared at the magazines on the low Formica table in front of us. Battered copies of *Field and Stream*, *Parenting*, and *Better Homes and Gardens* were not likely to tempt us, and I closed my eyes and slumped down in my chair. I found myself daydreaming about Christmas trees: white ones with golden ribbon and golden decorations, green ones with red flocked cardinals stuck on the branches, trees covered with big Italian glass ornaments and artificial icicles, dripping with tinsel. It was a shock to open my eyes and see long legs in front of me, legs covered in a dark suiting material. Barney Simpson dropped into a chair opposite us. His hair looked even rougher than it had when he'd come to my hospital room. I wondered if he'd ever tried cream rinse on it, to make it a bit more tameable.

"I have to confess," he began, "I put a flag on your statement so Britta would call me when you came in."

"Why?" Tolliver asked. I sat up and tried not to yawn.

"Because I thought you might bolt without coming to the meeting tonight if I didn't catch you here and remind you to come," Simpson said with every appearance of frankness. "Britta told me the computers had been down when you were checking out this morning, so I decided to take advantage of the opportunity."

"You belong to the same church? Doak Garland's church?"

"Oh, I make an appearance every few Sundays," he said, not a bit abashed by something most southerners would be ashamed to admit. "I have to confess that I don't have a great attendance record. I like to sleep in on Sundays, I'm afraid."

He seemed to expect me to supply him with a comforting reassurance along the lines of "Don't we all?" or "We miss a lot of Sundays, too." But I didn't say anything. This may have been childish on my part. Tolliver and I don't ever go to church. I don't know what Tolliver believes, at least not in detail. I believe in God; I don't believe in church. Churches give me the cold chills. The only reason I'd been in a church in the past five years was to go to a funeral. Having the body that close was very distracting. It buzzed at me during the whole service. If this had been Jeff McGraw's funeral, rather than a kind of memorial service for all the lost boys, I would never have agreed to come to it.

"Abe Madden is due to speak," Barney Simpson said. "That should be interesting. Sandra hasn't said much, but it's common knowledge that Abe wouldn't pursue the boys' disappearances with anything like the purpose Sandra wanted when she was a deputy. And it's also no secret that's one reason she was elected sheriff."

Barney Simpson gave us a serious nod, his big black glasses reflecting the overhead fluorescents.

"Then I guess it should have a little more controversy than the usual memorial service," Tolliver said. "Our bill is ready, you said? Your computers are back up and running?"

"Yes. We're backing up everything this evening so we

won't lose anything in the upcoming ice storm. I guess you've been listening to the weather, like everyone else around here. Did you-all find a place to stay?"

"Yes, we did," I said.

"Back in the motel, I guess. You-all were lucky to find somewhere."

"No," Tolliver said. "They were all out of rooms."

He went over to the window to check on the bill while Barney looked at me expectantly, waiting for me to tell him where we'd found a place to stay—but I didn't. I wasn't sure why I was being so ornery. A bop on the head will only excuse so much. I forced myself to be polite.

"Is there a Mrs. Simpson?" I asked, though I simply could not have cared less.

"There was," he said, regret tingeing his voice with gray. "We came to a parting of the ways a few years ago, and she and my daughter moved to Greenville."

"So you get to see your daughter sometimes."

"Yes, she comes back to stay with me and visit her junior high buddies every so often. Hard to believe she's in college now. Any children for you?"

"No," I said, shaking my head.

"Well, they're a mixed blessing," the administrator said in a consoling voice, as if to assure me I didn't have to grieve at not having any.

I stood and moved over to Tolliver, who was getting a receipt from Britta.

"Could I take you two to supper?" Barney Simpson asked, and we tried not to look too astonished.

Tolliver glanced at me quickly to get my reaction to this

very unexpected invitation, and he said, "Thanks, but we already have plans. We appreciate your offer, though."

"Sure, sure."

Britta had closed her window and I could see her silhouette behind the glass as she rose and began putting on her coat.

The hospital was as closed as a hospital gets.

We left then, heading out the front door with the receipt and Simpson's goodbyes. "What a lonely guy," I said.

"He has a thing for you," Tolliver said gloomily.

"He does not." I dismissed the idea without a second glance at it. "He didn't care about me at all. I didn't represent a woman to him, one little bit."

"Then why'd he want to be our best friend?"

"I guess it was the newness of us," I said. "He may not have the chance to meet that many people. I bet his job pretty much holds him down. We're variety."

Tolliver shrugged. "Whatever. Where you want to eat?"

"This is Doraville. What are our choices?"

"It's too cold for Sonic. There's a McDonald's and there's a Satellite Steaks."

"That'll do."

Satellite Steaks was very much like Golden Corral or Western Sizzlin'. On this cold night, with the prospect of a memorial service and bad weather to anticipate, everyone in Doraville had had the same idea. There were some easily identifiable strangers who had to be with the news crews, and there were a lot of locals (who probably didn't come in during the summer tourist season), and there were travelers from the interstate. The place was jammed. Manfred and

Xylda were at a table for four. Without consulting Tolliver, I went right over to their table and asked if we could share.

"Oh, please," Xylda said. She had maybe a ton of makeup on. Her encounter with the media at the barn seemed to have galvanized her into going the extra mile. Her eyes were positively Cleopatran, and she'd actually tied a scarf around her head à la a gypsy, with her brilliant red ringlets flying out from under it to form a shocking contrast with her pale, plump, wrinkled face. I sat beside her and got a big whiff of stale perfume. Tolliver had to sit by Manfred, which wouldn't hurt him. And Manfred had to smell better than his grandmother.

"How are you feeling?" Manfred asked. He really looked anxious.

"I'm doing good," I said. "My head feels better. The arm is a pain."

"I heard you two checked out of the motel. I figured you'd be long gone."

"Tomorrow or the next day," Tolliver said. "We're just waiting to see if the state guys have anything else to ask us. Then we'll be on our way. You two?"

"I need to stay until tomorrow afternoon, at least," Xylda said in a whisper. "There are more dead people to come. And the time of ice is near."

Now, that I understood. "That's what the weather says. There's going to be an ice storm."

"We're hoping to get out of town ahead of it," Manfred said quietly. "Grandma don't need to be away from a big hospital any longer than we can help it. I'll be taking her back home as soon as I can." I looked at him sideways and read clearly the grief written on his face. It made me want to give him a big hug.

Xylda looked like she was listening to a faraway voice. I was seriously concerned about her. Before, she'd been in the likeable fake category, though she'd always had her moments of true brilliance. They'd just been too few and far between for her to make her living off of them. Now she appeared to be "on" all the time. The stretches of shrewd reality that had helped her earn a living (if fraudulent) wage seemed to be fewer and farther between.

I wondered what Manfred would do when she was gone. He was very young and he still had all his options open. He could go to college and get a regular job. He could apprentice in a circus. He could assume the hand-to-mouth existence of petty fraud and chicanery that Xylda had led. This wasn't the time or place to quiz him about his future plans, when the big stumbling block to any of them sat beside me spilling salad dressing down her blouse.

Xylda said, "That boy is going to be a murderer." Fortunately her voice was quite low. I knew she was talking about Chuck Almand.

Speaking of a young man with options open. "Not for sure, though. He could still save himself. Maybe his father will find a good therapist for him, and he'll work out all his kinks." I didn't believe it, but I should at least sound like I thought it was possible.

Manfred shook his head. "I can't believe they didn't arrest him."

"He's a minor," Tolliver said. "And there aren't any witnesses against him except his own admission. I don't think jail would do him any good, do you? Maybe just the opposite, in fact. Maybe in jail he'd find out how much he enjoyed hurting people."

"I think in jail he'd be on the other end," I said. "I think he'd get hurt a lot, and maybe come out ready to give it back with interest."

We all mulled it over. The waitress bustled up to take our orders and to ask Manfred and Xylda if they needed more to drink. They both accepted, and it was a few minutes before we could resume our conversation.

"I wonder if there's a kid like that in every community," Tolliver said. "One who likes to cause pain, likes to have the power over smaller creatures."

"There was someone like that in our school in Texarkana?" I asked. I was surprised.

"Yeah. Leon Stipes. Remember him?"

Leon had been six feet tall when he was in the sixth grade. Leon was black, and he was on the football team, and he scared the hell out of the other teams we played. I suspected he'd scared the hell out of most of the players on his own team, too.

I explained Leon to Xylda and Manfred. "He liked causing pain?"

"Oh, yeah," said Tolliver grimly. "Oh, yeah. He really did. In practice, he'd nail people he didn't have to, just to hear them yelp."

I shuddered with distaste. With one hand, I opened my purse and pulled out my bottle of vitamins. I pushed it over for Tolliver to deal with. He removed the childproof lid and shook one out. I took it.

"How are you feeling?" Manfred asked. "The arm hurting?"

I shrugged. "The pain medicine works pretty well," I said. "In fact, I'm wondering if I'll fall asleep in the memorial service."

"You'll be much better soon," Xylda said, and I wondered if she was basing that on foresight or on optimism.

"What about you, Xylda?" I looked at her curiously. "Didn't I hear you were in the hospital last month?" There's an Internet group for those of us who work in the paranormal field. I check it out from time to time.

"Yes," she said, "but it's bad for my spirit, the hospital. Too much negative there. Too many desperate people. I won't go in there again."

I started to protest, caught the warning glance Manfred gave me. I shut up.

"I don't blame you," Tolliver said. "Harper's just trailing negative thoughts, and she was only in there for a couple of days."

I could have kicked him, if I could have summoned the energy. I stuck out my tongue.

Tolliver and Manfred talked about car mileage while we ate, and Xylda and I thought our own thoughts. When Tolliver left to go to the men's room and Manfred was paying their bill, she said, "I'm going to die soon."

I was affected enough by the pain medicine to accept this calmly. "I'm sorry to hear you think so," I said, which seemed safe enough. "Are you scared?"

"No," she said, after a moment's thought, "I don't believe

124

I am. I've enjoyed my life and I've tried to do good, for the most part. I never took money from anyone who couldn't afford it, and I loved my son and grandson. I believe my soul will enter another body. That's very comforting, knowing the essential part of me won't die."

"Yes, it must be," I said, pretty much at a loss as to how to carry my end of the conversation.

"Your questions will all be answered," she said. "My sight is clearer the closer I come to the end."

Then I said something that surprised even myself. "Will I find my sister, Xylda? Will I find Cameron? She's dead, right?"

"You'll find Cameron," Xylda said.

I bowed my head.

"I don't know," Xylda said after a lengthy pause, and I raised my face to stare at her, trying to figure out what she meant. Manfred was coming back to the table to leave a tip. Tolliver was in line at the cash register. We were in a cone of strangeness together. "But there are more important things for you to think about first," Xylda continued.

I hardly understood how anything could be more important than finding my sister's body. I slid out of the booth and started struggling into my coat, while Xylda began scooting to the outside. Manfred helped me get my right arm into its coat sleeve and draped the coat over my left shoulder. He bent slightly and gave me a kiss on the neck as he did so. He did this so casually that it seemed churlish to make a big deal out of it. In fact, it wasn't until I saw Tolliver's face that the light kiss really registered on me. Tolliver was absolutely inclined to make a big deal out of it, and I gripped his arm with my good hand and began marching toward the door, forcing him to come along.

"It was nothing," I said. "I wasn't even thinking about it. He's just a very young man with a sick grandmother." I'm not sure what sense that made, but at the moment it just slid right out of my brain and then my mouth. "We're just going to this meeting now. Come on, or we'll be late."

Somehow we both ended up in the right car and Tolliver turned on the motor to get the blessed heater started. He pulled my seat belt across me with unnecessary force, and I squeaked because my arm hurt.

"Sorry," he said, not sounding very sorry at all. "He rubs me the wrong way. He just crawls around you. All that stuff in his face and God knows where else! Just waiting to touch you."

Instead of keeping quiet and letting things die down like I ought to have done, I said, "Isn't it okay that someone likes me?"

"Sure! Just not him!"

Tolliver would rather I got together with Barney Simpson or the Pastor Doak Garland? "Why not?"

There was a long moment of silence while Tolliver struggled with that question. "Because he, well, he actually stands a chance with you," he said. "Other guys don't because we're always traveling and you aren't going to see them again, but he understands the lifestyle and he has to travel, too, with Xylda."

I opened my mouth to say, *So you don't want me to have anyone?* But a power beyond me shut my mouth. I didn't say

126

anything. This was closer to the bone than I'd imagined Tolliver would get, and I was scared to take it any further.

"He's younger than me." I had to say something.

"Not too young," my brother said. We'd changed sides in the Manfred argument, I realized. Suddenly, I was trying not to smile. I realized the pain pill I'd taken at the cabin was definitely working. I had the blooming warm sense of well-being, the chatty feeling of affection for all mankind. If I ever became addicted to any pharmaceutical, pain pills would be my drug of choice. But I didn't plan on becoming addicted. Once the pain was gone, the pills would be. I had to watch myself, after the example my mother had set me.

"The trick to avoiding these pills is not to get hurt," I said seriously.

Tolliver had a little trouble catching up to this conversational line, but he got there. "Yes, you don't want to end up in the hospital again," he said. "For one thing, you can't do your share of the driving while you're on them."

"Oh, yeah, like you care," I said.

He smiled. I felt better. "But I do," he said.

The lot of Mount Ida Baptist Church was already full of cars. One of the local cops was directing the overflow parking. Tolliver asked if he could drop me off right in front of the church, and the cop nodded. I got out of the car awkwardly and stood just inside the vestibule, waiting. As other people passed me and went in, I glimpsed Twyla sitting at a table just inside the door. She had a clear plastic box in front of her, a box with a slot cut in the top.

There was a sign on the front of the box that read "Please

help our families bury their children." It was already half full of bills and change.

Twyla glimpsed me, too, and made a beckoning gesture. I maneuvered through the doors and went to sit in the vacant folding chair beside her. She leaned over to give me a half hug.

"How you doing, girl?" she asked.

However I was doing, it had to be better than Twyla. Everything wrong with me would heal. Not so, her. "I'm okay," I said. "They've got you working, I see."

"Yep, they thought it would be more effective if a relative sat here," she said. "So here I am. If you say six of the boys were local, we need at least four thousand dollars for each burial, so our goal is twenty-four thousand. We got these up all over town, but this is a poor place. I think we'll be lucky to get six thousand through these collections."

"How do you expect to make up the rest, or do you think that just won't happen?"

Twyla looked grim. "I think it won't happen. But we're doing the best we can. Maybe if the poorer families can just make a good down payment on the funerals through these donations, each individual family can pay the rest on time."

I nodded. "Good idea." Emboldened by the pain medication, I said, "It's too bad the media don't chip in. After all, they're profiting by the deaths as well, aren't they? They should donate something."

A fire lit in Twyla's eyes. "That's a good idea," she said. "I wonder that I didn't think of it. What happened today at Tom Almand's? I'm hearing some mighty funny things. That boy of his in trouble? Hey, Sarah," she said, lifting her round face to a woman coming in. "Thanks for helping," she added as the older woman dropped a couple of dollars into the slot.

"There are too many people around to talk about it," I said quietly. No one had asked me not to discuss the macabre nature of the findings at Tom Almand's, but I didn't want to be broadcasting it. Chuck Almand would be a pariah soon enough. I wouldn't hasten the process. Though some country people tend to be more practical about animals than city people, plenty of the inhabitants of Doraville would be disgusted at the pain inflicted on cats and squirrels and the odd dog . . . especially if the cats and the dog turned out to be somebody's pets. "But he's not a boy you'd want to have dating your daughter or grand-daughter."

"The sheriff says we won't get the bodies back for a week at least, maybe longer," Twyla said. "It seems hard that we finally discover Jeff, but we can't bury him."

"At the same time," I said, "you want every bit of evidence that can tie his death to the killer."

"I don't like to think about him getting cut up," Twyla said. "I can't think about it."

I didn't know what to say, and the fuzzy golden goodwill the pill lent me did not give me any inspiration. I decided it was best to keep silent. I looked over the crowd in the pews. Mount Ida was a larger church than I'd imagined from the outside. The pews were gleaming with polish, and the carpet was new, too. At the front of the church were easels with enlarged photographs of the dead boys, each with a spray of flowers at the base. I would have liked to look at them, since

I'd touched on each of these young men in my very own way, but going up there would have seemed rude and pushy.

There was a knot of law enforcement uniforms in one of the front pews. I recognized Sheriff Rockwell's hair, and I thought I also saw Deputy Rob Tidmarsh, who'd discovered the animal graves.

Somehow the Bernardos had beat us here. I glimpsed Xylda's unruly red head a few pews up and to the right and Manfred's platinum spikes beside her. From the rear view, the two didn't stand out so much. There was plenty of dyed hair in evidence, and several spiky hairdos.

Tolliver came in, his face pinched with cold. He dropped a twenty into the slot. He was surprised to find me seated by Twyla, but he leaned over to shake her hand and to tell her how sorry he was. "We appreciate the use of your cabin," he said. "It made a big difference, having a place to stay." I hadn't even thought of thanking her, and I was angry with myself.

"I'm very sorry Harper got hurt," Twyla said, and I felt better when I realized I wasn't the only one who'd forgotten to mention something fairly major. "I hope they catch who did it, and I'm sure it was the same bastard who killed our Jeff. This is something else I forgot," she said, pressing a check into my hands. I nodded and slid it into Tolliver's chest pocket. We started down the aisle to find a place to sit.

We paused by a pew with some free space in the middle, and when the pew's settlers saw my cast, they were kind enough to all shift down to let us sit on the end. I said "Thank you" several times. It felt good to settle down on the padded pew shoulder to shoulder with Tolliver. We were far enough away from the door to avoid the effects of the constant gusts of cold air with each entrance.

Gradually the murmurs died down and the crowd became silent. The doors didn't open and close anymore. Pastor Garland came out, looking youthful and somehow sweet. But his voice was anything but sweet, or peaceful, as he read the scriptures he'd selected for the occasion. He'd picked a passage from Ecclesiastes, he told us, and he started to read. He began, "To everything there is a season . . ."

Everyone around me was nodding their heads, though of course Tolliver and I didn't recognize the scripture. We listened with great attention. Was he saying that it had been time for the boys to die? No, maybe his emphasis was on "a time to mourn." That was now, for sure. The rest of his readings were from Romans, and the thread that ran through them was about maintaining your own integrity in a world bereft of it. And they were eerily appropriate.

There was no point in saying the murders were events the congregation had to accept philosophically. There was no point in saying the people of Doraville had to turn the other cheek; it wasn't the community's cheek that had been struck. Its children had been stolen. There would be no offering up of other children to be killed, no matter how much scripture was quoted.

No, Doak Garland was smarter than he appeared. He was telling the people of Doraville that they had to endure and trust in God to get them past the bad time, that God would help them in this endeavor. No one could disagree with that message. Not here, not tonight. Not with those faces at the front of the congregation, staring back. As I watched, a deputy ceremoniously added two more easels, but these were left blank. The two boys who were strangers. I felt touched.

"These are the children of our community," Doak said. He gestured to the faces. Then he pointed to the two blank easels. "And these are someone else's children, but they were killed and buried right along with ours, and we must pray for them, too."

One picture was the stern one boys always take for their high school football picture. The scowling boy, looking so very tough . . . I'd seen him in his grave, beaten and cut, tortured beyond his endurance, every vestige of manhood stripped from him. Suddenly the tragedy of it seemed unbearable, and as Doak Garland's voice rose in his sermon, tears flowed out of my eyes. Tolliver fished some Kleenex from his pocket and patted my face. He looked a little bewildered. I'd never reacted like this to a previous case, no matter how horrific.

We sang a hymn or two, we prayed long and loud, and one woman fainted and was helped out into the vestibule. I floated through the service on a cloud of pain medication, every now and then weeping with the emotion that could not be contained. When the usher—the hospital administrator, Barney Simpson—came by with the plate to pass for further donations toward the burials, a man two pews ahead of me turned his head as he handed his neighbor the collection plate, and I saw to my amazement that Tom Almand had come to the service. He had brought his son with him, and that hit me wrong. The counselor should have stayed home with the boy. Chuck was laboring under such a terrible burden, he shouldn't be in a place where the atmosphere was sheer grief and horror. Or did he need to be reminded that other problems were worse than his? I was no counselor. Maybe his dad knew best.

I reached across myself to squeeze Tolliver with my good hand. He looked at me inquiringly. He was restless, and I could tell he wanted to be anywhere but here. I nodded my head to indicate Tom Almand and Chuck, and after scanning the crowd with a blank face, Tolliver gave me a significant look to let me know he'd spotted them. As if he could feel our gazes, Almand turned a bit and looked straight at us. I thought he would look disgusted, or angry, or anguished. What does the father of such a child feel? I didn't have a clue, but I was fairly sure it would be a painful mixture of emotions.

Tom Almand looked blank. I couldn't even be sure he recognized me.

Okay, that was freaky. I would have added forty more dollars to the collection plate if I could have heard what Almand was thinking.

"Huh," Tolliver said, which put it in a nutshell.

Then the collection was over, and everyone settled back into receptive silence. But a stir went through the crowd when a stubby man in a bad suit rose from the front pew and went to the lectern.

"Those of you don't know me, I'm Abe Madden," he said, and there was another little ripple of movement. "I know that some of you blame me for not realizing sooner that those boys were being killed. Maybe, like some of you think, I let what I *wanted* get in the way of what I *should*. I wanted those

boys to be okay, just out sowing a few wild oats. I should have been looking harder for them, asking harder questions. Some in my own department told me that." He might have been looking at the current sheriff when he said that. "Some in my department thought I was right. Well, we know now I was wrong, and I ask your forgiveness for a great mistake I made. I was your servant while I was in office, and I let you down." And he went back to his seat.

I'd never heard anything like that before. What it must have cost the man in pride to do that . . . I couldn't even imagine. Tolliver was less impressed. "Now he's confessed and asked for forgiveness," he whispered. "Can't anyone point fingers at him anymore; he's paid his debt."

A member of each family spoke, some briefly, some at length, but I heard very little fire and brimstone. I expected some homophobic stuff, given the nature of the murders, but I didn't hear any. The anger was directed at the rape, not at the sexual preference of the rapist. Only two family members spoke of vengeance, and then only in terms of the law catching the responsible party. There was no lynch talk, no fist shaking. Grief and relief.

The last speaker said, "At least now we know this is at an end. No more of our sons will die." At that, I saw a sudden movement in the Bernardos' pew. Manfred was gripping Xylda by the arm, and her face was turned toward his. She looked angry and urgent. But after a few seconds, she subsided.

We might as well have left then, for all I got out of the rest of the service. I was drowsy and uncomfortable, and I wanted nothing more than to lean my head on Tolliver's shoulder and fall asleep. That would clearly be the wrong thing to do, so I focused on sitting up straight and keeping my eyes open. At last the service was over, and we sang a closing hymn. Then we could go. I stepped out of the pew first since I was on the end, and a grizzled man in overalls took my hand. "Thank you, young lady," he said, and then began making his way out of the church without another word. He was the first of many people who made a point of touching me: a light hug, a grip of the hand, a pat on the shoulder. Each contact came with a "Thank you," or a "God bless you and keep you," and each time I was surprised. This had never happened to me before. I was sure it would never happen again. Doak Garland embraced me when we reached his spot at the door, his white hands light on my shoulders so he wouldn't hurt me. Barney Simpson, towering over me, reached out to give me a light pat. Parker McGraw said, "Bless you," and Bethalynn wept, her arms around her remaining son.

No one asked me a single question about how I'd found the boys. The faith of Doraville seemed to hinge on the acceptance of God's mysterious ways and the strange instruments he selects to perform his will.

I was the strange instrument, of course.

eight

~~~

THERE were a couple of cars behind us on the long road out to Pine Landing Lake. Of course, the little hamlet of Harmony was past the lake, and there were other people in residence at the lake itself, so I told myself not to be crazy. After we turned off, the other cars continued on their way. Tolliver didn't comment one way or the other, and I didn't want to sound paranoid, so I didn't say anything.

We hadn't left on an outside light—in fact, I wasn't even sure if there was one—and I tried to mark the location of the stairs before Tolliver cut the ignition. We had a few seconds before the headlights turned off, so I hurried as much as I could to start up while I could see my way. There was a noise from the underbrush, and I said, "What the hell is that?" I had to stop and look, and then I saw a lumbering small shape scoot across the driveway and into the thicket between ours and the next vacant cabin, barely visible through the thick growth of trees and brush.

"Coon," Tolliver said, relief clear in his voice. Just then the headlights cut out and we made our way up to the cabin in an anxious silence. Tolliver had gotten the key out, and after some fumbling he managed to turn it the right way. My fingers scrabbled on the wall, trying to find the light switch. Contact! In a split second, we had the miracle of electric light.

The fire had died down in our absence, and Tolliver set about building it back up. He was really into being Frontier Man, and I suspected he was feeling very macho. Not only was his kinswoman wounded (me), requiring his care and attention, but he had to provide fire for me. Soon he would start to draw on the walls about hunting the buffalo. So I was smiling at him when he turned around, and he was startled.

"You ready for bed?" he asked.

"I'm sure ready to put on my pajamas and read," I said. It was pathetically early, but I was exhausted. He opened my suitcase and got out my flannel sleep pants and the long-sleeved thin top that had come with them. He'd given the set to me for Christmas, and it was dark blue with silver crescent moons on the pants and silver sparkles on the top. I hadn't quite known what to say when I'd opened the box, but I'd grown to like them.

"Are you going to need me to help?" he asked, trying hard to keep any trace of embarrassment out of his voice. We were pretty matter-of-fact about brief glimpses of each other that sometimes occurred when we shared a room, but somehow his assisting me with my clothes was a little more personal.

I ran through the process in my head. "I'll need help getting my shirt off," I said, "and unhooking my bra." A nurse had helped me get it on that morning.

I went into the very rudimentary bathroom, which was several degrees colder than the main room since it was farthest from the fireplace, and began the unexpectedly complicated task of getting my clothes off and my pajamas on. My socks defeated me, though. We'd put out some towels before we left, and I scrubbed my face, which would just have to do for tonight. After a few groans and some cursing, I had my pajama bottoms on, my shirt half off, and I backed out of the bathroom so Tolliver could help with the rest.

There was a long moment of silence. Then he said, "There's a lot of bruising on your arms and ribs," and his voice was tight.

"Yeah, well," I muttered. "When someone hits you with something big, that's what happens. Get the bra, okay? I'm freezing."

I barely felt his fingers as he took care of the hooks. "Thanks," I said, and scurried back into the bathroom. When my mission was accomplished, I gathered up my discarded clothes and brought them out with me, shoving my shoes ahead of me with my foot. I'd kept my socks on. It was just too cold to take them off.

Tolliver had turned down my sheets and blankets for me, and propped up the pillows. My book was on the bedside table; but my bad arm would be toward that side. I hadn't thought about that when I'd picked the usual bed.

He held the covers up while I maneuvered myself into bed. Then he covered me up. Oh, even on this lumpy old bed, being on my back felt divine.

"I'm all tucked in," I said, already feeling sleepier. "Gonna read me a story?"

"Read your own damn story," Tolliver said, but he was smiling, and he bent over to give me a kiss. "You've been a real trouper today, Harper. I'm proud of you."

I couldn't see what I'd done that day that had been so outstanding. I said so. "It's just been another day," I said, my eyelids drifting shut.

He laughed, but if he said anything in response, I missed it.

When I woke up, it was daylight. I hadn't even had to get up to use the bathroom during the night. Tolliver was still asleep in the bed to my left. There weren't any curtains up over the big windows in the cabin—maybe they'd been taken down for the winter, or maybe the family just dispensed with them out here—and I could see trees outside. I turned my head and looked over the hump that was Tolliver to peer out the glass doors onto the big porch outside. Was it a porch, or a balcony? It was on the second floor of the structure. . . . I decided it was a porch, and I could see that it was no weather to stand outside on it. The sky was clear and beautiful, and the wind was blowing; it looked cold, somehow. If the weatherman had been correct, this would be the high point of the day.

Maybe we would get to leave today, start up to Pennsylvania. It would be just as cold there, if not colder; but maybe we could dodge the predicted winter storm. I would never see Twyla Cotton again, probably. Maybe I would see

Chuck Almand again on the news in a few years, when he got arrested for killing someone. His dad would cry and wonder what he'd done wrong. After we left Doraville, the town would get back to its business of mourning its dead and accommodating its media visitors. The funeral directors would have an unexpected surge in profits. The hotels and restaurants would, too. Sheriff Rockwell would be glad to see the last of the state boys. They'd be glad to leave Doraville and return to wherever they were based.

Manfred and his grandmother would go back to their home in Tennessee. Sometime in the next few months, Xylda would die. Manfred would be on his own, begin his own career of providing psychic insights to the ignorant and the educated. Sometimes he'd be sincere, and sometimes he wouldn't. I thought about Tolliver's surprising paranoia concerning Manfred. I smiled to myself. It was true I found Manfred intriguing, if he wasn't exactly my inner pinup poster. His confidence that he could please me, and his conviction that I was desirable . . . well, what woman doesn't enjoy that? That's pretty potent. But as far as actually following through on it . . . it was probably more fun to flirt with Manfred than actually carry the attraction to the next level. Though I wasn't much older than him in years, in other ways I felt I was way too much his senior.

I really needed to get up to visit the bathroom. With a reluctant sigh, I worked my way out of the covers and sat up. This low bed was not good for such maneuvering, and it was hard keeping quiet, but I wanted to let Tolliver sleep as long as he could. He'd had the harder row to hoe the day before, having to take care of me.

Finally, I was on my feet and heading to the bathroom. That necessary task done, I brushed my hair one-handed, with a very lopsided result, and brushed my teeth a bit more efficiently. I felt better immediately. When I opened the door as quietly as possible, I saw that Tolliver wasn't moving, so I padded over to the fireplace and eyed the remaining embers. Carefully, I added more wood, trying to keep the arrangement tight but with ventilation as Tolliver had done. To my gratification, the fire picked right up. Hah!

"Good job," said Tolliver, his voice heavy with sleep. I eased into one of the two ancient wooden chairs he'd arranged in front of the fire. Its faded cushion smelled of damp and some long-ago dog. Of course the family would put their castoffs out here. No point buying special furniture for a place where they came to relax, where they'd be coming in wet from swimming. Also, the cabin was pretty vulnerable to theft, and who wants to tempt thieves with something valuable? I told myself how grateful I was to Twyla for letting us stay here, for free and away from the reporters. But at the same time, I admitted to myself that I'd much rather be in the motel, at least from a comfort standpoint.

Tolliver had his cell phone plugged in and charging, and now it rang.

"Crap," he said, and I agreed with the sentiment. The last thing I wanted to do was talk to anyone.

"Hello," he said, and after that all I heard was, "I guess we can," and "Okay," very noncommittal stuff. He hung up and groaned.

"That was the SBI agent, Klavin. He wants us to come into the station in an hour."

"I have to have coffee before I face any cops," I said.

"Yeah, no shit." He got out of bed and stretched. "You sleep okay?"

"Yeah, I don't think I moved all night." I did some stretching myself.

"I'll go shower. What are you going to do about that?"

"I'll have to take a sort of sponge bath, I guess. I can't get these bandages wet." That was another thing that was going to grow old very quickly.

"Okay, I'll hurry." Tolliver can take the quickest showers of anyone I know, and he was out and toweling his hair while I was still trying to assemble a set of clothes for the day. I managed to get my pajamas off by myself, and I managed to clean myself—more or less—but getting dressed was a real ordeal. I was trying to balance modesty with need, and it wasn't an easy achievement. Putting on my underwear turned out to be literally a pain in the butt, and I had to maneuver endlessly to get my bra up my arms and get my boobs in the cups so Tolliver could hook it.

"Geez, I'm glad I don't have to wear one of these things," he grumbled. "Why don't they fasten in front? That would make more sense."

"There are some that hook in front. I just don't have any."

"You give me your size, I'll get you some for your birthday."

"I'd like to see you shopping in Victoria's Secret."

He grinned.

We had a few extra minutes to go into McDonald's for their alleged pancakes. I pay lip service to hating McDonald's, but the pancakes were good and so was the coffee. And God, it was so warm in there. The windows were steamed up. The place was full of burly men in bulky jackets, mostly in camo patterns. They all wore big boots and had freshly shaved faces. Some of them would be going to work out at the crime scene, and some of them would be going about their usual business. Even the presence of death wouldn't stop life as usual in Doraville. That was a comforting thought, if one I'd had about a million times before. A job like mine makes you a big "river of life" person.

I hated to leave the homey atmosphere of McDonald's— okay, I guess it's pretty bad if you think McDonald's is homey—for the unpleasant interview ahead. But we wanted to be on time, and we hoped they would let us leave town after. Tolliver had left our stuff at the cabin, though. He said it wouldn't take long to swing back by and throw our stuff into the suitcases if we were allowed to leave. And we'd have to straighten up the cabin a little and return the key.

We ran the gauntlet of the press since we had to park in front that day. There wasn't a friendly officer at the gate to the rear parking lot to let us through, and we hadn't thought about calling ahead. The ranks of the fourth estate seemed a little thin today, and I wondered if the forensic people were still digging at the barn. I got through the re-maining light crowd with a few "No comment"s, and they didn't dare follow us into the station.

When we were settled at the table in a conference room, carefully nursing our extra cups of coffee we'd brought with us, we had quite a little wait. Spread out on the table was a big map marked "Don Davey Property." The drawing was liberally marked up. From where we sat, Tolliver had a hard time reading the print, but I gave him a superior sneer and read the labels.

"The first grave is marked 'Jeff McGraw,' and all the others are marked with the name of the boy that was in there," I said. I caught myself talking in a very low voice, as if I could disturb the dead. "The two graves where the boys weren't local, they have names on them, too. Maybe there was ID on the bodies. The northernmost one reads 'Chad Turner,' and the other one is 'James Ray Pettijean.'" I scooted my chair a little closer to Tolliver's. "I guess they're all being autopsied now," I said. It really didn't make any difference what happened to the body after the soul was gone; it was dross. Somehow, there being so many of them gave me the cold grue.

"There wasn't anything *remaining* at the grave site?" Tolliver asked, careful of the fact that ears might be listening.

"No," I said, just as carefully. No souls, no ghosts; and there's a big difference. I've seen souls lingering around fairly fresh bodies every now and then. I've only seen one ghost.

Pell Klavin and Max Stuart came in just then. The two SBI agents looked very tired. I wondered if there were more agents coming to help them. The two men dragged out chairs and slumped in them, right across from us; between us lay the map.

"What can you tell us that we don't already know?" Stuart said.

I was irritated that he didn't even try to observe a common courtesy, but then I thought of poring over the dead boys' biographies all night, and I excused the two agents. I wouldn't have been inclined to offer meaningless courtesies, either.

"Probably nothing," I said. "All I do is find bodies. I'm good at that, but I'm not a detective."

"We can't keep finding them like this."

"That's all of them, I think. That's surely all the dead on that piece of property."

"How do you know he hasn't buried a few somewhere else?"

"I don't. But there's no cutoff date."

They both leaned forward, eager for an explanation.

"There's a wide spread of death dates," I said. "There's years' worth of killing, at least six. And the McGraw boy's only been dead three months. Unless the killer's been active for a very long time, chances seem good that all his victims are there together. He may have an earlier burial ground. He'll start a new one, for sure. But I'm thinking that one probably has all the past few years' victims in it." I shrugged. Just my opinion.

Stuart and Klavin exchanged glances.

"Oh, and all the ones that are there, they were all killed in the same place," I said. "So it seems to me if that's the favored killing spot, all the bodies are there."

Stuart looked pleased. "Yes, we think they all died in the old shed there on the property."

I was glad we hadn't opened the sagging doors while we were there. I didn't want to know what it looked like inside. From my moments with the dead, I had too clear an idea as it was.

"Is . . . is there another site you'd like me to check?" I dreaded them saying yes—but Max Stuart shook his head.

"We don't know how you do what you do," he said. "If we hadn't seen the results, we'd never believe you. But we've seen all the bodies, and we've heard how you found them, and no amount of investigation can find any link you ever had with any living soul here. So we have to believe you actually have some uncanny ability. We don't know its dimensions or its limits. Is there anything you can tell us about these boys?"

That must have been incredibly hard for him to say. I started to deny it automatically, but then I thought again. I'd explain as closely as I could. "I see the moment of death," I said. "I see their bodies in the grave. Hold on," I said, and I shut my eyes, gripping the arm of my chair with my good hand and hugging the bad arm close to me. The clothes had been thrown down into the grave. . . .

"Most of them had crosses, right?" I said. Klavin started. Stuart glanced back at the board, as though this was printed right above the boys' names. "But this is a religious community, and that may be a coincidence." I looked back at the bodies, staring down into the earth in my memory. Oh, there. "Broken bones," I said. "Some of them have broken bones."

"Not from the torture?" Tolliver asked me.

"Well, yeah, some fresh ones from the torture. But at some time in the past, at least four of them had broken a bone." I shrugged.

"Does that mean they were all abused as children? Is that the common thread?" Agent Stuart bent forward, as if he could pull the answer out of my head. "What did these boys have in common? Why were they picked?"

"I don't know. I see what I see in a total flash: body, emotions, the situation. Once I saw the dead guy's pet, or maybe I just picked up on that from the dying person's thoughts. I don't see the person who caused that death."

"Just tell us everything you do know," Klavin said.

I looked from one to the other, suspiciously. They would listen, sure, and then give me those long-suffering looks that said they didn't believe a word I'd said. I'd had investigators tell me that before. "Oh, please, any little detail will help. . . ." Then it was like, "Oh, that's all you can do? What good is that?"

"We promise we'll be respectful," Klavin said, interpreting my look correctly. "We realize you've had trouble with law enforcement agents in the past."

I thought about it. I thought about the check Twyla Cotton had tucked into my hand the night before, the check that was over and above the amount we'd agreed upon for finding her grandson. I thought about the families crowded into the church, the grief and fear. Balanced against ridicule from men I'd never see again, that ridicule seemed like nothing.

So I took a deep breath, closed my eyes to help me concentrate, and looked into one of the graves again. I picked the one closest to the road. I pointed at it on the drawing. "This is Tyler," I said. "He's been tortured. His skin was cut off in strips. He was raped. Clamps were put on his testicles. He was ready to die and welcomed death, because he knew no help was coming. The cause of death was strangulation. Some time in the recent past, he'd broken his leg."

There was a quick intake of breath from one of the agents. I didn't open my eyes to see which one. Tolliver took my hand, and I gripped his hard. In my mind, I walked to the next grave. "Hunter," I said. "Whipped, fucked, branded. He thought someone would come, right until the end. Lived for two days. Hypothermia." Hunter had died in weather like this, cold and damp. The November abduction, I guessed. "No broken bones. He had . . . scoliosis." I saw the curve of his spine, shining below me.

It went on, the litany of torture and death. Sex and pain. Young men, used up and discarded. The two transient boys had had no particular bone problems, but the locals had . . . except for Jeff McGraw and Aaron Robertson. So that was fifty percent. The broken bones were a dead end.

They'd died of a variety of reasons. Most of the reasons were oddly passive, like the strangling and hypothermia that had killed Tyler and Hunter.

"Passive?" Klavin sounded indignant. He pulled a white handkerchief out of his pocket and patted his nose. He'd caught a cold probing around the killing site. "Abducted, tortured, raped. That sounds pretty damn active to me."

"That's not what I'm trying to express," I said. "They were let to die. They weren't stabbed or shot or poisoned, something that would cause instant, sure death. Hunter was just left there, and he died. Maybe weather interfered with their visits, maybe he—the killer—was bored with him. The strangulation—well, you can change your mind at the last few seconds on that, too."

"I see what you mean," said Stuart. "Like the death was kind of an afterthought, or an experiment."

"Like the pleasure didn't come with the death, but with what lay before," I said. "The pain was the attraction. And once they were all used up, and there wouldn't be any more reaction from them, they were no good anymore." But that wasn't quite right. Stuart's comment about it being an experiment was closer to the thought I was trying to express.

Tolliver looked nauseated.

"That's not what we're getting from the other psychic," Klavin said in challenge. "She says that the killer sat and watched for the moment of death, taking an 'orgasmic' pleasure from it."

"Then Xylda's probably right," I said instantly. "I'm not a psychic, and she is. Or maybe . . ." But then I stopped. Both the agents were looking at me with that expression I knew so well. It said, as clearly as if they'd spoken out loud: *Watch her. She's going to back and fill and try to dovetail her imaginings with the story the other freak told us.*

"Did you ever think," I said very slowly, very reluctantly, "that there might be two killers?"

They were both goggling at me. I can't interpret the living nearly as well as I can the dead. I'd done well with the two state agents so far, but I had no idea what their faces were saying now.

"That's all I can tell you," I said, and I got up to leave. Tolliver hastily got to his feet, too. "Can we leave town?" I asked. "Whenever we choose?"

"As long as you let us know how to reach you, you and your brother can hit the road," Stuart said, in a tone that implied he'd be glad to see the back of us.

"I'm *not* her brother," Tolliver said. He sounded as angry as if they'd been arguing about it for the previous hour.

Stuart looked surprised. "All right, then. Whatever," he said, shrugging. "You two can go."

I was so astonished by Tolliver's outburst that I had to fumble to gather up my purse and follow him out. He almost left me in his cloud of dust. He proceeded clear on out of the station, with me trailing behind. With a little awkwardness with the doors, I was slowed down enough that I just reached him when he got to our car. He was standing with his hands on the hood, glaring down at the gray paint. The remaining newspeople were shouting at us, but we completely ignored them.

I had no idea what to say. I just stood there and waited. I would have gotten in the car, but he had the keys in his hand. The mist in the air began to get heavier, become almost-rain. I was miserable.

Finally he straightened up, and without a word to me, he clicked the doors open. I stepped down from the curb to the door on the passenger side, opened it and got in, pulled it closed. Thank God it was my left arm that was out of whack. Still silently, Tolliver leaned over me to pull my seat belt around and click it shut.

"Where?" he said.

"The doctor's office."

"You hurting?"

"Yes."

He took a deep breath. He held it for a minute. Let it out. "I'm sorry," he said, leaving it open as to what he was sorry about.

"Okay," I said, not really sure what ground we were

walking on. I had a few ideas. Some of them were more frightening than others.

Tolliver had pinpointed the location of the doctor's office earlier on one of his drives to and from the hospital. Dr. Thomason's red brick office was small, but the parking lot contained at least six cars. When I went in, I anticipated a long wait. The man who was not my brother went up to the window, told the woman behind it who I was and that I'd seen the doctor at the emergency room.

"We'll have to work her in, hon, it may take a little bit," she said, reaching up to push her glasses back on her nose. Then she patted her helmet of sprayed hair lightly, to make sure it was still in good shape, I guess. Tolliver was working his old magic. He brought back a clipboard with forms to fill out.

"Apparently, we'll have plenty of time to do this," he said, for my benefit. I was in a blue molded plastic chair against the far wall, and he came to join me. In the waiting room with us were a young mother and her baby, who was blessedly asleep, an elderly man with a walker parked in front of him, and a very nervous teenage boy, who was one of the tribe of foot jigglers.

A nurse in teal came to the door and called, "Sallie and Laperla!" The young mother, hardly more than a teenager herself, got up with the infant carrier cradled in her arms.

"I wonder if she knows La Perla is a brand of underwear," I murmured to Tolliver, but that barely got a smile from him.

The boy scooted down the line of chairs until he was

within conversational distance of us. "You the one found the bodies," he said.

We both looked at him. I nodded.

Now that he'd told me who I was, he was stumped to think of something else to tell me. "I knew all them," he said finally. "They was good boys. Well, maybe Tyler got into a little trouble now and then. And Chester, he wrecked his dad's new Impala. But we went to youth group together, at Mount Ida."

"All of you?"

" 'Cept Dylan, he's a Catholic. They got their own youth group. But the rest of the churches, they all go together at Mount Ida."

Ordinarily, I'd be bored stiff by this conversation, but I wasn't today.

"Did you read the stories in the paper today?" I asked.

"Yep."

"You ever met those two boys from out of town?"

He looked surprised. "No, never," he said. "I never heard of 'em. I think they were hitching or something. They were from way far away."

I hadn't read the whole story. "Way far away" to this boy might mean Kentucky or Ohio. He meant only that the two out-of-towners weren't from North Carolina.

The young mother came out, her baby crying now. They stopped at the window for a minute, then went out the front door. I could see the rain increasing. She would have to run for her car. The nurse called the old man, who got slowly and carefully to his feet. He shuffled through the door to the inner sanctum preceded by his walker, which had sliced-open tennis balls fixed on the front feet. It gave the walker a jaunty air. As soon as he was through the door, the nurse also called, "Rory!" Our companion jumped to his feet and hurried back.

Now that we were by ourselves, I thought Tolliver would talk to me, but he leaned back and closed his eyes. He was shutting me out on purpose, and I didn't know what to make of it. If he was just in a snit over some unknown issue, then I could be in a snit right back. If I'd hurt him somehow, or he was harboring some personal grief unknown to me, then I wanted to help him. But if he persisted in being a butt-head, then he could just stew in his own juice.

I leaned my own head against the wall, closed my own eyes.

We probably looked like prize idiots.

After about ten minutes of this, the old man made his way out, and Rory sped past him to hold the door open. "Allergy shot!" he called to us cheerfully as the old man shuffled past. I didn't know if he was explaining about his own visit or the old man's, but I nodded in acknowledgment.

The nurse opened the door yet again. She was a pretty, trim woman of about forty-five, with dark hair and bright blue eyes. She was so healthy and cheerful that I felt better just looking at her. "Miss Connelly," she said, and looked at us curiously.

Tolliver leaped to his feet and reached down to help me get up. This was just plain weird. I took his hand, and he hauled. The nurse showed us back to our designated waiting room. She weighed me and measured me and took my blood pressure, which was just fine. Then she began to ask me questions. It was mostly a repeat of what was on the forms, and the stuff from the hospital.

"So you just wanted to see Dr. Thomason today to get him to check up on your injuries?" She sounded a little dubious.

"Yes, I'm having more pain than I'd expected, though that may be because I'm so very, you know, depressed."

"Oh, I guess in your line of work, that would be . . . understandable."

"But surely—excuse me—you must be feeling the same way, here in Dr. Thomason's office."

"Because most of the boys were patients of ours? Yes, it's a sad thing. A sad, sad thing. You never think something like that would happen to anyone you know. And we knew all those boys, though a couple were patients of Dr. Whitelaw's."

"And Jeff's grandmother said he'd been in here recently," I lied.

"Oh, you must have misunderstood her. Jeff goes to Dr. Whitelaw."

"I must have, sorry."

"No problem. Let me tell Dr. Thomason you're ready." She sped out on her soft-soled nurse's shoes, and before I could think everything through, Dr. Thomason breezed in. "Hello, young lady. Marcy tells me you're not feeling as well as you'd hoped. You've been out of the hospital—let's see— just since yesterday? That right?" He shook his head, as though keeping track of the passing time was an incredible task. "Well, let's have a look at you. No fever, blood pressure good," he muttered, checking what Marcy had written on the chart. He ignored Tolliver as if Tolliver weren't there.

Dr. Thomason looked and thumped, and felt, and listened. He asked questions very quickly, hardly seeming to give himself time to absorb the answers . . . as if he did not believe I would tell him the truth, or as if he weren't interested in the truth. He came to stand right in front of me. Since I was up on the examining table, his eyes were slightly lower than mine, and as he looked up at my face his eyes looked almost luminous behind his gold-rimmed glasses.

He smiled at me. "You seem fine to me, Ms. Connelly. You're doing well as anyone could hope, after being attacked the way you were. No cause for alarm. You're healing right on schedule. Still got plenty of pain pills, I hope?"

"Oh, yes," I said.

"Good. If they were all gone, I would worry about you. I think you're good to go. You're simply not going to feel wonderful for a while."

"Oh. Okay, then, thanks for seeing me."

"Right. Good luck. You're cleared to travel." And he strode out, white coat flapping around his legs. He was delighted that I was leaving town, there was no two ways about it. Tolliver came over to help me down from the examining table, and we left in silence, paying on the way out. I glanced at the big filing cabinet in the receptionist's area. If I were a daring detective, I would think of way to get the receptionist and the nurse out of the way and look through the files of the dead boys. But I wasn't, and there wasn't an excuse on this earth that would get the receptionist, the nurse, and the doctor out of the way long enough for me to do more than roll open the relevant drawers. Women did this all the time in movies and on television. They must have better scriptwriters. Real life didn't afford chances to examine private records unless you just broke in at night and read them, and I wasn't about to do that. My need to know who had done this would only carry me so far. I wouldn't risk going to jail myself.

And, I asked myself, why was I even concerned? The law enforcement people on hand were trained and efficient, and they had all the labs and their own expertise at their beck and call. They would find who'd done this, I had very little doubt. And the deaths would cease. Someone would go to jail after a long and lurid trial.

"There's something nagging me about this," I said. I had to break the silence or burst. "There's something wrong about this whole thing."

"Something wrong, aside from eight dead kids?" Tolliver's voice was level, but his words were edgy.

"Yes. Something wrong."

"Like what?"

"I just think that someone's in danger."

"Why?"

"I don't know. There's just . . . where are you going?"

"Back out to the cabin."

"Are we leaving?"

"The doctor said you were good to go."

I turned on the car radio. After the warmth of the morning, the temperature was dropping sharply, just as predicted.

"And what's the weather news, Ray?" asked a female voice on one of the local stations.

"In a few words, Candy, the news is . . . stay home!

There's an ice storm on the way, and you don't want to get caught in it. The highway patrol is advising all motorists to stay home tonight. Don't try to travel. Wait until the morning, and get another road advisory then."

"So, Ray, we should bring in a lot of firewood and rent a lot of old movies?"

"Yeah, you can watch 'em until your electricity goes out!" Ray said. "Get out your board games and flashlights and candles and stock up on water, folks."

They went on for two more minutes, advising people in the area on how to weather the storm.

Without saying a word, we stopped at the little Wal-Mart.

"Stay in the car," Tolliver said roughly. "You'll just get jostled." It was really crowded, and people were coming out with carts full of emergency stuff, so I didn't argue. We keep a throw blanket in the back of the car all winter, and I pulled it around me as he made his way inside.

Since there were only two of us to provide for and since we didn't plan on staying in the area any longer than we could help, Tolliver didn't have that much shopping to do. Nonetheless, it was at least forty-five minutes before he came out of the store with his buggy.

When we got back to the lake, we parked right by the stairs, about halfway down the steep drive. I decided I could help by moving one thing at a time from the car trunk to the middle of the stairs up to the living quarters, with pretty much a level swing of my arm. Then Tolliver could come down a few steps and get the stuff and put it away. It saved him a little work, and I felt like I was contributing. But I was shaking by the time we finished.

There was one more thing I needed to do. As a last-minute precaution, I backed the car up the sloping driveway and parked it parallel to the road. It wasn't a neat job since I was driving one-handed, but least we wouldn't have to negotiate an iced-over slope. I locked the car and went down the driveway and up the steps, moving carefully. The first licks of moisture were in the air.

Ted Hamilton came over a little later to make sure we'd heard the news about the weather. His wife, Nita, came with him, and she was just as small and slim and spry as her husband. They both seemed pretty excited by the prospect of the oncoming ice storm.

Tolliver had brought up so much wood that I thought we might have to leave Twyla some money to pay for it. The older couple nodded approvingly and settled in for a nice conversation. We unfolded the remaining two chairs, which had been leaning up against the wall. They were cloth spectator chairs, and they smelled a little off, but at least there were chairs. I could only offer the Hamiltons bottled water and a chocolate chip cookie, after we'd thanked Nita for her wonderful casserole, which we planned on finishing up for supper.

"Oh, no, we're fine," Nita said, speaking for Ted and herself after a glance in his direction. "You know, we've always been worried about that pine growing behind this cabin."

"Why?" I asked.

"Pine roots are so shallow, and it overhangs this cabin," Ted said. "Pretty poor planning. I said something to Parker about it last summer, but he just laughed. I hope he's not sorry he didn't listen."

Okay, they were that kind of people.

"We're out here year-round, not like the people who just come here when it's good weather and everything's going well," Nita said. As if they were the people who really stuck with the poor lake when things weren't going so good. The true friends.

"We'll just have to hope the pine can handle the ice," Tolliver said. "Thanks for making us aware of it." He maybe spoke a little dryly, because Ted's face tightened up a bit.

"I hope it stays up, too," Ted said. "Hate for something to happen to you two. Specially since you're visiting."

"We're lucky to have you two out here," I said, to smooth over Ted's ruffled feathers. "I think I'd be scared if we were out here by ourselves."

That made Ted and Nita both happy. "We'll be right next door; don't forget to call us if you need us. We got all kinds of emergency gear, anything you might need."

"That's really good to know," I said, and they finally, thank God, rose. We kept assuring each other we were so happy to have the other there until they were really down the stairs and on their way back to their own cabin.

We had brought in a radio we kept in the trunk, and we turned it on. The weather news was still the same. The police news was still the same. I guess I'd harbored some wild hope that they'd arrest someone, some secret suspect. Or maybe someone would just walk in to confess, unable to bear the burden of guilt any longer. I said as much to Tolliver.

"A guy that could do this so often, to kids he knew," Tolliver said, "he's not going to walk in and say he's sorry unless he craves the attention. He's going to be pissed off that he can't do it again, that he has to relive all his old good times instead of making new ones. And you're the one responsible for that."

I stared at Tolliver. This was what had been griping him.

"I don't think so," I said, as calmly as I could. "I think he came to the motel in a fit of anger, sure enough. But I'd think right now he'd be most concerned about keeping his skin intact and remaining at large. He's not going to do anything that would draw him to police attention. He's going to lie completely low."

Tolliver thought that over; I'll give him that. "I hope so," he said, sounding unconvinced. He went to the window and looked out into the darkness. "Can you hear it?" he asked.

I went to stand beside him at the window. I could hear a *plink-plink-plink* as the ice hit the glass. In the light that spilled from the window and the big security light, considerately aimed straight down, that the Hamiltons had fixed high on a pole, we could see tiny bits of ice hurtling toward the ground. It was eerily pretty. I had never felt so isolated in my life.

It didn't stop while we got ready for bed. I was tired, but not nearly as achy as I thought I would be. My head was okay now, and my arm was at least much better. I was able to cope with getting undressed and into my pajamas with less help, though Tolliver still had to do the bra-unhooking. We both read for a while; as Tolliver remarked, if we still had electric light we should use it. He was reading an old Harlan Coben, and I was reading Gavin de Becker's *The Gift of Fear*. Finally, I got too sleepy to keep my eyes open, and the bed had gotten warm around me, and I laid down the book and closed my eyes. Some time later, I heard Tolliver snap off the lamp between the beds, and then the only light that came in the room was a faint glow from the Hamiltons' security light. I'd been too exhausted to notice it the night before, and I didn't really think about it now . . . until I woke some time later and that light had vanished. The cabin was in absolute pitch darkness. The wind was howling around the corner of the cabin like a banshee, and I heard an odd sound in the wind.

"What is it?" I asked, and I heard myself sounding terrified.

"It's the frozen branches brushing together," Tolliver said. "I woke a few minutes ago and I've been listening. That's what I decided."

I scare pretty easy where Mother Nature's involved. "Okay," I said, but I didn't sound any calmer.

"Come over here, I'm closer to the fire," Tolliver said. "Bring some blankets."

I got out of the bed faster than I would have believed possible. My bare feet thudded on the boards as I yanked the blankets off my bed and brought them over to Tolliver's. I tossed them over the bed awkwardly. I slid in beside him and could hardly wait until the covers settled back over us. My teeth were chattering with cold and fear.

"Here, here," he said, and put his arms around me. "You were just out of the covers for a second or two."

"I know," I said. "I'm a chicken. I'm a wuss." I burrowed into his warmth.

"You're the bravest person I know," he said, and when I

pressed my face into his chest, he said, "Are you listening to me?"

I pulled away enough to say, "Yeah, I'm listening."

"I'm not your brother," he said, in an entirely different voice.

For a second, I didn't hear the roar of the wind around the cabin or the ominous shaking of the ice-laden branches. "I know," I said. "I know that."

And he kissed me.

I'd loved him for so long. Though everything might change, would change, I couldn't help but kiss him back.

It was a long kiss, a hard kiss. I'd seen him walk out so many doors with other women, and finally he was with me.

He started to say something, but I said, "No, don't." I kissed him again, my own initiation. That seemed to answer his question, if that was what he'd been going to ask. "It's you," I said, as he kissed my throat. I had my good hand under his sweatshirt, touching the precious skin of his back, his ribs, the almost flat nipples. I rubbed my face in the hair on his chest and his breath caught in his throat. His hands were not idle, either, and when they found my breasts he made another, altogether different noise. I thought I would weep with joy.

"The shirt's got to come off," he said, and we worked to do that. "Your arm?" he asked.

"Okay, don't worry about it," I whispered. "Just don't lie on it and it'll be okay." I felt like I could get hit with a shovel all over again and I wouldn't care right now. My body and my heart were fully engaged for the first time. His hands seemed to know where to go and what to do when they got there. We knew each other so well in every other respect, it seemed only natural that we would easily understand each other's desires in this new activity. We already knew the appearance of each other's bodies, but not the textures or specifics; now we set out to learn those. His phallus was long, not as thick as some I'd encountered. He'd been circumcised. He had a slight upward curve. He was very sensitive around his balls. I loved touching him in places I'd never had the right to touch him before, and he loved being free to touch me between my legs. He loved it, and his fingers could be very clever.

"I wish I could see you," he said, but I was glad for the dark. It made me a little braver, and I concentrated on my sense of touch, so I didn't have time to think. If I'd had time to think, it wouldn't have gone nearly as wonderfully as it did.

As it was, when we'd finally gotten off enough clothes, when I was sure neither of us was going to back down, when he finally entered me, it was the happiest moment of my life. I let go of my safety, and I said, "I love you."

And Tolliver said, "Always."

nine

~~~

"I wish you had some Kleenex," I murmured. I was resting on his chest. Our clothes were somewhere under the covers with us, or at least most of them were.

"Just use my sweatshirt," he said in a lazy voice, and I stifled a giggle.

I felt around us, maybe tickling him a little in the process, and located what felt like his sweatshirt. "I hope you weren't teasing, because I'm going to use it," I said.

"Go right ahead." He kissed the top of my head.

So I dried myself off a little, and patted him, too.

"Hey, be careful, that's my favorite body part," he murmured.

"Mine, too," I said, and he laughed. I felt his belly heave up and down. It was wonderful.

"I didn't think we'd ever do it," he said, sounding suddenly serious.

"Me, either. I thought I'd keep on watching you go off with waitresses."

"Or that cop, the one in Sarne. He really scared me. To say nothing of Manfred."

"Really?"

"Oh, yeah. I mean, the piercings and the tattoos, that's a lot to put up with, but he's so gone on you. And his grandmother won't live forever. I had a feeling Manfred would say that when Xylda passed away he'd be free to escort you around, and you'd want me to have the normal life you're always trying to shove on me, and you'd dump me and hire Manfred to be your manager, and I'd have to go find a job somewhere away from you."

"That's not going to happen, right?"

"Not if I have anything to say about it. And I do, right?"

"I believe I remember telling you how I felt about you."

"I could stand to hear it again."

"Uh-uh. You first."

"I love you. I don't love you like I should love a sister. I love you like a man loves a woman. I want to be inside you again, right now. I want to have sex with you over and over."

I had to stop myself from squeaking, *Really?* I took a deep breath. "Why?" I said, which might have been worse.

"Because you're beautiful and smart," he said instantly. "Because you always try hard, no matter what you're doing. Because you're honest, and because I've wanted to see your boobs for years now, and damn it, it's dark in here and I can't."

"I got to see your dick one time, when you got out of the shower and the door wasn't shut tight," I said. "It was a year ago."

"Oh, and you been dreaming about it ever since," he said hopefully.

"Well, actually . . . yes. But don't get a swelled head."

"That's not the head that's swelling."

"So I feel." I licked my thumb and ran it over the lower head.

"Oh, God."

I did it again.

He just drew in his breath this time. "Keep doing that," he said.

So I did, and then he found something to do to me that I liked, and we traded like that until we were ready to join again. This time was even better, and we reached the climax at the same time. I thought we would pound each other into pieces. This time he fell asleep almost as soon as we were through, and after I'd used his sweatshirt again, I did, too.

I was so deeply asleep the huge crash came as a complete surprise to me. In fact, it scared me so much I almost started screaming.

"Tree came down," said Tolliver. "It was a tree. Hold on, baby, it wasn't on us."

We scrambled into all our clothes. Tolliver rejected the sweatshirt with the simple remark "Damp," and found his suitcase by patting the area where it was supposed to be. He fished out another one, he told me, and I heard him fumbling around further. I'd gotten out of the bed on the other side and I was feeling the floor for my boots.

With lots of "Oops" and "Where are you? I found the flashlight," we finally connected and went to the window. Tolliver switched the flash on, and we looked outside. It was one of the big searchlight kind, and he'd gotten it at Wal-Mart that afternoon. It showed us that the pine tree the Hamiltons had been so worried about had indeed fallen under the weight of the ice. But due to some force we couldn't fathom, it had fallen at an angle and blocked the Hamiltons' driveway instead. I had an awful feeling their car was under it.

"Does their roof look okay?" I asked. But we couldn't tell.

"I guess I have to go to over and check on them," Tolliver said.

"I'll come," I said.

"No, you won't. Not with a broken arm, you're not getting out there to walk around on slick ice. If there's something wrong over there, I'll come back and get you," he said. "Hey, how's your arm feeling? We didn't bump it too much?"

"No, it's pretty good."

"So I'll be back in a few minutes."

I really couldn't argue with his reasons for wanting me to stay behind. It made sense.

I waited in the cold cabin while Tolliver worked his way down the ice-slick stairs and began a slow progress across the front yard of our cabin and over to the Hamiltons' place. I poked the fire and added a log, and then I pulled a chair over to the window and wrapped myself in a blanket.

Half of me was intent on following the light held in Tolliver's hand, while the other half was standing a little distance apart screaming, "You just slept with Tolliver! You just slept with Tolliver!" in tones of mingled horror and delight. Only time would tell if we'd just (literally) fucked up the best relationship we'd ever had—or if we'd opened the door to greater happiness.

Even thinking that felt sappy. But God, it might all be okay. I snapped out of this incoherent internal babbling to realize that Tolliver was having a hard time getting to the door of the Hamilton house because of the tree branches.

I opened the window, with a lot of effort. One-handed, it was a bitch.

"You need me to come help?" I called. My voice was startling.

I felt Tolliver was restraining himself from saying that was the last thing in the world he needed. "No, thanks," he called back, with wonderful restraint. Even hearing his voice made me catch my breath. There was something different about it, there was. Some tension that had kept him taut and stretched had snapped. I was as moony and dreamy as a girl who'd had her first French kiss, and I made myself enter the here and now.

The Hamiltons' door was opening, and I could see Ted Hamilton. He was wearing a hat, which looked ridiculous but actually was pretty smart, considering how much of your body heat you lose through your head. He and Tolliver exchanged a few words, and then Tolliver began making his way back over to our temporary home.

I opened the door when he reached the top of the steps, and he propelled himself inside.

"Oh, God, it's cold out there," he said, and he made a

beeline to the fire. He piled on a couple more pieces of wood and stood there for a moment, his face as close to the fire as he could get it without actually singeing his mustache. He closed his eyes with the bliss of the warmth.

"Were they okay?"

"Yeah. Mad. Ted said a few words I think he'd been saving up since the Korean War. I was glad I'm not a member of the McGraw-Cotton family. He actually said he was gonna sue."

"Wonder if he'd have a chance in court."

Tolliver held out a hand, tipped it one way then another. "I want to say that would be ridiculous, but you know how the justice system can be."

We fell silent, looked at each other.

"Are you sorry?" he asked.

"No. You?"

"We should have done it a long time ago. You kept saying I should leave you. I didn't know if that was what you wanted or not. I finally decided to sink or swim. You were thinking what?"

"I was thinking I loved you so much that I shouldn't keep you around me, because you must not find out I felt that way. I thought you might think it was gross or sick. Or . . . you might feel kind of sorry and responsible for me, which would be worse."

"As far as I'm concerned, you're the original lemons-into-lemonade girl," he said. "You get struck by lightning, and instead of wailing and moaning about it and applying for disability, you discover a usable skill and figure out a way to make it work for you. You've got the brains and the charisma to make it in your very own business."

"Charisma," I said scornfully.

"You do, or hadn't you noticed the way men like you?"

"Adolescent boys like me," I said. "That's not exactly a big plus."

"Not just adolescents," Tolliver said. "They just don't know how to hide it."

"You're saying I'm a guy magnet? Get real."

"Not in the sense that someone like, I don't know, Shakira or Beyonce is. You're not a blond shake-your-booty kind of girl, but you've got your very own attraction, and believe me, men feel it."

"As long as this man feels it," I said. I looked up into his face.

"You made me stop breathing there for a minute," he said.

I looked down and smiled. "At least you know everything bad about me already."

"I didn't know you made that sound when you came," he said, and I did a little not-breathing all my own.

"I didn't know you had that slight curve in your dick," I countered.

"Yeah . . . ah, how does that . . . I mean, is that okay?"

"Oh, yeah," I assured him. "Touches something wonderful inside me."

"Oh? Hmmm."

"And I wondered, if you were up for it . . ."

"Yeah?"

"You'd maybe touch it again?"

"I think you could persuade me. If you went to great lengths."

"Would you like me to go down on you?"

By the light of the flickering fire, I could see his pupils dilate. "Oh," he said.

"Lick you? Like this?" I extended my tongue and did a little flickering of my own.

"That would do the trick," he said hoarsely. "Jesus, Harper, I don't understand why we don't have guys following us from town to town just to watch you do that."

"Because I've never done it for anyone but you," I said. "You don't think I'd say something like that to anyone else, do you?"

"Please," he said. "Please do that for me. And no one else."

I knelt before him carefully, and pulled down his sweats and the long underwear he'd pulled on before his excursion to the Hamiltons'. Somehow, him still having clothes on seemed to make what I was doing even naughtier.

I looked up to make sure he was looking as I made good on my promise. Oh, yeah. He watched my every move as if I'd hypnotized him.

"Oh, my God," he said. He reacted in a very gratifying way.

In my limited experience, men were always so glad to get sex, they were pleased with it no matter how inexperienced their partner was. They weren't there to run a critique group. They were there to have an orgasm. Provided you put their penis in the correct hole and made enthusiastic noises, they went away happy. It was like signing up for basic cable. That was what you'd sign up for if you were getting it for a person you didn't know well.

"For you, baby, HBO," I said, and made him moan.

*   *   *

I woke the next morning to brilliant clear light coming through the bare windows. I blinked and shuddered. I burrowed deeper under the covers, closer to the other body in the bed. Tolliver! I was in bed with Tolliver and we were naked. I sighed with bliss and kissed his neck, which was the easiest thing to reach.

"I guess I have to stop calling you 'sis' now," he said, his voice heavy with sleep.

"Uh-huh."

"I guess Manfred is shit out of luck."

"Uh-huh."

"I guess the chainsaws we hear mean that there are people outside the cabin cutting up the tree, and we don't have any clothes on."

"Oh . . . no."

"Yeah, hear 'em?"

I did. Wouldn't you know that even though there were fifty empty cabins and houses around this lake, we'd be in the one that had neighbors? And I was going to have to get out of the warm bed to go to the bathroom, and I'd have to flush it by pouring water in. Yuck. And I definitely needed a sponge bath, for which I'd have to stand naked in the freezing bathroom, since there weren't any curtains on the windows and the stupid Hamiltons were out there trying to free their car from the clutches of the tree.

"I hope their car is a pancake," I said.

"You don't mean it."

"No. Yes. Sort of." I laughed. "I just don't want to get out of the bed."

"Do you think they'll stomp up the steps and look in?"

"Oh, yes, any minute." His hand found mine under the huge pile of blankets and he gripped my fingers tightly.

"I don't want to leave this bed, either," he said and kissed me. His hand released mine to skim across my ribs. "But I'm exhausted, too."

"Oh, poor thing. Did I wear you out?"

"I'm a shadow of myself."

"That's funny, you feel substantial enough," I said, rubbing my hand across his (okay, flat and muscular) belly.

"Woman, I need fuel," he said. "If I'm going to keep up with your insatiable demands."

"You haven't even met insatiable yet," I said. Then I dropped the smile. "I can't believe we did it, Tolliver. This is all I ever wanted."

"Me, too. But my metabolism is telling me to eat first and talk later."

I kissed him. "So shall it be." I slid my sweatpants back on and made a dash for the bathroom. Fifteen excruciatingly cold minutes later, I was more or less clean, and I was wearing several layers of clean clothes. I had on two pairs of socks and some rubber boots that Tolliver had pulled off the shelf at Wal-Mart the day before. While Tolliver took his turn in the bathroom, I looked on the shelves above the stove to find a cheap metal pan. I put some water in it and set it on a level place in the large fire. When there was a chance the water was fairly warm, I used Tolliver's folded-over sweatshirt to get the pan off the fire and I poured the hot water into two mugs with powdered hot chocolate in them. We had some Pop-Tarts. Sugar would help restore our energy.

Tolliver smiled when he saw a little steam coming up from the mugs. "Aw, that's great," he said. "Wonder Woman." We sat in the two chairs closest to the fire and drank and ate while we listened to the battery-powered radio. The roads were in terrible condition, and though the temperature would rise above freezing by the midafternoon, roads wouldn't be clear until the next morning. Even then, they'd be patched with ice. Power crews were out repairing downed power lines, which should be reported, and checking on isolated farms. Citizens were urged to check on their elderly neighbors. I glanced out the window. "The Hamiltons are okay, Tolliver," I said.

"Have you tried your cell phone?" he asked.

When I turned it on, I had a few messages.

The first one was from Manfred.

"Hey, Harper, my grandmother got real sick late yesterday, and she's in the hospital here in Doraville," Manfred said. The second message was from Twyla, hoping we were okay out there at the cabin. The third message was from Manfred. "It would be great if you and Tolliver would stop by; there are some issues about Grandmother I'd like to talk about," he said, very much as though he were trying to sound adult but not quite achieving it.

"That sounds bad," I said. "That sounds like turning-off-the-machines bad."

"Do you think we can make it into town?" Tolliver said. "I'm not even sure we can make it up the driveway."

174

"Did you not notice that I moved the car before the storm hit? It's up by the road."

"Where anyone trying to drive on that narrow road can bash it?"

"Where we won't have to get up an icy slope in it and possibly end up in the lake." Apparently, happy sex and our altered relationship didn't preclude our occasional squabble.

"Okay, that was a good idea," he said. "We'll see if we can get into town around noon, when whatever's going to melt has melted."

Somehow we never got around to talking further about what had happened between us, and somehow that was okay. Tolliver got restless, which I'd expected, and he bundled up and went outside to help Ted Hamilton for an hour or two. When he came back up the stairs, I could hear him stomping snow and ice off his boots. I was reading by the fire, and I was getting a little stir-crazy. I looked up expectantly, and he came over and bent to give me a casual kiss on the cheek, just as if we'd been married for years.

"Your face is freezing," I said.

"My face is frozen," he corrected me. "Did you call Manfred? We saw a car go by while we were out there working, and they made it okay."

"I'll call him now," I said, and found I had to leave a message on Manfred's voice mail.

"Probably has it turned off while he's inside the hospital," Tolliver said.

I opened my mouth to ask a few questions about our new relationship, and once again I saw the wisdom of closing it. After all, why would Tolliver know any more about it than me?

I relaxed and let the tension drain away. We would make this up as we went along. We didn't have to send out announcements. I did have a sudden awful thought. "Ah, this new thing we've got may be a little confusing for our sisters," I said.

I could tell from the expression on Tolliver's face that this hadn't occurred to him. "Yeah," he said. "You know . . . you're right about that. Mariella and Gracie . . . oh, God. Iona."

Our aunt Iona—well, strictly speaking, my aunt Iona— had gotten guardianship of our two half sisters, who were much younger than us. Iona and her husband were raising the girls in as different a way as possible from the life they'd led with my parents. And in a way, they were absolutely right. It was much better to be brought up as a fundamentalist Christian than as a kid who didn't know what a real meal was, a kid at the mercy of whatever scum our parents let into the trailer. Because that was the way I'd been brought up after my preteen years. Mariella and Gracie were well clothed, well fed, and clean, They had a stable home to come back to every day, and they had rules to follow. These were great things, and if their early years led them to rebel against this regimen now and then, well, so be it. We were trying to build bridges to the girls, but it was uphill work.

Iona's reaction to our new relationship hardly bore thinking about. "Ah, I guess that's a bridge we'll have to cross when we come to it," I said.

"We're not hiding anything," Tolliver said, with sudden firmness. "I'm not going to even attempt it."

That had a very nice permanent sound to it. I'd been sure how I felt, but it's always nice to know your partner is feeling the same way. I let out a silent sigh of relief.

"No hiding," I said.

We ate peanut butter sandwiches for lunch. "Ted's wife probably whipped up a four-course heart-healthy meal on a woodstove," I said.

"Hey, you eat heart healthy most of the time."

My eating habits had gone by the wayside while we stayed in Doraville, for one reason or another. I'd have to resume them soon. With variable health problems like I had, it paid to stave off as much as I could by following good rules.

"How's your leg?" Tolliver asked, following the same train of thought.

"Pretty good," I said, extending my right leg and rubbing the quads. "I can tell I haven't been running in a few days, though."

"When do you get to leave off the cast?"

"Five weeks, the doctor said. We'll have to try to be in St. Louis then, so I can check with our doctor there."

"Great." Tolliver smiled so broadly that I knew he was thinking of several things that would be much easier when my arm healed.

"Hey, come here," he said. He was sitting on the floor in front of the fire, leaning back against a chair. He patted the floor between his legs, and I eased myself against him. He put his arms around me. "I can't believe I can do this now," he said. If my heart could have wagged its tail, it would have. "It's okay to touch you. I can touch you as much as I want. I don't have to think twice every time."

"Were you really thinking twice?"

"I thought I might scare you off."

"Same here."

"Idiots."

"Yeah, but now we're okay."

We sat there in contentment until Tolliver told me his leg was asleep, and we figured if we were ever going to try to go into town, the time was right.

Ten

SEVERAL times during the trip into town, I was almost sorry I'd turned on my cell phone and gotten Manfred's message. That was the most frightening driving experience I've ever had. Tolliver managed it, but he said every bad word in his vocabulary, even a few I didn't quite understand. We met one other car on our journey, and it was filled with teenage boys, who all have a built-in death wish. As soon as I thought that, I remembered the boys in the frozen ground, and I was sorry.

There were mighty few visitors' cars parked in the hospital parking lot. Snow had covered the sodden yard around the little building, so it looked almost pretty. When we went in, the reception lady was not at her desk, so we wandered back until we found a nurses' station. We inquired there about Xylda Bernardo.

"Oh, the psychic lady," the nurse said, looking a bit impressed. "She's in ICU. Her grandson is in the ICU waiting area, if you want to see him." She gave us directions, and we found Manfred sitting with his head in his hands. He was in one of those waiting areas that's just a little nook lined with chairs and littered with coffee cups and old magazines. It looked as though the hospital cleaning staff hadn't made it in this morning. That wasn't good.

"Manfred," I said. "Tell us what's happening with Xylda?"

He raised his head and we could see his eyes were red. His face was tear-stained.

"I don't understand," he said. "She was better. She kind of collapsed last night, but this morning she was better. The doctor had been in to see her. The minister came and prayed with us. They were going to move her to a regular room. Then she just—I left just for a minute, just to get some coffee and use the phone—and when I came back she was in a coma."

"I'm so sorry," I said. There's really nothing you can say that'll make the situation any better, is there?

"What does the doctor say?" Tolliver asked. I sat beside Manfred and put my hand on his shoulder. Tolliver sat at right angles to us and leaned forward, his elbows on his knees. I looked at his face, so serious, so focused, and I felt a wave of love that almost knocked me over. I had to concentrate to get my mind back on Manfred and Xylda's misfortune.

"It's the same doctor that saw you, Harper," Manfred said. "The guy with white hair. He seems okay. He says he doesn't think she's going to wake up. He doesn't know why she took such a turn, but he says he's not surprised. It's all . . . it doesn't seem definite enough. No one's telling me exactly what's happening with her. I thought medicine was sharper than that now."

"Have you called your other relatives?"

"My mother is on her way. But in the traffic conditions between Tennessee and here, there's no way she'll get here before Grandmother passes away."

This was awful. "Your mom's relying on you to make the decisions?"

"Yeah. She says she knows I'll do the right thing."

What a great thing for a mother to say, but what a huge responsibility.

"I was hoping," Manfred said after a long moment, "if you could go in to see her, you'd be able to give me some advice." He was looking at me when he said this, and he said it very seriously. I understood what he meant, after a moment. He wanted to know if her soul was still there.

Okay. I was cringing inside, but I nodded.

He showed me the door to the ICU unit, which of course was quite small at such a little hospital. I thought Xylda would benefit from going to somewhere larger with more machines—isn't that what it boils down to?—but there was no way to get her there. Nature had overthrown technology once again. That seemed amazing to me, as I looked at all the machines Xylda Bernardo was connected to. They silently recorded everything that was going on inside her; and yet, when Manfred wanted to know something as basic as whether or not his grandmother's soul was still attached to her body, he had to ask me to do it.

I held Xylda's limp hand for a moment, but it wasn't

necessary for the task that had been set me. Xylda's soul was still there. I was almost sorry. It would have simplified the decisions ahead for her family if her soul had already departed.

Barney Simpson stuck his head in the door and looked at me quizzically.

"I thought we'd kicked you out," he said, keeping his voice low out of respect for the quiet figure on the bed.

"You make visits to the patients in the ICU?"

"No, to the families of those patients. I saw someone in here, so I came to check."

"I'm just standing in for her grandson for a minute," I said.

"You're a good friend. This is the other lady, right?"

"Xylda Bernardo. The psychic. Yes."

"She told the law enforcement people about Chuck Almand."

After a second, I nodded. That was more or less true. "Yes."

"What an extraordinary talent," Simpson said. He ran a hand over his bushy dark hair, trying to tame it, but he didn't have any luck.

"She's definitely out of a different mold," I said. I took a step toward the door. I wanted to report back to Manfred. Simpson stood back to let me pass. A nurse went by us as she entered Xylda's room. "You again," she said to Simpson. "Can't get rid of you today."

"Nope. My car's iced in," he said, smiling.

"Oh, so your stay isn't voluntary," she said.

"I'd love to go home."

So would I.

By the time I reached Manfred, Barney Simpson had continued on with his round of visiting.

"She's still intact," I said. Manfred closed his eyes, whether in dismay or gratitude I couldn't imagine.

"Then I'll wait in there with her," he said. "Until she goes."

"What can we do for you?" Tolliver asked.

Manfred looked at him with an expression that almost broke my heart. "Nothing," he said. "You've claimed her, I can see. But having you two as friends is good, and I'm really grateful you made the effort to get into town to see us. Where are you staying?"

We told him about the lake cottage. He smiled at the story of the Hamiltons. "When you two leaving?" he asked. "I guess the cops have cut you loose?"

"I guess we'll leave tomorrow," I said. "But we'll come by the hospital to check on you before we go. Sure there's nothing I can get you?"

"Since the hospital still has electricity," Manfred said, "the shoe may be on the other foot. You can get hot food here. The cafeteria is open."

The phrase "hospital cafeteria" didn't sound very appetizing, but "hot food" did. We coaxed Manfred into going with us, and we ate hot biscuits with gravy poured over them, and some hamburger steak, and some green beans. I had to swear to myself I'd do double running the next week.

At the last minute, I almost turned back to stay with Manfred. He seemed so alone. But he said, "There's no point in you staying here, Harper, as much as I appreciate the offer. There's just sitting and waiting here, and I can do that on my own. My mother should be here tomorrow morning, if the roads clear. I'll step out of Grandmother's room from time to time to check my voice mail."

I gave Manfred a hug, and Tolliver shook his hand. "We'll come if you need us, man," he said, and Manfred nodded.

"I don't think she'll last the night," he said. "She's tired out. But at least she had a last moment in the sun yesterday. She told me she thought the boy definitely killed the animals, but that something else was going on there, too."

"Like what?" I'd been moving away, but now I turned back to face Manfred. This was bad news.

He shrugged. "She never told me. She said the whole property was surrounded by a swamp of evil."

"Hmmm." Well, "swamp of evil" sounded pretty bad. What could Xylda have meant? See, this is what makes me nuts about psychics.

"She used a different word."

"Than what?"

"Than swamp. She called it a . . . miasma? Is that a word?"

Manfred wasn't stupid, but he wasn't much of a reader, either. "Yeah, it is. It means, like, a thick unpleasant atmosphere, right, Tolliver?"

Tolliver nodded.

Had I missed something, like a body? Had I made a mistake? The idea was so strong, so shocking, that I hardly noticed the bitter cold as we made our way to our car. "Tolliver, we've got to go back to that property."

He looked at me as if I were nuts. "In this weather, you want to go poke around private property?" he asked, getting all his objections in one sentence.

"I know the weather is wrong for this. But Xylda . . ."

"Half the time Xylda was an old fraud, and you know it."

"She wouldn't be about this." A thought occurred to me. "Do you remember when we were in Memphis, she said, 'In the time of ice you'll be so happy?'"

"Yeah," he said. "I do remember that. And it is the time of ice and up until you wanted to go trespassing, I was happy." He didn't look happy. He looked worried. "As a matter of fact, I wanted to go back to the cabin and stoke up the fire and get happy again."

I smiled. I couldn't help it. "Why don't we just ask?" I said.

"Just ask this guy if we can look over his property again? Just ask him if he snuck some bodies in there while we weren't looking? Because there's a miasma of evil around it?"

"Okay, I get your point. I just think we have to do something."

Tolliver had started the car the minute we got in and the heater was finally working. I bent over a little to let the hot air blow directly on my face.

"We'll go by, have a look," he said, very reluctantly.

"Then we'll follow your plan about the cabin."

"Okay, that part sounds good."

We traced our route of yesterday and alternately slid and bumped our way through the nearly deserted streets to the back of Tom Almand's property. The area where all the police and media vehicles had parked was a churned-up mess, the black mud hardened into a sea filled with black crests. Tolliver parked where it would be very hard to see our car from the house. I got out of the car and moved carefully to the barn. What had I missed there?

Inside the barn, the air was cold and still and stale, and

there were several holes in the dirt floor. This was where the sacrificed animals had been exhumed. I thought about the boy, Chuck, but then I banished the picture of his sad eyes from my mind, and I concentrated on opening myself to the vibration that came uniquely from the dead—the human dead.

When I opened my eyes, Chuck Almand was standing in front of me.

"Oh, God, you scared me, boy!" I said, raising a gloved hand to my throat.

He was wearing heavy boots and a heavy coat, a hat and gloves and a scarf, so he was appropriately dressed for the weather, at least.

"What are you doing here?" he asked. "Did you think you'd missed something?"

"Yes," I said. I had no reasonable story to tell. "Yes, I wondered if I'd missed something."

"You thought there might be dead people here?"

"I was checking."

"There aren't any. They're all dug up, out at Davey's old farm."

"You don't know of any others?"

His eyes flickered then, and I heard someone else outside. Thank God.

The door of the barn opened, and my brother came in. "Hey, Chuck," he said casually. "Honey, you finished?"

"Yeah, I think so," I said. "Negative results, like we expected."

Chuck Almand's light, bright eyes were fixed on me. "Don't be scared of me," he said.

"I don't believe I am," I said, trying to smile. And it was true I wasn't exactly frightened of the boy. But I did feel very uncomfortable around him, and I was concerned about him in an impersonal kind of way.

Then I heard another voice calling from outside, "Chuck! Hey, buddy, you in there? Who's here?" To my bewilderment, Chuck's face changed in the blink of an eye, and the boy punched me in the stomach as hard as he could. His lips moved as he hit; I saw them on my way down to the floor.

"Get out of here!" he screamed as I stared up at him from my kneeling position on the cold dirt. "Get out! You're trespassing!"

Tom Almand dashed in, the door to the old barn creaking and groaning as it kept moving after he'd shoved it. "Son, son! Oh, my God, Chuck, what did you do?"

Tolliver was at my side, helping me up. "You little son of a bitch," he said to the boy before me. "Don't touch her again. She wasn't doing anything to you."

I didn't say anything, I only stared up into his eyes, my good arm across my middle. He might hit me again. I wanted to be ready this time.

But the only thing that happened was a lot of talk. Tom Almand apologized over and over. Tolliver made it clear he wasn't going to let anyone else pound on me. He also made it clear that he didn't want the boy anywhere around me again. Tom thought we shouldn't have been trespassing. Tolliver said the police had been glad to welcome us here to this same spot the day before. Tom informed us that it wasn't the day before and that we needed to get the hell off his property. Tolliver said we'd be glad to, and he was lucky we weren't calling the police to report his son's assault on my person.

I sagged against Tolliver as he helped me out to the car. He was in a complete state. He was trying so hard not to say "I told you so" that he was practically bursting at the seams. But God bless him, he managed not to say it.

"Tolliver," I said, when we were safely in the car and on our way back to the cabin.

He stopped in mid rant. "Yes?"

"Right after he hit me, before he started yelling at me, the boy said, 'I'm sorry. Come find me later,'" I said.

"I didn't hear him say that."

"He said it real low, so you wouldn't hear. So his dad wouldn't hear."

"He said you should *come find him*?"

"He said he was sorry. Then he told me to come find him later."

"So is he schizophrenic? Or is he trying to persuade his dad that he is?"

"I think he's trying to persuade his dad of something, I'm not sure what."

The rest of the drive back to the cabin, we were silent. I don't know what was in Tolliver's head, but mine was busy trying to understand what had just happened.

When we parked at the top of the slope again, we noticed that the Hamiltons' place was silent and still except for the smoke rising from the chimney. Maybe they were taking a nap. That sounded like a good idea.

"I'm not pleased with myself, thinking like a seventy-year-old," I grumped as we made our way down the drive to the steps up to the door.

"Oh, I bet we'll think of something to do that the Hamiltons aren't doing," Tolliver said, in such an intimate voice I felt all of my blood rushing to a critical point.

"I don't know; the Hamiltons are pretty hale and hearty for people in their seventies."

"I think we can give them a run for their money," Tolliver said.

We started right away, and with pauses to throw some more wood on the fire and lock the door, we managed to make a good effort. I don't know how the Hamiltons' afternoon went, but ours went just fine. And we did eventually get the nap.

That night we made more hot chocolate and ate more peanut butter. We also had some apples. I like to think we would have talked to each other just as much if the electricity had been working, but maybe we wouldn't have. There's an intimacy to being alone together in the near darkness, and every time we made love I felt surer of him, and our new relationship became more solid. Neither of us would have taken the step off the edge of the cliff if we hadn't been after more than yet another one-night stand.

"That last waitress in Sarne," I said. I gave him a narrow-eyed stare. "That was the one I really minded, and for a couple of weeks I couldn't figure out why."

"Well, two things. I was hoping you'd come in on us, clobber the woman, and throw her out and tell me I was your one and only; and barring that, I was horny," Tolliver said. "Plus, she offered. Okay, that's three things."

"I was tempted," I admitted. "But I never felt I could risk it. I kept thinking, What if I ask him not to, and he asks me why not? What can I say back to him? No, don't do it, I love you? And you would say, Ohmigod, I can't travel with you anymore."

"I was thinking you'd say the same thing," he said. "You'd say that you couldn't be with someone who wanted to go to bed with you all the time, you had to have a clear head to do your job, and you didn't want to fog it up with dealing with lust. After all, you picked fewer bed partners than me."

"I'm a woman," I said. "I'm not gonna go around sleeping with whoever wants to sleep with me. I need a little bit more than that to go on."

"Not all women are like that," he said.

"Yeah, well, lots of them are."

"Do you hold it against me? Those random women?"

"Not as long as you're disease free. And I know you are." He got tested as regularly as he could, and he always used a condom.

"So," he said, "we're together now."

He was asking a question. "Yes," I said. "We're together."

"You're not gonna go with anyone else."

"I'm not. You?"

"I'm not. You're it."

"Okay. Good."

And just like that, we were a couple.

It seemed strange to get ready for bed and then climb into Tolliver's.

"We don't always have to sleep in the same bed," he said. "Some beds are going to be narrow and even lumpier than this one. But I want to sleep with you. Really sleep."

I wanted to really sleep with him, too, and it was easier than I thought. In fact, hearing his breathing beside me seemed to help me doze off faster than I normally did. I hadn't slept in the same bed with anyone for a long time; and maybe not for a whole night since I'd shared a bed with my sister Cameron. When I'd stayed with a guy, I often hadn't made it through till morning.

I did wake up a few times during the night, record my new situation, and fall right back to sleep. On one of these moments of wakefulness, I saw that my phone was vibrating against the floor by the bed. I reached down and scooped it up.

"Hello?" I said quietly, not wanting to wake Tolliver.

"Harper?"

"Yes."

"She died, Harper."

"Manfred, I'm so sorry."

"Harper, maybe someone killed her. I wasn't in the room."

"Manfred! Don't say that out loud. Don't say that where anyone can hear you. Where are you?"

"I'm standing outside the hospital."

"Why do you think that?"

"I think that because she was getting better. The nurse even said she thought Grandmother was going to speak. Then she died."

"Manfred, you need us to come in?"

"Not until morning. It's too bad out there. There's nothing

you can do. You stay in bed. I'll see you in the morning. My mother should be here then, too."

"Manfred, you need to go back to the motel and lock the door. Don't eat or drink anything at the hospital, all right?" I tried to think of more advice to give him. "And don't be alone with anyone, okay?"

"I hear you, babe." He sounded barely conscious. "I'm getting in the car now, and I'm going to drive to the motel."

"Hey, call me when you get there."

He called again within ten minutes to tell me he was safely locked in his room. Furthermore, he'd seen some reporters who were up drinking, and he'd told them someone had been following him. So they were as alert as drinking people could be, and they all professed to be disgusted that someone was following him around on such a sad night. Somehow they all knew already that Xylda had passed. Maybe they were paying one of the hospital staff to be a news clearinghouse.

None of this woke Tolliver, which surprised me until I recalled he'd been outside helping Ted Hamilton earlier. Plus, we'd had our own share of vigorous indoor exercise.

It was after three in the morning when I talked to Manfred the last time. I lay awake praying for him for a few minutes. Since I knew he was safe, and Xylda was beyond my help, I slept again.

eleven

SOMETIME during the night, or rather toward the early morning, the electricity came back on. I'm sure it happened after dawn, because it didn't wake us up. I was lying there wondering why the lamp across the room was on, when I realized the miracle of electricity was once again visiting us. I had mixed feelings about electricity, for obvious reasons, but on this day I was glad to see it. I stuck a toe out from under the mound of blankets, and it didn't freeze immediately. I smiled. This was really good. And my arm was much better.

I hauled myself out of bed and went into the bathroom. I brushed and sponged, and changed my clothes, managing to do everything but deal with the bra. That I just left off. It wasn't that noticeable anyway since I was wearing both a tank top and a sweatshirt, so who was going to know?

The police, that's who. Just as I was trying to figure out how to put on clean socks, there was a knock at the door. I realized I'd heard the feet coming up, I'd just been thinking so hard about dressing myself I hadn't paid attention.

I was glad I was awake to answer the door, especially since I'd introduced Tolliver as my brother to the police chief, and she was here right now, and only one bed was in use. It was credible that I could have gotten up first and made my bed, and I just didn't want to have to explain or endure the horrified stare I'd get otherwise.

Sandra Rockwell had bigger fish to fry than worrying about our sleeping arrangements, as it turned out. Tolliver sat up and looked as she pushed past me into the cabin, looking around her as she did so. "Sheriff," I said, "what's up?"

Sandra looked under the beds, in the bathroom, and then she opened the trapdoor and went down in the storage shed underneath. When she came up, she looked more relaxed, if not any happier.

"Okay, I'm not happy with you doing this," I said, and Tolliver barely bothered turning his back while he pulled off his sleep pants and pulled on his jeans. She gave him a good enough look that I knew she could replay the moment later, and I felt like whaling her one.

"Have you seen Chuck Almand?" she asked.

I was very surprised, which was a massive understatement.

"Not since yesterday. We saw him then. Why would we have seen him? What's happened to him?"

"Can you tell me exactly what happened?"

"Ah. Okay. I wanted to be sure I hadn't overlooked

anything in the barn. It just seemed like one of those loose ends, you know? So I went back. I knew it was a stupid thing to do, but I hoped I could just slip in and out without anyone knowing. Chuck came in while I was in there. He got mad at me, and hit me."

"Hit you?" But she wasn't surprised, not at all. She'd heard all this from Chuck's father, no doubt.

"Yeah, he slugged me in the stomach."

"I imagine you were pretty angry about that."

"I wasn't happy."

"I'll bet your brother wasn't happy, either."

"I'm right here," Tolliver said. "No, I definitely wasn't happy. But his dad came in, and the boy just seemed so disturbed, we left."

"And you didn't call us to report the whole thing?"

"No, we didn't. We figured you-all had more important things to be doing." She knew we hadn't called. She was just underscoring all the mistakes we'd made. I felt worse and worse. Going back to the barn had been my fault, my bad decision, and if the boy was gone, maybe that was my fault, too.

"So no one knows where he is?" Tolliver asked. "Since when?"

"One of the other counselors from the health center came by, maybe an hour after the incident in the barn, as close as I can make out. This is a close friend of Tom's, and he wanted to talk to Chuck to see if he could help." The sheriff made a face. She didn't believe counseling would make any difference in Chuck's case, it was clear. "So Tom starts looking for the boy to get him to talk to the counselor, but Chuck wasn't there. So the counselor insisted Tom call the police. He did, and then he began calling Chuck's friends. No one had seen the boy."

"You haven't had any luck finding someone who saw him around town?"

"No luck. But we thought he might have tried to find you, to finish what he'd started. Or to apologize. With a kid that messed up, who knows what he was going to do."

Deputy Rob Tidmarsh came in, stomping his feet just like the sheriff had done. "Didn't see nothing, Sheriff," he said.

So she'd been distracting us while her minion checked out the property. Well, there was nothing to find, and there was no point getting angry about it. She'd done what she had to do.

"We might need to call our lawyer," I said.

"I've got him on speed dial," Tolliver said.

"Or maybe," Rockwell said, overriding our voices, "you found Chuck and decided to punch him back." She was looking at Tolliver as she said this, as if I were accustomed to sending Tolliver to do my punching.

"We were here all night," Tolliver said. "We got a phone call at—what time did Manfred call us, Harper?"

"Oh, about three," I said.

"What evidence is a phone call on a cell phone?" Rockwell asked. "And did Manfred talk to you?" She was looking at Tolliver with no friendly face.

"He talked to me, but Tolliver was here."

"He won't say he talked to Tolliver, then."

"Well, he may have heard him in the background. But he didn't talk to him directly, no." Calling our lawyer in Atlanta was beginning to seem like a possibility we should bear in mind. Art Barfield had made a mint off us lately, and I was sure he wouldn't mind making a little more.

"I'm not in the habit of abducting boys," Tolliver said. "But of course there's someone here in town who is. Why are you looking at me instead of trying to find out who took all the other boys? Isn't it far more likely that that's who's got Chuck Almand? And if that's so, isn't the boy running out of time?"

I figured Sheriff Rockwell was grinding her teeth together in frustration, from the tensed look of her face.

"Do you think we're *not* looking?" she said, almost biting the words out. "Now that he doesn't have the use of his usual killing ground, where would he have taken the boy? We're searching every shed and barn in the county, but we have to check out all other possibilities. You were one of them, and a pretty likely one at that."

I didn't think we were so damn likely, but then, we'd had the run-in with Chuck and his dad. There was something more I could tell the law.

"He told me he was sorry," I said to the sheriff.

"What?"

"The boy said he was sorry. For hitting me. He told me to find him later."

"Why? Why do you think that was? What sense does that make?" The tall deputy was looking over Rockwell's shoulder at me as though I'd started barking.

"At the time I just thought—I have to say, I thought it was just some kind of mental illness talking. He looked so strange when he said it."

"And what do you think now?"

"I think . . . I don't know what I think."

"That's not a hell of a lot of help."

"I'm not a psychologist, or a profiler, or any kind of law enforcement person," I said. "I just find dead people." *I just find dead people.* Chuck knew that. And he'd said, "Come find me."

"Then we should get you out searching, too," Sandra Rockwell was saying.

I was sitting there in the grip of a horrible idea, wondering how I could have possibly thought only a day ago that the world might be better if someone took Chuck Almand out right now. That was before I'd seen his secret face, the face he wore when he told me he had to hit me.

Tolliver started to say something, stopped. I looked at him. It wasn't the time to remind them that I got paid for this work. His instinct to hold in his words had been a good one. No, I wasn't reading his mind. We just know each other very well.

"Where do you want me to look?" I asked, and my voice was coming from far away.

That stumped her for a moment. "You'd know if the body was new, right?" she said.

"Yeah."

"Then we'll just take you everywhere we can think of," she said.

I thought of Manfred sitting at the hospital, or in his hotel room, hoping we'd show up. I thought of the road out of town, out of this situation. But weighing that against the life of a boy, what could I say? Which Rockwell knew, of course.

"You're ready to go, right? We'll swing back later and pick up Mr. Lang here," the sheriff said.

"No, I think *not*," I said right back. "I'm not going anywhere without him." Though it would be better if Tolliver went to help Manfred, if we had to be separated. But then . . . no. It was better if we stayed together. I was going to be selfish about this.

Tolliver vanished into the little bathroom while I made the sheriff useful by asking her to help me with my shoes. Tidmarsh tried not to snort, but he didn't quite succeed. Sheriff Rockwell was game, and my hiking boots were laced up and tied in a neat bow in no time. I took my pills for the day and picked up the cabin a bit while we waited. I tried to bank the fire so it could be revived. The electricity might be back on, but there was certainly a chance it would go off again. The fireplace was still essential. I had a gloomy feeling we'd be spending another night here.

Manfred would be better than I at solving this problem. Maybe if he went to the house, or to the barn where we'd last seen Chuck, he could trace the boy somehow. On the other hand, it would be inhumane to ask Manfred to work just now. And he might not be up to it. He'd told me several times his psychic sense was weaker than his grandmother's. I thought he was wrong, but that was what he believed.

I called him, since we were waiting, anyway. Manfred sounded sad but collected. I explained the situation to him, and he said that he'd heard from his mother again, that she was making better time now that the roads were clearing up. "We'll see you later," I said. "You hang in there, Manfred."

"I don't trust anyone here," he said. "I don't trust the doctor, I don't trust the nurses, I don't think the hospital guy is on the level. Even the minister gives me the creeps. You think I'm being paranoid? You think there's really something wrong here?"

"That's hard to answer at this point," I said.

"Oh, right, the sheriff's there," Manfred said dismally. "I just can't throw the feeling off, Harper. Something's really wrong here."

"In Doraville? Or specifically at the hospital?"

"I'm just not sharp enough to say," he said after a long pause. "I don't have the gift like my grandmother did."

"I think you're wrong. I think all you need is some experience," I said. "I think you do have it in you."

"You don't know how much that means to me," he said. "Listen, I've got to go now. I've got an idea."

That didn't sound good. That sounded like he was about to do something on his own. Young men on their own in Doraville didn't fare well. I tried to call him back right away.

He did pick up, finally. "Where are you going?" I asked. Tolliver had come out of the bathroom, finally, clean and dressed. He stood frozen in place by the anxiety in my voice, his dirty clothes in his hands.

"I'm going to look for the boy," Manfred said.

"No, don't go without someone with you," I said. "Tell us where you're going."

"You might get in trouble again."

"Hey, we've got the sheriff, remember? Where you going?"

"I'm going to that barn again. That's where I have to go."

"No, wait for us, okay? Manfred?"

"I'll meet you there."

But it would take us a lot longer to get there, since we were starting from the lake.

I told the sheriff what the situation was, and she went ballistic. "We've searched the barn," she said. "We've gone over and over it. That dirt floor is empty, the stalls are empty, there's no loft. It's an empty wooden building with walls so thin there couldn't be a hidden space in there. There aren't even any more dead animals, I'm almost a hundred percent sure, and you told us yourself there aren't any bodies there."

"No dead ones," I said. Then I said, "No dead ones . . . at least there weren't any . . . oh, shit. We got to get there." The feeling of dread that had blossomed in my head now bloomed in full. I didn't speak to anyone again.

We got into the patrol car and onto the road within five minutes. There wasn't much traffic and the roads were a hell of a lot clearer, but it was still a good twenty-minute drive into Doraville, then another ten minutes through the town to the street where the Almands lived.

Instead of creeping up to the barn from the rear of the property as we'd done yesterday, we pulled into the driveway by the aging frame house, and I got out as quickly as I could. My muscles were sorer today than they'd been the previous day, and I was skipping the pain medicine, so I was feeling everything I did.

Tolliver put his arm around my waist to help me along, and we stumbled down the remains of the drive that led beyond the house to the barn. I could catch a glimpse of Manfred's car on the track that ran behind the property.

And I felt the vibration, the stirring in my head. A very fresh body. "Oh, no," I said, "oh no no no." I began to run, and Tolliver had to grip me under my shoulder to keep me up. The sheriff caught fire when she saw my distress and she and the deputy pulled ahead of us easily. She drew her gun, and I don't even know if she realized she was doing it.

We all screeched to halt when we entered the dilapidated barn.

Tom Almand was standing in front of the stalls at the rear of the barn. He had a shovel in his hands. About three yards in front of him, Manfred was keeping to his feet with great effort. He was bleeding from the head. Manfred had his own weapon, a short-handled spade. It was so shiny and new I suspected Manfred had bought it that very morning, maybe on the way to the barn. He hadn't gotten in a lick yet.

"Tom, put the shovel down," the sheriff said.

"Tell him first," Tom Almand said. "He came in here to attack me."

"Not true," Manfred said.

"I mean, look at him, he's a freak," Tom said. There was a snarl on his narrow face. "I live here."

"Tom, put down the shovel. Now."

"There's a human body here," I said. "There's a body here *now*." I just wanted to be clear they understood. I just wanted them to get that asshole Tom Almand out of the way.

Manfred took two more steps back from Tom, and put his spade on the floor.

And Tom ran at Manfred with his shovel raised to strike.

The deputy shot him first, and missed. Sheriff Rockwell managed to get him in the arm, and he screamed and crumpled.

Tolliver and I stood against the wall while the deputy rushed forward to cover the bleeding counselor, and Manfred fell to his knees, his hands clasped to his head; not to indicate surrender, but because his head was injured.

We started forward to help our friend, but the sheriff said sharply, "Stay back! Stay out of the scene!" and we did. She was calling for ambulances on her radio, and when the shovel was beyond Tom Almand's reach, she handcuffed him despite his bleeding arm, and searched him very thoroughly. No weapons. She told Tom Almand about his rights, but he didn't respond. His face was as blank as it had been at the church the other night. The small man had gone somewhere else, mentally.

"Do you still feel a body?" she asked when that was done. It took me a second to realize she was talking to me, I was so wrapped up in the tension of what had just happened, the fear that Tom Almand would charge someone again, the possibility of Manfred being critically injured. I didn't worry about Tom's arm wound at all. He might bleed out before the ambulance arrived, and that would be fine with me.

"Yes," I said. "There's a very fresh body. Can I show you where?"

"How close do you have to come to this man?"

"I have to go to the first stall."

"Okay, go."

I very carefully worked my way around the tableau of bleeding men and law enforcement to get to the opening to the stall. I stepped inside on the old straw and began kicking it aside. It kept falling back into its original position, so I began picking up handfuls and tossing them over the side of the stall. "Tolliver," I said. He was at my side immediately, helping. The shovel or the spade would have come in handy, but I knew better than to suggest it. "Isn't this a latch?" I asked.

Tolliver said, "I wish we had a flashlight," and one landed on the floor beside us. Sheriff Rockwell had had one on her belt. Tolliver turned it on and aimed it at the boards at our feet.

"Trapdoor here," Tolliver said, and the deputy cursed. I guessed he'd been one of the ones who'd searched the barn.

Tom laughed, and I looked out at the tense group of people in the barn. For about a dime, the deputy would have kicked him in the head. His body language spoke loud and clear. I could hear emergency vehicles approaching, and I wanted to open the trapdoor before they got here and there was even more confusion.

Tolliver found the latch quickly. It was very strong, I guess to hold out against battering from below.

We did need a shovel to open it, and without asking Tolliver went across the barn to take Manfred's. We stuck the spade in the little opening and pried. After Tolliver got it up a little, I held the spade with my good hand while Tolliver grasped the edge and swung back the trapdoor. It was very heavy, and we found out why—there was insulation liberally tacked on the underside, which would muffle any sounds from below.

I looked down into a kind of pit, maybe six by six. Probably eight feet deep, it was reachable by a steep wooden ladder. The dead body of Chuck Almand lay at the foot of the ladder. He was staring up at us. The boy had shot himself in the head. What drew the eye first was the terrible damage to Chuck's head.

Behind the corpse there was a naked boy chained to the wall. His mouth was duct-taped shut. He was whimpering behind it, and he was looking over his shoulder and up at us with an expression I never want to see again. He was spattered with Chuck's blood and I suppose some of his own. There were cuts on his body, and the blood there was crusted and black. The cuts were swollen and red with infection. He had no blanket, no jacket, nothing, and he'd been in the pit with the corpse all night.

I ran out of the barn and vomited. One of the ambulance drivers rushing in stopped to check on me, and I just waved my arm to indicate the interior of the barn.

After a few minutes, Tolliver came out. I was leaning against the peeling wood, wishing I were anywhere but here.

"He killed himself so you'd find him," Tolliver said. "So you'd find out what his father was doing."

"So I'd have a corpse to find," I said. "Oh, Jesus, he took such a chance. What if I hadn't come back?"

"What if Manfred hadn't decided he had to check the barn again?"

"Do you think Tom Almand's known where Chuck was all this time, since he reported him missing?"

"No, but I guess he didn't have a chance to come out here to check. That other counselor asking to see Chuck made Tom report him missing." Tolliver shuddered. "I never want to see anything like that again."

"He sacrificed himself," I said. I couldn't get my thoughts together. "And it was almost—almost—for *nothing*."

"He wasn't thinking good," Tolliver said in a massive understatement. "And he was just thirteen."

The stretchers went by, Manfred's first, his face white as death and his eyes open and blank.

"Manfred!" I called, just wanting him to know that someone who knew him was near, knew what he had done. But his face didn't change.

Tom Almand came out next, his eyes closed, his lips in a strange smile. He was now handcuffed to the stretcher by his good arm, and there was a bandage on the arm that had been shot. I hoped he'd been shot good, and I wondered if Sheriff Rockwell had been truly trying to hit his arm. It had been an alarming moment, but then, that was what law enforcement people trained for, right?

Maybe the arm was best. Maybe the people he'd wounded the most, or the survivors he'd wounded most, could get something out of his trial and conviction. Surely he'd be tried and convicted, wouldn't he? We could follow it in the national news. The media loves a serial killer trial, whether the killer being tried is gay or straight, black or white or brown. There's no discrimination in that field.

I realized I was thinking crazy, and I also realized we had no place here. But the two SBI agents were running across the back lane like the barn was on fire with a baby inside, and they weren't about to let us go. Stuart and Klavin weren't out of breath, because they were fit agents, and they stood right in front of us. "You're here again," Agent Stuart said. He had on proper gloves and an L.L. Bean heavy outdoor-guy coat, and gleaming boots that went halfway up his calves. If he didn't look like the little mountaineer! Klavin was a bit more downscale, with a battered water-proof coat that had seen several years of use and a knit cap that had earflaps.

"He killed himself," I told them. They would want to know.

"Who?" I thought Stuart was going to shake me, he was so anxious to know everything.

"Chuck Almand. He killed himself with a gun."

Klavin said, "Who was in the ambulance?"

"Tom Almand and Manfred Bernardo," Tolliver said.

They looked at each other blankly. "The kid's dad and the psychic's grandson," Tolliver said.

"She died last night," Stuart said.

"Yes, she did. And her grandson almost died today," I said.

"The last victim is alive," I said, and they were in the barn so fast you couldn't see them for the smoke.

"Why haven't they brought him out?" Tolliver leaned and looked in, but then he gave up. He didn't want to go in that barn again, and neither did I.

"Maybe they can't get him unlocked," I said. Tolliver nodded. That seemed reasonable.

"Wonder who he is," Tolliver said after a long moment. The weather might be much better than it had been, but it was still cold standing out there, and we had nothing to do.

I turned to Tolliver and hugged him. His arms slid around me, and we stood there in the bright cold day, clinging to each other. "We'll find out," I said, my lips against his neck. "It'll be in the papers, or on the news." The tortured body, slumped against the wall, the bloodstains everywhere. The poor dead boy on the floor of that miserable pit. *Jesus, God. This is not what you intended people for.*

I hadn't thought in Christian terms for a long time, and I was surprised to find myself thinking in them now. And I hadn't rebelled, either, hadn't had the "Why, God?" thoughts. Those were bad, those were pointless. Of course, I'd never found such atrocities, so closely linked, in adjacent graves.

"Chuck saved that boy's life," I said numbly. "He provided a dead body for me to find."

"Do you think he really cut up those animals?"

"Maybe his dad made Chuck do it, hoping Chuck would follow in his own footsteps. Maybe Tom thought if Chuck was guilty of *something* he'd be less likely to report his dad."

"Xylda seemed pretty sure Chuck did it."

"I'd hate to think she was wrong in her last big reading."

"Me, too." Tolliver sounded grim. "You think her loathing of him was what drove Chuck to tie everything up this way? I mean, everyone at the same time looking at him with such disgust, such dislike? And his dad acting right along with them. When he knew better, and the boy knew that."

"Chuck was a hero. He survived living with a father that killed boys for fun."

"But he didn't tell anyone."

"Maybe he didn't know, until the animals were dug up. Maybe then he realized his dad was the one killing the boys, or maybe Tom told him then. Like, 'Everyone thinks you're evil and sick now, so I'll show you something really evil and sick! Like it?' "

"Or maybe he knew all along," Tolliver said, more realistically. "Maybe he kept silent because he loved his dad, or was scared of his dad, or because he kind of liked torturing the animals and felt he and Tom were two of a kind. Maybe he even helped, with the boys. There must have been times it would have been handy to have an extra pair of hands. Some of the boys were big, and heavy. Football players. Adolescents who'd gotten their growth. Frankly, someone as little as Tom Almand, I don't know how he managed it."

"But Chuck put a stop to it." I buried my face in Tolliver's jacket. He ran his fingers through my hair, taking care to avoid the shaved spot on the left side of my head. He patted me. It was intensely comforting.

Finally they brought the last victim out. He was covered with blankets, there was an IV running already, and he was strapped to the gurney. His eyes were closed, and tears were leaking down his filthy face.

"What's your name, son?" Sheriff Rockwell was asking.

"Mel," the boy whispered. "Mel Chesney. From Queen's Table, up near Clearstream."

"Mel, how long have you been down there?" said Klavin, keeping pace on the other side.

"Two days," he said. "Two days. I think."

And then he said, "I can't talk about it."

I didn't blame him at all.

The boy had been there yesterday when we'd had our confrontation with Chuck. If Chuck had just told us then . . . but his father had come in, and maybe he simply couldn't. I wondered if Mel Chesney had been in the hole when the police were digging up the animals. Oh, God, that was too bitter to think about.

I was sure every law enforcement person on the scene was wondering the same thing. Mel Chesney had been down there for hours by himself and then with a corpse, thinking all the while he was going to be tortured to death. It was almost a miracle he hadn't died of hypothermia.

No one tried to stop us as we began going to the sheriff's car. But we couldn't go back to the cabin and get our stuff unless someone drove us. The sheriff said, "Rob, take them to the station." Rob Tidmarsh raised his forefinger to tell us he'd be one more minute.

Rockwell glared at us as if we were an annoying detail she had to clear off her slate before she turned her attention to more important things, and I think that was exactly the case. "We got to process this scene, and it's gonna take a while," she said. "You two go sit at the station, and when I can spare someone to run you out to the lake, I'll send 'em back to get you."

"Rob can't take us on out there?"

"Rob's going to pick up more film while he's at the station. The state forensic boys are going to be here as soon as they can get here, but we want our own pictures. Rob'll be coming right back here, and for now, this is the most important spot in Knott County. So you two are gonna have to cool your heels for a while."

We'd been doing plenty of that.

There was no help for it. No matter how irritated we might feel—and I for one felt plenty irritated—Rob was going to dump us at the station.

"Will they take the boy to the local hospital?" I asked the deputy.

"No, they'll take him on to the bigger hospital in Asheville," Rob said. "The SBI guys insisted. We got good doctors here." He sounded deeply resentful.

"I got good treatment here," I said. Admittedly, I wanted to be on Rob's good side in case we could get him to take us out to the cabin later. But it was the truth. I was willing to believe, a small town like this, the hospital wouldn't have the big diagnostic machines larger hospitals could acquire, but I seemed to be mending fine, and the nurses had been very kind, if very busy.

Rob relaxed a little.

There's always something strange about riding through town in a cop car when you're seated in the back with a wire mesh between you and the driver. It just makes you feel guilty of something, and you feel awfully conspicuous. When we pulled in back of the station and got out, the media swarmed around the back of the station wanting to know if we'd been arrested. Damn it. I wasn't in the mood to put up with this. I couldn't understand why the vicious swarm hadn't migrated to the old barn.

"We kept radio silence and used our cells," Rob said when I asked him. He seemed completely open now, and he made a point of walking by my side and holding open the back door to the station, making it clear to the watching reporters that I was in favor.

Inside, there was chaos. The news was spreading in the building and it was only a matter of time before it would flow outward.

Rob looked as if he didn't know what to do with us once we'd gotten to the sheriff's office, so he stuck us in one of the interview rooms, told us where the snack and drink machines were, and said there were some magazines in the waiting area if we wanted to go get them. He was obviously in a tearing hurry to collect the film and get back out to the latest crime scene, so we nodded and he took off.

There ensued several hours of boredom. We could have been on the road getting the hell out of Doraville. We could have been in bed together enjoying our new relationship, an idea that got Tolliver's vote. (I would have enjoyed some aspects of that, but truthfully, I was pretty sore in unexpected places, and my arm had been too busy for a cracked arm.) Or we could have been making money on another job. But instead, we sat in the drab room.

For a change of pace, we made a foray to the station waiting room out front. We commandeered all the magazines, bought junk food from the machines, and tried to stay out of the way.

After four hours, the sheriff came back. She, Klavin, and Stuart came into the room with a couple more chairs, and we went over everything all over again.

"And you really think this boy Chuck killed himself so you'd find the other boy?" Stuart asked for the fifth time.

I shrugged. "I don't know what was going through his mind."

"He could have written a note, he could have called us, he could have called you, for that matter, and said, 'My dad has put a boy in a hidden room,' and that would have solved the problem."

"That wouldn't have solved the problem for him," Tolliver said.

"He was an adolescent boy," I said. "He was full of drama and horror and guilt and sorrow. I guess he was trying to atone for himself and his father."

"So what do you think, Ms. Connelly? Do you think he tortured the animals willingly?"

"If he did, that enjoyment horrified him." I didn't think there was a simple explanation of Chuck Almand's behavior. I thought at the end he'd tried to do the right thing, but his thinking processes hadn't foreseen the possibility that he could come out the other side of the horror of his situation, come out and heal and recover. He just hadn't lived long enough to believe that he had a future after his dad's arrest, and he wanted his dad to stop killing. At least, that was the way I interpreted Chuck's actions.

They talked at us for a long time, trying to pry things out of us that weren't there to be gotten. "And don't tell anyone anything you saw in the barn," Klavin said. "Not until we get the case completely locked."

That was easy to promise. We had no desire to talk about what we'd seen.

I had some doubts that the case was all wrapped up, but I kept them to myself. After all we'd done, they still weren't

213

going to listen to my speculations. But doubt niggled at me, and I had that feeling of incompleteness.

Now we had to find Manfred and his mother, who must be wondering what she'd done in her previous life to merit the punishment she was taking.

I asked the sheriff where Manfred was, and she surprised me by telling me he'd been kept here at the Knott County Hospital. He'd asked to stay here, she said.

"I can understand that," I said to Tolliver as we climbed into Rob's patrol car again. He'd finally been detailed to take us back to the cabin. "Otherwise, it would complicate his mom's life so much, and if he can get the care he needs here, that's better than moving him up to Asheville."

"The doctor said he'd be okay here," Rob said from the driver's seat.

"Okay, that's good," I said. Then I remembered that Manfred had suspected someone had killed his grandmother during the night. Maybe it wasn't so good that Manfred was in this hospital after all. Shit. More to worry about.

So when we got back to the cabin, we packed everything—just in case—and put it in the car—just in case. We put out the fire. We hung the cabin key from the rearview mirror so we wouldn't forget to return it to Twyla—just in case. Then we drove back into Doraville. We'd taken the opportunity to freshen up, since we'd had so little time that morning, and we felt better now. My arm was aching because I'd been more active that day than I should, and I took a pain pill. I felt almost ashamed to pop one, there were so many other people who were suffering far worse than I; but the only pain I could ease was my own.

"Can I just keep driving?" Tolliver asked as we came to the major intersection in Doraville. Straight ahead would take us out of town. Turning left would take us to the hospital.

"I wish," I said. "But I think we have to make sure Manfred and his mom are okay. Don't we?"

Tolliver looked stubborn. "I bet Manfred's mom is tough. She'd have to be, with Xylda for a mother. I bet they're fine."

I gave him a sideways look.

"Yeah, okay," he said, and took the left turn.

Twelve

MANFRED'S mother, Rain Bernardo, was a younger version of her mother. The resemblance was only physical, I discovered. Rain was not the least bit psychic, and she hadn't had any special rapport with Xylda. Rain worked in a factory and had risen to management level. She was proud of that. She was proud of being a single mom. She was dismayed that Manfred had followed in Xylda's footsteps and not hers. But she loved her son, and she'd loved her mother, and she was pretty subdued at Manfred's bedside. "Subdued," for Rain, meant she only talked fifty words a second instead of a hundred.

She had the family red hair, and she had the curves of her mother, but in Rain's case they weren't nearly as generous. In fact, Rain was a very attractive woman, and I was pretty sure she hadn't seen her fortieth birthday yet.

We were there when the first of the usual callers came in. Barney Simpson was more solemn than I'd ever seen him, and I wondered if he was a friend of Tom Almand's. After Barney had asked his usual questions about his patient's comfort and contentment with the treatment he was receiving in the hospital, he lingered. I wondered if he was admiring Rain. After all, he was a divorced guy.

"I'm very sorry about your mother," Barney told Rain. "She was a colorful lady, and I know you'll miss her. She made quite an impression on this little community in the short time she was here. She'll be long remembered."

That was a model of tact, I thought. Though Manfred was lying there pale and in pain, a twitch of a smile crossed his face.

"I appreciate your saying that," Rain said, not to be outdone in courtesy. "Thank you for taking such good care of her. Manfred said you came by to see her. Her health was so poor that both Manfred and I know she was due to go anytime, and we don't blame the hospital for anything." She cast a quelling look at Manfred, who had closed his eyes, absenting himself from the whole conversation.

"Manfred thinks she should have an autopsy," Rain said. "And she hadn't been under a doctor's care here in Doraville. Though of course she had doctors in Tennessee, and she saw her cardiologist right before she left for Doraville. What do you think?"

Dr. Thomason came in then, said, "It's raining outside, folks," and shook a few droplets off his umbrella. "Just rain, not ice," he added reassuringly.

"It's good you came in here now," Barney said. "Let me

tell you what we've been talking about." Barney repeated Rain's question. "What about it, Len?" he asked.

"Depends on what we hear from her doctor in Tennessee," Len Thomason said, considering. "If her doctor there is of the opinion that her death was expectable, not a surprise, no questions to be answered about it, then I think it would be reasonable to assume we didn't need an autopsy, and that's what I'll recommend to the coroner. On the other hand," he went on, raising both his hands to show us "caution," "if that doctor isn't satisfied—and he knew her best—we'll have to check into it."

Dr. Thomason had put it in such a matter-of-fact way that you felt quite sane and reasonable after listening, and you were sure this was the right course. That manner of his must have been invaluable to his practice. It was almost enough to make me ashamed I'd suspected he might have had something to do with the boys' deaths. Now, as I watched him smile gravely at some question of Rain's, I could only imagine all over again how easily Len Thomason could persuade a boy to go with him anywhere. Everyone trusts a doctor. There were a hundred things he could have said to induce a young man to go off with him. Right now I couldn't think of any, but I was sure given time I would.

Even Barney Simpson, who didn't seem like the most lighthearted of individuals, perked up around Dr. Thomason. I remembered he'd gone in to talk to Xylda the night before; no, he'd peeked in and gone away. He hadn't even gone into the room.

Doak Garland was across the hall, praying with some relatives outside a room with an "Oxygen in Use" sign on the door. Anyone would go with him, too. He was so meek and mild, so pink and polite.

Why was I even worried about further suspects? Tom Almand had been arrested. The case was closed. It was hard to believe one man could cause so much misery. Even Almand's own son had died of his evil. There was something about the whole thing that felt—unsealed, uncompleted.

I was sure that Tom had had an accomplice, a partner in crime.

Once I admitted this to myself, the idea wouldn't go away. While Tolliver talked to Barney Simpson, and Rain discussed Manfred's injury with Dr. Thomason, I picked out the reasons I suspected this. I had them all in my head when I looked up to meet Manfred's eyes. I felt Manfred connect with me. Suddenly Manfred said, "Mom."

Startled, Rain turned to the bed. "What, honey? You feeling okay?"

"I've been thinking," he said. "I won't argue with you about the autopsy if you'll let Harper touch Grandmother and tell us what she sees."

Rain looked from Manfred to me, and I could tell from her compressed lips that she was trying to hide revulsion. She not only hadn't fully believed in her mother's talent, she had loathed it. "Oh, Manfred," she said, really upset, "that won't be necessary. And I'm sure Harper wouldn't want to do that."

"I'll know how she died," I said. "And I'm sure cheaper and less invasive than an autopsy."

"Harper," she said, giving me a face full of disappointment. She struggled with herself for a minute, and I felt sorry for her. Abruptly she swung toward Dr. Thomason. "Would you mind very much, Doctor? If Harper—sees—my mother?"

"No, not at all," Dr. Thomason said. "We medical people long ago realized that there's more to this earth than we see in our practice. If that would bring comfort to your son, and you're agreeable . . ." He seemed sincere. But then, a sociopath like the one who'd killed the boys would seem very normal, right? Otherwise, people would have spotted him a long time ago.

"Have you heard anything about the boy who was taken to Asheville?" I asked.

"Yes, I have." Thomason nodded several times. "He's not talking, not at all. But they don't think his life is in danger. They think he'll recover. Most of his silence is psychological, not physical. That is, his tongue and voice box are in working order. Lungs, too. Well. Miss Connelly, the body is at Sweet Rest Funeral Home on Main. I'll call them after I leave here, and they'll be expecting you."

I inclined my head. I wasn't looking forward to this, but I did want to know what had taken Xylda into the other world. I owed her that much. And Manfred, too.

"How long do you think Manfred will need to stay in the hospital?" Rain asked.

Dr. Thomason, who'd been on the point of leaving the room, turned to give Manfred an assessing look. "If all his vitals stay good, and he doesn't run any fever or have any other symptoms that scare me, tomorrow should be good," he said. "How about you, young lady? Your pain better?" he asked me suddenly.

"I'm doing much better, thank you," I said. Barney Simpson had been trying to find a break in the conversation to take his leave, and he said "See you later" to everyone in the room and strode out the door.

Maybe it was the pain, maybe it was the shock to his nerves the past week had been, but out of the blue Manfred said, "Well, when's the wedding?"

There was instant silence in the room. Dr. Thomason completed his own departure in a hurry, and left Rain looking from the bed to Tolliver and me, almost as astonished as we were.

I'd known Manfred wouldn't be happy, but I hadn't thought he'd be angry. I told myself to bear in mind his many shocks of the past few days. Tolliver said, "We haven't set a date yet," which was yet another surprise I hadn't wanted.

Now I was mad at everyone. Rain was gaping, Manfred was looking sullen, and Tolliver was really furious.

"I'm sorry," Rain said in a brittle voice. "I thought you two were brother and sister. I misunderstood, I guess."

I took a deep breath. "We're no relation, but we spent our teen years in the same house," I said, trying to keep my voice gentle and level. "Now, I think, Manfred must be tired. We'll just go over to the funeral home. Sweet Rest, I think the doctor said?"

"Yes," Rain said, "I think that was it." She looked confused, and who could blame her?

As we strode out of the hospital, Tolliver said, "Don't let him spook you, Harper."

"You think Manfred saying the word 'wedding' is going

221

to spook me?" I laughed, but it didn't sound amused. "I know we're okay. We don't need to take any big jumps. We know that. Right?"

"Right," he said firmly. "We've got all the time in the world."

I wasn't in the habit of feeling so sure about that, since I spent a lot of time with surprised dead people. But I was going to let it slide for now.

This funeral home was one of the one-story brick models, with a parking lot that would fill up way too quickly. I've been in hundreds of funeral homes, since lots of people don't make up their minds until the last minute about asking me in. This would be one of the two-viewing-rooms kind, I was willing to put money on it. After we walked into the lobby, sure enough there were two doors facing us, each with a podium outside with a signing book waiting for mourners. A sign on a stand, the kind with removable white letters that stick into rows of black feltlike material, said that the viewing room on the right contained James O. Burris. The one on the left was empty. There were also rooms to our right and left; one of those would be for the owner. The other would be for a co-owner or assistant, or it would maybe be employed as a small reception room for the bereaved family.

And here came the funeral director herself, a comfortably round woman in her fifties. She was wearing a neat pantsuit and comfortable shoes, and her hair and makeup were also on the comfortable side.

"Hello," she said, with a kind of subdued smile that must be her stock-in-trade. "Are you Ms. Connelly?"

"I am."

"And you're here to view the remains of Mrs. Bernardo?"

"I am."

"Tolliver Lang," Tolliver said, and held out his hand.

"Cleda Humphrey," she said, and shook it heartily. She led us to the back of the building, down a long central hall. There was a rear door, which she unlocked, and we followed her across a bit of parking lot to a large building in the back, which was really a very nice shed that was brick, to match the main building. "Mrs. Bernardo is back here," she said, "since she's not going to be buried here. We keep our temporary visitors in a transition room back here."

"Transition room" turned out to be Cleda Humphrey's comfort-speak for "refrigerator." She opened a gleaming stainless steel door and a draft of cold air billowed out. In a black plastic bag on a gurney lay Xylda. "She's still in her hospital gown, with all the tubes and so on still attached until the autopsy decision is made," the funeral director said.

Shit, I thought. Tolliver's face went very rigid. "At least her soul's gone," I said, and I could have slapped myself when I realized I'd spoken out loud.

"Oh," said the cheerful, motherly woman. "You can see 'em, too."

"Yes," I said, really startled.

"I thought I might be the only one."

"I don't think there are many of us," I said. "Does it help in your job?"

"When they're gone like they should be," Cleda said. "If I see one lingering, I try to call in their pastor to read a prayer. Sometimes that does the trick."

"I'll have to remember that," I said faintly. "All right. Let me do my thing." I closed my eyes, which wasn't necessary but did help, and to get the best impression possible, I laid my hand on the bag. I could feel the chill flesh under the surface.

I feel so bad, I'm so tired. . . . Where's Manfred? What's that man doing here? Looking at me. So tired . . . sleep.

My eyes flew open to meet the funeral director's curious blue gaze.

"Natural death," I said. It wasn't murder if someone else just stood there and watched. I'd had no sense of touching, or any other kind of contact. Someone, some man, had watched Xylda in her last moments, but that was hardly surprising. It might have been the doctor or a nurse. There was no way to tell. However, the image I got was chilling—someone calmly and dispassionately watching Xylda die. Not aiding, but not preventing, either.

"Oh, good," Cleda said. "Well, I'm sure the family will be glad to know that."

I nodded.

The black bag went back into the transition room.

In a somber silence, we retraced our steps across the parking lot and through the corridor back to the front doors of the funeral home.

"I guess you're braced for a huge amount of business," Tolliver said. "When the bodies of the—the young men— are released." I was sure he'd been going to say "victims."

"We're going to be pretty busy, yes, sir," she said. "One of those boys was my nephew. His mama, my brother's wife, she can't hardly get out of bed in the morning. It'd be one thing if someone had grabbed him and killed him—that would be bad enough. But to know he lived for a while, and got hurt so bad, and got used so unnatural, that just kills her."

There was no possible response that would be helpful, because I thought she was exactly right. To know your loved one was cut and burned and raped *would* make the fact of his death much worse, and there was nothing to be done about it. I'd always figured my sister Cameron had been raped before she'd been killed, without ever having proof of either. And just imagining it might have happened was pretty damn awful. I thought the act of rape itself was unnatural, regardless of the gender of the victim. But an emotional time like this was no time to debate the issue.

"We're really sorry," I said.

"Thank you," Cleda Humphrey said with dignity, and we let ourselves out.

"She was pretty decent," Tolliver said as we got into the car. "Probably the most relaxed funeral home person we've ever dealt with."

That was certainly true. "She seemed to take us pretty much in stride," I said.

"Nice change."

I nodded.

Pastor Doak Garland pulled into the parking lot in his modest Chevrolet just as Tolliver was putting the keys in the ignition. He approached the car, so Tolliver turned the key and pressed the window button.

"Hello again," Doak said, bending down to look at us.

"What are you busy doing?" I asked, hoping he wouldn't ask us about our own visit to Sweet Rest.

"Well, one of the bodies is already being released tomorrow, Jeff McGraw's, so I'm here to talk to Cleda about the service. I think we'll need extra traffic control, so I've already been to the sheriff's department, and I think Cleda needs to be prepared for an extra visitation night."

"This is going to take it out of you," Tolliver said. "There are a lot of services coming up."

"Well, I wasn't the minister for all these boys," Doak said with a gentle smile. "But the whole community will turn out for each funeral, so we're all in for a hard time. And maybe we should be. How could this happen in our midst, and we knew nothing?"

That was too big a question for me. "Wouldn't some of that be due to the former sheriff, Abe, um, Madden?" I said. "Wouldn't some of that be due to his policy of pretending the boys were runaways instead of missing and in danger? He seemed willing to shoulder his share of the blame at the memorial meeting the other night."

Doak Garland looked taken aback. "Maybe we shouldn't be into pointing fingers," he said, but he didn't say it with any force. It was clear he wasn't thinking about Abe Madden's role in the terrible drama for the first time. "You really think that had a bearing?" he said.

"Of course," I said, surprised. I didn't know Abe Madden. I didn't have to be careful of his feelings or his reputation. "If his attitude toward the vanishing boys was really the one I've heard described, then of course it had a bearing.

Possibly if the investigation had gotten under way quicker, we'd have a few more kids walking around alive."

"But will assigning blame make this any easier?" Doak asked rhetorically.

I decided to take the question literally. "Yes, it will, for everyone but Abe Madden," I said. "Assigning blame does help people feel better, in a lot of ways. At least in my experience. Plus, if you can correct the behavior that led to the problem, the problem might not repeat itself." I shrugged. Maybe, maybe not.

I'll say this for Doak Garland, he didn't just whip out a platitude, as some men of the cloth were prone to do. He mulled the idea over. "There's a lot in that," he said. "But really, Ms. Connelly, that's just assigning a scapegoat to bear the sins of all of us."

I thought in my turn. "Okay, there's something to that, too," I admitted. "But there is blame to be assigned here, and the former sheriff should shoulder at least some of it."

"As he did," Doak Garland said. "In fact, it would be a good idea if I dropped by to see him. He may be thinking the same way you are."

I wondered if the pastor was trying to make me feel guilty in turn, but I didn't. I don't like to see people get depressed or shunned, but I knew that in my own experience, you had to assume responsibility for your own actions before you could move along with your life.

We didn't have any more to say, I felt. I raised my eyebrows at Tolliver, and he said, "Pastor, we've got to be going." Without further conversation, we rolled up our windows and pulled out of the parking lot.

"Where are we going?" Tolliver asked. "I mean, I can drive around aimlessly, but since there are still patches of ice . . ."

"I'm hungry, what about you?" I asked, and that was easy to answer. All the businesses in Doraville appeared to be open now, and people were going about their affairs with an air of relief. I felt relieved, too. We could get out of here just about any time now.

"What if we just left?" Tolliver said. "We could be on the interstate going in the right direction in an hour. We could find twenty restaurants."

I was surely tempted. We were sitting in the parking lot of the McDonald's again, and I stared at the golden arches, trying to feel something besides resignation.

"We have to return the key," I said, stalling.

"Yeah, a five-minute delay."

"Will they let us?"

" 'They' being the SBI guys? Sandra Rockwell?"

"Any of the above."

"What could they want us for?"

"We haven't signed a statement about yesterday."

"Yeah, true. We might need to stop by the police station for forty-five minutes and do that. Okay, let's go get a burger, and then we'll tie things up."

I wanted to leave, really I did, but there was something nagging at me, or maybe two or three things nagging at me. But I kept reminding myself I wasn't a police officer, and I wasn't responsible. On the other hand, if I suspected something, I should mention it to someone who'd take me seriously.

228

I hardly registered standing in line with Tolliver, whom I had to stop thinking of as my brother. We were way past that now. And I realized that now I could touch him in public. Now he knew how I felt. He felt the same way. I didn't have to hide it anymore. It was awful how strong the habit of standing away from him, not touching him, not watching him, had become once I was afraid of losing him if he realized that I loved him. Since the ice storm, I could watch him all I wanted, and he would enjoy it.

"Do you remember us talking yesterday about what Xylda said in Memphis? That in the time of ice, we would be so happy?" I asked him.

"She did say that. We agreed that Xylda wasn't a fraud, at least not all of the time."

"I think that as she got older, she got closer to the bone," I said.

"I don't know if that daughter of hers will ever believe it."

"Rain just wants everything to be normal," I said. "Maybe if I'd been brought up by Xylda, with all her ups and downs and spiritual moments, I'd be the same way."

"I think the way we were brought up was bad enough."

He was right about that. Being raised by Xylda would have been a cakewalk compared to living in the trailer in Texarkana.

I thought again of the sacrifice Chuck Almand had made as I sat alone at our table, waiting for Tolliver to bring our order. I'd gathered the napkins and straws with one hand, transported them, and returned to get the ketchup packets. I stared down at the table, which was clean, and wished I never had to go into another fast-food place in my life, before

I returned to the subject of Chuck, niggling at the puzzle of his behavior.

Tolliver put the tray on the table, and I began taking my food off. At least I could eat this food one-handed. Without asking, Tolliver tore open three ketchups for me and squirted them on my French fries.

"Thanks," I said, and went back to thinking. But this was no place to tell Tolliver what I was worried about, even if I could put it together—not here, where every soul in Doraville who wasn't at school or at work was crowded in together sharing germs and eating food that was bad for them. I lost my appetite quickly, and piled my trash back on the tray.

"What's wrong?" Tolliver asked. He did care, but I could hear the undertone of anxiety, maybe of irritation. He wanted to leave. Doraville gave him the creeps and the deaths of all those young men was giving him nightmares.

"After we leave here, let's go out to the death site," I said. "I'm really, really sorry," I added when I saw the expression on his face. "But I need to."

"We found the bodies," he said, in as low a voice as he could manage. "We found them. We did what was required. We got our money."

We so seldom disagreed, or at least we hardly ever felt so strongly about our disagreements. I felt sick.

"I'm sorry," I said again. "Can we just leave here, and talk about it?"

In a stiff silence Tolliver dumped our trash into the receptacle and thumped the tray down on top. He held the door for me when we left, and unlocked the car and got in the driver's side, of course, but he didn't start it up. He sat there waiting for an explanation. He'd almost never done that before. Usually, whatever I said went. But now our relationship had changed in deep ways, and we didn't yet know the new balance. It had shifted, though. Now I had to explain, and I accepted that. It hadn't always been comfortable, being Queen of the World. I'd gotten a little too used to it, too.

In the past, I would simply have told him I needed to see the site again, and he would have driven me there without asking me any further questions. At least, most of the time. I pulled my left leg up on the seat and twisted so my back was to the passenger door. He was waiting.

"Here's my thinking." I took a deep breath. "In the story we've got now, the way it looks, Chuck Almand was helping his dad secure the boys. His dad was bringing him along in the family business by showing him how to kill cats and dogs and other small animals, so Chuck would grow up into a big serial killer like Papa Tom. Right?"

Tolliver nodded.

"But that thinking is wrong," I said. "If Chuck was helping his dad, if we accept the idea that it would take more than two people to subdue the boys—"

"Gacy worked alone," Tolliver said.

That was true. John Wayne Gacy had tortured and killed boys in the Chicago area, and he'd acted alone. Plus, in the pictures I'd seen, he hadn't looked like any really fit guy. "He got them to put on handcuffs, right?" I said. "Told them they were trick handcuffs and he'd show them how to take them off, and then they turned out to be real?"

"I think so."

"So he had a gimmick, and so might Tom," I said.

"And Dahmer acted by himself."

"Yeah."

"So I don't think you're making such a point."

"I'm thinking there were two people." It would have been much easier to subdue a healthy adolescent male if there were two abductors. And maybe the boys had been kept alive for a time so two men could enjoy them, each in his own way. "Maybe one got off on the sex, one on the torture, or each on some personal combination of the two. Or maybe one just enjoyed the death. There are people like that. That's why the boys lived for a while. And we know they did. So the killers could have equal time with their victim."

"And you're sure about this."

"I can't say a hundred percent sure. I think so."

"Based on what?"

"Okay, maybe based on something intangible from their graves," I said. "Maybe just my imagination."

"So—there was Chuck. And Tom made Chuck help him."

"No. I don't think so. That's where I was going when we started talking about Gacy and Dahmer. See, the animals were pretty fresh. But the boys have been vanishing for five years, right? More or less. The animals, well, none of them had been dead for longer than a year, looked like. Warm summers here, lots of bugs."

"So what's the bottom line?"

"Tom's helper wasn't Chuck. It was someone else, someone who's still at large."

Tolliver looked at me with a completely blank face. I had no idea what he was thinking or whether he agreed with me.

I held my hands out, palms up. "What?" I said.

"I'm thinking," he said. He turned on the car while he thought, which was good, because it was feeling pretty chilly. Finally he said, "So, what to do?"

"I have no idea," I said. "I need to run in to tell Manfred his grandmother died on her own. Though there was someone there who didn't do anything about it."

"What?"

"Someone watched her die. Someone didn't call for help. Not that I think it would've done any good. But . . ." I shook my head. "That's just creepy. She knew someone was standing and watching."

"But not harming her. And not helping."

"No," I said. "Just watching."

"Could it have been Manfred himself?"

I snatched at the idea. That would make sense. Manfred wouldn't necessarily have known Xylda was passing. "No," I said reluctantly, after I'd thought about my connection with Xylda's last moment in the funeral home cooler. "No, it wasn't Manfred. At least, if it was, Xylda was beyond recognizing her own grandson, and I didn't get any sense of that much disorientation from our connection."

Tolliver dropped me off while he went to gas up the car. I strode through the hospital like I worked there, and I got to Manfred's room to find he was by himself. Trying not to look too relieved—Rain was probably a nice woman but she was a lot of work—I went directly to his bedside and

touched his hand. Manfred's eyes sprang open, and for a second I thought he was going to yell.

"Oh, thank God it's you," he said when he'd grasped who I was. "What did you find out?"

"Your grandmother died of natural causes," I said. "Ah— do you remember standing in the doorway to her room and looking at her for any length of time?"

"No. I always went right in and sat in the chair right by her bed. Why?"

"At the moment she died, someone was standing in the doorway watching her."

"Did they frighten her?"

"Not necessarily. Surprised her. But that didn't cause her death. She was in the process of dying."

"You're sure." Manfred didn't know what to do about this random piece of information. Neither did I.

"Yes, I am. She died a natural death."

"That's great," he said, much relieved. "Thanks so much, Harper." He took my hand, folded it in his warm one. "You did that for me and it had to be awful. But now we don't need an autopsy, she can rest in peace."

Xylda's resting in peace had nothing to do with whether or not she had an autopsy, but I decided it was best to let the subject die a natural death, as natural as Xylda's.

"Listen to me," I said. His face hardened at my tone, which was serious.

"I'm listening," he said.

"Don't be alone here," I said. "Don't be alone in Doraville."

"But the guy was arrested," Manfred said. "It's done."

"No," I said. "No, I don't think it is. I don't think anyone

234

would actually snatch you from the hospital, but if they let you out, you stick right by your mom all the time."

He could see I was dead serious. He nodded—reluctantly, but he nodded.

And then Manfred's nurse came in the room, and she said it was time for him to get up and walk, aided by her, and I had to go stand out front to wait for Tolliver.

Barney Simpson was on his way to the front of the hospital with a sheaf of papers, and I happened to fall into step beside him.

"I would have thought an administrator would be chained to a desk," I said. "You're all around the hospital."

"If my secretary were well, I would be in my office almost nonstop," Simpson agreed. "But she's off. One of the missing boys was a grandson of hers. And though it's going to be a long time before they get to bury the boy, it just seemed right to let her have a day or two off to be with her daughter."

"I'm real sorry for all the families."

"Well, at least there's one happy family. The folks of that boy that was under the stall should sure be having a good day today."

He gave a nod and veered off into a smaller hall lined with offices. Everyone in Doraville was affected by these crimes, though I guess the severity of the affection was lessened with your emotional distance from ground zero—the killing field above the town.

I felt a little foolish, now that I thought about it. It was nuts, warning Manfred. He was older. But he was small, and attractive, and right now he was vulnerable. He was a stranger, too, and wouldn't be missed as quickly as one of the local boys. It was nuts because if you looked at it logically, there was no way the remaining killer—a killer only I seemed to be worried about—would take another boy. Everyone was watching, everyone was wary, everyone was suspicious. At least, they had been. Now it was another story. The boogeyman was in jail, his tormented son was dead, the last victim was safe in the hospital and going to live. A happy ending for just about everyone. The people I heard talking about it were even not too unhappy about poor Chuck, because he would have been so messed up anyway by his father's death, and all the people assumed he'd had to help his father with the boys and the guilt of it had driven him to sacrifice himself. He'd redeemed himself, maybe.

I thought only part of that was the truth.

But if Chuck were alive, I wouldn't have given a nickel for his life. Because his dad's partner would suspect that Chuck knew his identity, even if the boy hadn't. So someone really was happy Chuck had died, and had good reason for being so.

I thought of all the good things I'd seen in Doraville, and all the nice people I'd met. There was a snake in the grass in this pleasant mountain village, and it was a pretty huge snake. Doraville didn't deserve to be singled out for such horror.

When Tolliver pulled up by me, I got into the car and without saying a word, he drove me up to Davey's old farm, the site of so many cold graves.

Klavin and Stuart were up there, and for once I wasn't

displeased to see them. They were measuring the area and making some more pictures of the orientation of the buildings to the road, the surrounding terrain, and whatever else took their fancy. We got out and watched in silence for a few minutes.

They were busy, and disinclined to talk to us. Each couple tried to pretend the other one wasn't there. The wind was blowing up here, and it was chilly, though the beautiful sun took the edge off. I had discarded my heavy coat and put on a blue hoodie, and I pulled the hood up around my face and tucked my hands in my pockets. Tolliver put his arm around me and kissed my cheek.

As if that had been a signal, the two SBI men approached us.

"Have you given your statement at the police station about yesterday?" Klavin said.

"No. We'll do that before we leave town. We just wanted to ask a question, see if you'd answer it," I said. "I suppose it'll be a long time before all the tests are finished on those poor boys."

Stuart nodded. "What were you wanting to know?" he asked. "I figure you're entitled to an answer or two, since you found them."

That was a refreshing point of view, and one with which Klavin didn't necessarily agree.

"I want to know if they were fed and cared for after they were taken," I said. "Or maybe they were sedated. I want to know if their lives were extended."

Both the agents froze. Klavin had been messing with a tiny digital camera, and Stuart had been loading some small machine into the back of their rented SUV. "Why?" Stuart asked, after they'd resumed moving. "Why do you want to know that, Ms. Connelly?"

"I wonder if there was more than one person involved in torturing these boys," I said. "Because I really suspect that Tom Almand wasn't working alone, that he had a killing buddy who helped subdue the poor boys. Some of them were big boys, you know. Tom Almand was a little man. So, did he have some story that made them trust him enough to put themselves into a situation they couldn't get out of? Or did he have a strong right arm that would be sure they got that way?"

The two men looked at each other, and that was enough.

"You gotta tell people," I said. "They all think they're safe, and they're not."

"Look, Ms. Connelly," Stuart said, "we got half the team in jail. We got their killing floor. We got their dump site. We got their survivor, safe and guarded. We even got their backup place for stashing victims, for whatever reason they had it: maybe they prepared it in case they heard this place was being sold, maybe they realized the road up here might become difficult in the winter. Then they'd use the place in the Almand barn. We figure this because there aren't as many bloodstains at the barn. There isn't all the parapher-nalia we found in there." He nodded toward the old shed to the left of the Davey house.

"We want to catch this other bastard real bad, Harper," said Klavin. "You don't know how bad. But we don't figure he's going to be grabbing anyone anytime soon. You see what we're saying?"

No, I was too dumb to understand. "Yes," I said, "I see. And to a certain extent, I agree. It would be crazy for him to grab anyone else. But you see what *I'm* saying? He *is* crazy."

"But so far, he's managed to maintain a perfect façade," Stuart said. "He's clever enough, got enough sense of self-preservation, to keep on doing that."

"Are you sure about that? Sure enough to risk some boy's life?"

"Listen, the fact is, you don't have anything else to do with this investigation," Klavin said. He'd reached the end of his patience.

"I know I'm not a cop," I said. "I know I usually just come in to a town, do a job, and leave. And I like it that way. If I have to stick around, worse stuff happens. And then we have to stay longer. We want to drive out of Doraville. But we don't want anyone else to die. And until you catch this other killer, there's that possibility."

"But what can you do to stop it?" Klavin asked reasonably. "So far as we're concerned, after you give your statement about yesterday, you and your brother can leave. We have your cell phone number, and we know your home address."

"He's not my brother," I said. If Tolliver could tell people, I could, too.

"Whatever," Klavin said. "Hey, Lang, did you know your dad was in jail in Arizona?"

"No," Tolliver said. "I had heard he got out of jail in Texas, though." If they'd been trying to upset Tolliver, they had gone about it the wrong way.

"You two really got shanked in the parent department," Klavin said.

"No doubt about it," I said. He couldn't make me angry like that, either.

He looked a little surprised, maybe a little abashed.

"I can't figure you out," I said. "You can be decent when you want to be. But this shit about our parents, you think we haven't heard all this before? You think we don't remember what it was like?"

He hadn't expected me to clear the decks. Klavin clearly had issues.

"You two go on," he said, while Stuart watched him, a certain guarded look on his face. "Go back to town. Get your statements entered. Then leave. This case has too much cluttering it up. The psychic. You. Now that you've seen Tom Almand swing a shovel, I guess you know who attacked you. You gonna file charges?"

Oddly enough, I hadn't even thought about it. So much had happened since I'd been attacked that it had been low on my list of mysteries to solve. I took a moment to think about it. Theoretically, I was all in favor of Tom paying for the attack on me. But thinking realistically, how could we prove it was Tom? The only evidence against him was that he'd been known to hit someone else with a shovel, and he'd had reason to want to hit me—if you count the fact that I'd found his victims a reason, and I reckoned it was. I'd stopped his fun. At least, I'd thought so, until the trapdoor had swung open. I saw those boys' faces every time I thought about the trapdoor: the one face covered with blood and lifeless, and the other just as bloody and full of fear and a terrible knowledge.

I'd have to come back here to testify, and there really wasn't any more concrete evidence than there had been.

"No," I said. "Is Almand talking?"

"He's not saying one damn word," Klavin said. "He was actually pretty shocked about his son, I think, but he kind of shook it off and said the boy had always been weak."

"That's someone else's influence," I said. "Someone else's words."

"I think so, too," Stuart told us. He turned his back to us to look out over the acre of land that had yielded such a strange crop. "He's not going to talk in case he might trip up and expose his fuck buddy."

I was a little startled at Stuart going crude on us. But if I'd looked at those bodies and examined the inside of that shack as often as Stuart had, I might be pretty deeply upset . . . well, even more upset than I was already.

I wasn't sure why I was here. There were no ghosts, there were no souls, there was nothing left of the bones of the eight young men who had been put in the ground here. There was only the cold air, the gusting wind, and the two angry men who'd spent too much time observing too closely what horrors people could wreak on each other.

"What will you do with the shack?" I asked. Tolliver turned to look at it, along with Stuart.

"We'll have to dismantle it completely and remove it," Klavin said. "Otherwise, souvenir hunters will rip it to shreds. You can see the lab techs have removed the most heavily bloodstained areas for the lab's use. And all the instruments that were in there—the manacles, the branding iron, the pincers, the sex toys—they've gone to the lab, too. We brought a bunch of people up here."

Tolliver's mouth twisted in disgust. "How could he look in the mirror?" Tolliver said. It was rare for Tolliver to speak when we were in a professional situation like this. But men are less used to the idea of being raped than women are, and it strikes them with a fresh horror. With women, that horror comes right along with the female genitals.

"Because he was enjoying himself," I said. "It's easy to look in the mirror when life is fun."

Stuart turned to look at me, surprised. "Yes," he said. "He was probably happy every morning. Tom Almand pulled the wool over the eyes of almost every member of this community, for years. He's surely been pleased with himself every day of that time. The only person he couldn't fool, eventually, was his own son."

"So, he fooled everyone else?" I asked.

Tolliver gripped my hand. I squeezed his.

"His colleagues who have worked with him at the mental health center all say they've gotten along with him fine, that he was always on time, conscientious about keeping his appointments, fairly intelligent with his recommendations and referrals, and had only minor complaints by patients in the eight years he's been here."

I was impressed that they'd gotten together that much information in the limited time they'd had. I wondered if he'd been under suspicion from the beginning. Perhaps they'd gotten a head start on him, from a profile or something similar.

"But what about close friends?" I asked.

"He didn't seem to have any close friends," Stuart said. "Oh, he's been on the Hospital Expansion Board for the past six years; and so have Len Thomason and Barney Simpson, which makes sense. They're all health-care professionals, though from different aspects of the field. That minister got elected to the board last year, the one that conducted the memorial service. They've tried to get matching grants, federal money, private money, worked on fund drives, that kind of thing. Knott County really does need a new hospital, as you may have noticed."

All roads seemed to lead to the hospital. No matter what direction I started out in, I ended up at the front doors of Knott County Memorial.

"Has the boy spoken yet?" I asked, aware that pretty soon Stuart and Klavin would decide not to answer any more questions, just because.

"Not yet."

"And I know you've got him under very heavy, very careful guard?"

Klavin said, "You can believe that. Nothing will happen to that boy."

"His family come forward?"

"Oh, yes, they'd reported him missing the night before. And we found his car on the side of the road about a mile from the Almand house. He had a flat tire, and no spare."

"Well, that explains that. Considering the weather, he'd be glad to get a ride, no matter how nervous he was."

"Kids never think anything can happen to them," Stuart said grimly.

He'd found out different. He'd never be the same.

"Would you consider putting a guard on Manfred Bernardo?" I asked.

"He's older than the other boys," Stuart said.

"But he's part of the case."

"He's an adult, and he's in the hospital with plenty of people watching him," Klavin said gruffly. "Our budget's shot to hell."

"It's been interesting talking to you," I said. "Thanks."

"Did you know they were there?" Tolliver asked as we drove back to Doraville.

"No, I had no idea. I just wanted to look at the site again when it was clean."

"Clean?"

"No bodies. Just dirt and trees."

We drove in silence for a few minutes. Then I said, "Tolliver, if you knew you were going to be accused of murder in the next, say, three or four days—you weren't sure when, but you knew it was coming—what would you do?"

"I'd run," Tolliver said.

"What if you weren't quite sure?"

"If I thought there was a chance I wouldn't be picked out of the lineup, or whatever?"

I nodded.

"If I thought there was a chance I could hold on to my life, I think I'd try to stay around," Tolliver said, deep in thought. "Running is getting harder and harder with the rise of computers and the use of debit and credit cards. Cash isn't common, and people who use it are remembered. You have to show your driver's license for almost everything. It's hard to stay invisible in the United States, and it's hard to cross a border without a passport. If you're not a career criminal, it would be almost impossible to do either one."

"I don't think we're dealing with a career criminal here. I think we're dealing with an enthusiastic amateur."

Tolliver said, "Let's get out of here."

He was at the end of indulging me.

We'd had fights before, but they'd never had this element of the personal. But now we were more than manager and talent, more than brother and sister, more than survivors of a common hell.

And he was right. We had no business doing what the police were supposed to do, and God knows there were police enough to do it. But every time I thought of Chuck Almand, dead at thirteen because he wanted to lead me to discover what his life had been like, living with a man who tortured other boys for a pastime. . . . Then I told myself, *He succeeded. He got you there, and all the law enforcement people, which was what he surely intended. Let them take the weight of this now.*

"All right," I said. "Let's go."

Tolliver's shoulders relaxed. Up to that moment I hadn't realized how tense he'd been.

He was right.

We had to go to the police station to give our statements, and since there were still plenty of news crews around, we phoned ahead on the cell and asked if we could come in the back. We were denied permission. "It's already too crowded back there," the dispatcher said. "The state boys all have cars there, and a couple of the forensic guys, plus we have deputies working extra shifts. Park in the front, and we'll have someone watching out for you."

We had to park down the street from the station because of all the media, and we walked briskly through them, looking neither to the right nor the left. Luckily, we'd almost made it to the door by the time we were recognized. As the voices rose in questions I wouldn't answer, I focused on the door. I hoped it would be the last time we'd ever walk into that particular building. Deputy Rob Tidmarsh was standing there ready to swing the door open. He escorted us to what had been an interrogation room. In fact, it was the same one where we'd been such unwilling guests. It was now set up with a laptop computer and a young man who was ready to extract information from us. We gave him our accounts of the happenings in the barn, and he printed them out, and we signed them. All this took about an hour and a half, maybe twice as long as we'd estimated, and we saw Sandra Rockwell pass by about six times, but she didn't feel the need to speak to us.

There must be a lot to do, I thought as Tolliver talked to the young man, who was about our age. Chronologically. In a case of mass murder, there must be a million details to collect and put in order. I couldn't imagine being in charge of that. And then to have other people brought in over my head, people coming into my town and in front of my own employees taking the case away from me, or at least important aspects of it. . . . No wonder Rockwell didn't have time to stop to talk to us. Building a case against the man who'd killed eight boys and tried to kill another was way more important than stroking the ego of a woman who'd done her job and been paid for it.

Yes, no matter how connected I felt to the case, it was time for me to go. I'd never stayed as long, or maybe it just hadn't felt as long. I'd never found that many bodies at one event, either. This was a first for all of us.

What I felt like doing was prying open the heads of a few people myself, prying them open and looking inside, trying to locate the guilt I knew was in one of them. My conviction that there was a second murderer remained unshaken. But I couldn't think of a way to discover for sure who it might be, and Tolliver was right. It wasn't my job. I wished, for one deluded minute, that I was telepathic. I could just read a man's mind and fathom his guilt or innocence.

But that wasn't going to happen, and I wouldn't wish telepathy on my worst enemy. If I'd been psychic . . . well, after seeing the havoc even a mild gift had wreaked in Xylda's life, and seeing how isolated Manfred felt, I didn't want that, either. My own talent was so focused, so specific, that its use was very limited. And I'd passed the limit here in this little foothill town.

When we were through, we left out of the same door we'd entered, but in the meantime the newspeople had spotted our car and camped around it. Tolliver put his arm around me and we bulldozed through them. Even though my arm was in a cast and there was a bandage on my head, it was hard to get them to move aside. Maybe we'd been dodging them too much, and it had made them more determined to "get" us.

I could swear I recognized one newscaster. Then I realized

I had seen him on a national news network. "Have you ever found that many bodies in one place before?" he asked. It was such a pertinent question, and exactly what I'd been thinking about, that I said, "No, never. I never want to again."

The others started screaming louder. If I'd answered one question, I might answer more.

But then he made a huge mistake—he asked a "How did it feel?" question.

Those I won't answer. My feelings are my own.

After a few seconds of struggle to get the door open, of falling inside the car, buckling my seat belt, and locking the door, I was safe from more questions, and then Tolliver tumbled in the driver's door and got himself ready to drive. He put the car in gear and the knot of newspeople relaxed and spread apart to allow us to leave.

It was lucky for us they all stayed close to the police station, hoping for more tidbits from the police or the SBI agents. We were able to get to Twyla's house by ourselves. Twyla's car was the only one in the garage. I wondered how long it would be before she got to bury her grandson. And then there'd be the trial and all the surrounding publicity. Jeff McGraw wouldn't get to rest in peace for years, at least in the minds of his family.

Tolliver pulled in behind Twyla's car, left ours in park with the engine on, and scrambled out with the key to the cabin. He didn't say a word. Maybe he was afraid that if he said something, I would, too; I'd change my mind about leaving.

A car pulled in behind us as I waited. After a second, someone knocked on the window. I pressed the button to roll it down. Pastor Doak Garland stood there, as pink and innocent a man as I'd ever seen.

He said, "Hello again, Miss Connelly."

"Hi. I forgot to tell you what a good job you did at the memorial service. I hope you all took up a good bit of money toward the funerals."

"Praise God, I think we got about twelve thousand dollars together now," he said.

"That's great!" I was genuinely impressed. That was a huge amount of money in a poor community like Doraville. Divided among the six local boys, that wasn't much, especially when you considered the cost of an average funeral these days. But it would help.

As if he could read my mind, Doak said, "Three of the boys had burial insurance, so they won't need funds. And we're hoping to bring in at least three thousand more with a raffle. Twyla has very generously offered to match whatever we make for the raffle."

"That *is* generous."

"She's a great woman. Can I ask you a question just out of sheer curiosity, Miss Connelly?"

"Ah . . . okay."

"I'm not sure I've ever been in that old barn behind the Almand house. Where was the poor young man?"

"He was in a kind of—oh, wait, I'm not supposed to talk about it. Sorry, the cops made me promise."

"Well, you hear all kinds of things, you know," he said. "I just wanted to get the facts straight. Where's your companion?"

"He's coming right back out in just a second," I said.

Suddenly I felt very alone, though I was parked in a driveway on a suburban street. I jumped, pretending I'd felt my phone vibrate. "Hello?" I said, holding it to my ear. "Oh, hi, Sheriff. Yeah, I'm here at Twyla's, talking to Pastor Garland. He's standing right here, do you need him? No? Okay." I made an apologetic face at the minister, and he smiled and waved, and started into the house. I kept up the false conversation until he'd gone in the back door.

Half of me felt like a very big idiot, and the other half was simply relieved that he was gone. Where the hell was Tolliver? What was taking him so long?

I turned in my seat and began to undo my seat belt. I'd go in to find out what he was doing. I was really anxious. I had the uneasy feeling I'd overlooked something big.

Something about the ninth boy, the one who'd lived.

I stopped what I was doing and considered. He'd been identified. He was safe in the hospital in Asheville. He might never speak about what had happened to him, but I thought it was probable he would, when he got used to being safer and felt better physically. When he did begin to talk, he would identify the other killer, if in fact there was another one.

But what if he hadn't ever seen the other killer? What if he'd been kept in the stable because it had been Tom Almand, and Almand alone, who'd abducted him? Maybe it had been the first and only time Almand had made his son help him, and that was what had driven Chuck over the edge. Maybe Tom hadn't had a chance to share before he was discovered. So the accomplice had an even better chance of getting away with it.

And Doak Garland was not the man. He'd just asked me where the boy had been kept. If he'd been the other murderer, he would have known. If he'd just been trying to muddy the waters, he could have simply said nothing. It didn't make any difference what I thought. Why should he make such a point of asking me, unless he genuinely didn't know?

But someone had known, someone I'd talked to very recently. Someone had said the boy had been under the floor in the stall, or something to that effect. Who had it been? We'd seen so many people. Obviously, not Rain or Manfred; not any of the law enforcement people, they'd know and that would be okay. All right, who? Who had I talked to? The funeral home lady, Cleda something. No, not her.

I'd been sitting there with the door half-open, one foot out while I thought. With a suddenness that struck me dumb, a big SUV pulled in beside me, the door was ripped from my hands, and my arm was grabbed and I was out of the car. Then a big hand hit me right where the shovel had bashed me a long, long time ago, and then I was out.

Thirteen

I was in his vehicle by the time I was conscious enough to understand what was happening, and by then my mouth was taped shut and my hands were bound together. His blitz attack had caught me completely unawares.

Barney Simpson was hunched in the driver's seat, backing out of the driveway and taking off down the road like a maniac. The SUV lurched so violently that I slid to the floor. I had no means to stop myself. I landed on my bad arm, and the pain was excruciating. I would have screamed, but once again, he'd taken care of that.

There's something terrible about being right when being right means you get bitten on the ass.

I'd be lucky if that was all that happened.

He pulled over after five minutes. I still couldn't move, but I was trying to gather my energy. I had no idea where we were. Twyla lived in a suburb, maybe Doraville's only upscale housing development. Five minutes from it would take us almost anywhere: into the older part of Doraville or out into the country. Past Barney's head, I could see ice melting off a pine tree, one of a stand of trees. There are trees all over in North Carolina.

"We had it all," he said. He was looking down at me, and his big black-framed glasses magnified his eyes, so he was not just looking, but glaring. "We had it all, until you found them. I'd spot them at the hospital and mark them for the future, or Tom would see them out walking or hitching, and we would pick them up and then we'd just . . . use them up."

Oh, Jesus, I thought.

"We'd use every bit, all the pain, all the sex, all the fear. We'd consume them. Until they were nothing."

I was strangling behind the tape, gurgling and gasping.

"We had the second place, the place in the barn, in case we had two boys at the same time. It was like a holding cell. We'd never really had to use it. But I guess Tom just couldn't resist, even though the last thing he should have done was pick up another boy."

Having made his point, which was that I was the snake in their paradise, he put the SUV in gear and glanced in his rearview mirror. He pulled back onto the road.

"But Tom couldn't give it up, thought it would be his last time, I guess, and a hitchhiker, they're just like apples falling into your lap."

I couldn't just huddle there on the floorboard and fear. I had to think of something to do. I might manage to open the door and roll out, but the car was going so fast that I didn't think I'd survive. I would save that for a last resort. Dying that way would be better than dying the way the boys had.

Okay, it was time to fight. I kept telling myself that, but I remained so dizzy and disoriented that it was hard to make my muscles agree on an aggressive program. And then it was hard to get in position to make my blows count for something. My legs were free, because Barney hadn't had time to confine them, and also maybe he'd hoped I'd stay unconscious for longer. So I kicked at him, trying to get some force behind my legs, wriggling so that my back was braced against the door. Of course, the SUV swerved and he screamed at me, "I'm going to pull your skin off!" I knew he meant it literally. He didn't look like a hospital administrator anymore. He looked like what he really was: a man crazed with his own evil.

He struck at me, but he had to drive, so the random swings didn't connect with my legs often. If they did, they didn't have much force behind them because he was having to strain to reach me.

The pain in my arm was constant and increasing. In a way it was good, because it kept me awake and angry, and in a way it was bad, because it was draining my energy and my will. I even caught myself wanting to be careful of the healing injury. But there was no point in keeping the arm from breaking if I died soon after, I told myself stoutly, and I kicked with renewed vigor and rage.

"You crazy bitch!" he screamed. Well, *right back at you, buddy.* I was so pleased I had my hiking boots on.

I'd assumed sooner or later we'd be in the center of Doraville, but he swerved to the right, and I knew we'd turned onto one of the back roads that twisted through the county. We were going up into the mountains. That was the worst possible development.

He leaned way over, till his left hand was barely on the wheel, and he hit me in the face open-handed. I saw gray for a second. He looked very satisfied, when I could focus on his face again. He'd caused pain, and he liked that a lot. Also, I'd quit kicking. He could drive with both hands on the wheel. I debated with myself whether to let him drive safely and not get hit again, or to kick out and get hurt. I rested for a couple of minutes and decided it was time to try again.

I got his knee this time, and there was the familiar swerve, but this time he looked all around and pulled over again. Okay, this was a step for the worse. He flung open his door and dashed around the SUV while I was struggling to change positions so I'd be facing him. But I couldn't manage it, and he popped open the passenger door so suddenly that I fell out. He caught me by my hair, pulling the stitches in my scalp. I made a noise that would have been a scream if I could have opened my mouth. He dragged me out by the hair, out onto the narrow shoulder, gray with ice and snow slush. There was a steep slope down to the forest, patched with white. Beyond the forest, I glimpsed water.

I had to struggle desperately to keep from landing flat on the ground. I got my feet under me somehow, and tried to twist away, and he hit me again, this time with his fist, in the ribs.

Oh, God, it hurt.

Once I got my feet braced I rammed against him, trying to knock him down, but I only made him stagger a foot or two, and then he began beating me in earnest. I thought if I fell down he would kill me, but I didn't think I could stay up for long. I landed a lucky kick to his crotch, but when I brought my foot back down I slipped on the ice by the side of the road, and I toppled over. I rolled through snow and wet grass, down and down to the bottom of the slope.

He was no more dressed than I for something like this; in fact, he was even less prepared, because I was wearing boots and a heavy coat and scarf, and he was wearing a suit and that was it. His shoes went along with the suit, strictly in-door wear. By the time I got to the tree line at the bottom of the slope, he'd begun floundering down after me.

Getting up was very hard with my hands taped, but I was able to struggle to my feet, and I took off. It was terrible, making my way through the heavy brush and trees, with the ground slushy. But I had to put as much distance as I could between him and me.

Would he come down in the trees after me?

Yes, idiot. Of course he will. I heard his inarticulate scream of rage and then the sounds of him thrashing through the trees.

At least he was openly nuts now. At least he wasn't trying to reason. That was the only chance I had, his mental state.

Not that I was thinking. I was just running.

Plan, plan, plan, I needed a plan. The weather and terrain were all against me. If I trod in the patches of snow, all he had to do was follow my tracks. And it was very precarious, trying to hurry and also trying to avoid stepping in the snow. At least there were a few other tracks around; people had ridden their four-wheelers through here, and I could see another set of tracks, vague ones, a few yards away. I leaped between the snow patches, hoping that the ground would not show every print I made simply because it was wet. Maybe he wasn't any more of a woodsman than I was.

I felt the buzz of bones, very close. Instinctively I began tracking the buzz. The dead could not rise up and protect me, which would only have been right . . . but could they hide me? I couldn't have told you exactly what I was thinking, but I was comfortable with the dead.

The sky was darkening and visibility was getting worse even as I ran, bashing into trees and staggering to keep to my feet. I headed for the dead man. If no one had found him, maybe no one would find me. The feeling of him was fairly fresh, and I was so tired. But I kept on scampering, fast as a panicked squirrel.

The dead man was in the thicket right before me, an overgrown patch of short tree saplings, vines, and myrtle. The thicket was surrounded by pines, and there were pinecones littering the ground. I crouched to grab up a couple.

The live man trying to kill me was just a few yards behind me, though I couldn't see him. I could hear him, snorting and pushing through the growth. Half-standing, I threw one pinecone, then another. I threw them as hard as I could with my bound hands, and they made just a bit of noise a few yards away, when they hit the soggy ground. I didn't think Barney Simpson was any Daniel Boone. Maybe he would think he was hearing footsteps. There was a rocky outcropping close, and he might think my next steps had been on the rock surface. The dead man was waiting.

I hunkered down and tried to slow down my breathing. I sounded like a faulty bellows. *Please, Dead Guy,* I begged, *please be a hunter.*

God heard me. Or fate heard me. Or it was just the way it turned out. Dead Guy had a knife. It was in a sheath on his rotting belt. His camo was in shredded rags, stained with the fluids from his body. Some of his bones had been scattered, and the stomach area had been torn open and devoured by something. But Lyle—that was his name, Lyle Worsham—had a knife in that sheath. The Velcro yielded to my fingers, and then with some difficulty, I worked the knife out. It was rusted and pocked, but it was a knife—not the stout hunting knife I'd expected, though. The shape was strange to me. I awkwardly turned it in my fingers and tried to saw through the duct tape with it.

Before I was through, I was glad I had a coat on. My arms would've been a mess. And my first act was to rip the tape off my mouth. No silencing me.

Of course, then I crouched there without making a single noise. Where was he? Was he going to pounce on me any second? Had he given up to go back to the SUV? Was he even now fleeing the county? I didn't mind staying here until I was sure. I was cold and wet and scared, but I could be patient. I had old Lyle here with me. Had Lyle had a gun? He should have, right?

As it turned out, Lyle had been fishing, not hunting. There was a tackle box sitting on its side in two years' worth of downed leaves, and there was a creel that had once contained his catch. So now I knew why this knife had such a strange shape—it must be a filleting knife. He'd been to the lake to fish. Would the surface of the water have iced over? It had gotten above freezing this afternoon, and it had been sunny for a while. Now that the twilight was drawing in, the water might freeze again. I shivered. My vague idea of cutting across the frozen lake surface was simply stupid. My ignorance of the woods was probably equal to Barney Simpson's. Barney preferred indoor sports, like having sex with bound boys. I wonder what the former Mrs. Simpson had to say about Barney's sexual kinks.

My mind stopped wandering and focused at the faint noises I was hearing. Barney was trying for stealth, but he was a big man and he was wearing the wrong footwear. The snow crunched under his feet and he was breathing heavily. Me and Lyle, we were really quiet.

The next time I got abducted, I was going to have my gloves on, I promised myself. And a hat.

"Get out here, bitch," Barney called.

Mr. Simpson, I'm not satisfied with my treatment by your staff.

"There aren't any houses around here, and no one's going to come help you," he called, and he was closer to where I was crouched.

Could he possibly be *lying*? Why, yes, I thought he might be. The same way he'd been lying all along.

The glimpses I'd caught while I was running away had included a brief vista across a body of water, and the glimpse of some cabins; distant, but visible. Reachable. I was pretty sure of my location.

I thought I was very close to the southern shore of Pine

Landing Lake. I thought if I struck out through the trees, following the lake line northwest, I might find the cabin again. If I could go up and walk on the road I'd be sure, and walking would be easier and faster.

Now he was right outside the thicket. I bit my lip to keep from letting out my shuddering breath. With my right hand, I held the knife at the ready.

Hold it. Hold it. Don't say anything. And then his feet moved away.

The darkness couldn't fall fast enough to suit me.

He was the one who was in a hurry. Not me.

Lyle, you and me, we can wait forever, right?

And then he howled and pounced but he was howling and pouncing on the wrong shadow, and since I'd held still I was okay, I was okay. My arm was truly broken all the way through now, thanks to the beating by the side of the road, and my scalp was really bleeding, and my head was hurting like someone had dragged me out of a car by my hair, but I was okay. In danger of freezing in this position, though. I'd been in one position for too long, and I needed to move, needed to stretch a little, needed to shift my weight. But I was too scared.

He didn't have a gun, apparently. That was good. He could just shoot at bushes until he hit me; no, that would attract too much attention. Even in the rural South, random shooting will attract a certain amount of notice. But he might risk that, to kill me.

"This is ridiculous," he said, so close I almost shrieked. "I mean, after all, you must be nuts to react to a man talking to you that way. Kicking and screaming, fighting and biting. Who could expect anyone in your line of work to be sane, anyway? I was just trying to take you to the hospital when you started having a fit, that's all. Your overreaction caused me to panic. I took the wrong turn. Now here we are out in the middle of nowhere in very cold weather and you won't let me know where you are so I can get you the help you need."

The help I need is for someone to come along and shoot you, I thought. Barney was busy building a story, some kind of story that would enable him to hold on to what he had. He was doomed to fail. But then, he'd lasted this long, and it must be hard for him to believe it was the end.

And to think I'd suspected Doak Garland. Well, I shouldn't relax too soon. There might have been *three* of them.

And I really was thinking about that, so you know my mind was wandering. It was the cold and fear that were doing me in. I sharpened back up mentally just in time. I'd almost laughed at the picture of the whole town of Doraville being in on the kidnapping and the murdering. Like a Shirley Jackson short story!

And then he caught me.

Fourteen

HIS big hands grabbed my shoulders, and like so many young men had been, I was now in his power. Except I had a knife in my hand. He pulled me up and up, until I was almost off my feet. In the twilight it was hard to make out details but I could see the white of his shirtfront, where his unbuttoned coat flapped open, and I swung my arm as hard as I could. The knife went into his skin easily enough but skidded along a bone, maybe his rib, and he screamed as the blood welled through his shirt.

He dropped me and I ran. He caught up with me after a second, though; he was quicker to recover from the shock than I expected. He tackled me, and I twisted, coming up on my side and swinging the knife back. This time I got him in the shoulder and it went in much farther. He really did scream, and heaved off of me, scrambling to his feet. We were close to the edge of the lake then, and I saw a sign or two—we were in some sort of public fishing area. I backed up closer to the water because he was coming at me and I didn't have a choice.

He'd done all the talking up till now. "Come get me, you bastard," I said. "Come get me, rapist."

"They loved it," he said, amazingly. "They loved it."

"Sure," I said. "Who doesn't like being chained and burned and sliced before sex?"

"No," he said, panting, "not the boys. Tom. Tom and Chuck."

"Okay, you make me sick," I said. "You going to stand there and make me sick some more, asshole?"

And he charged. He can't have been stupid, because he had a good job and he did it well enough to keep it, but he was stupid that night because of the strain and the pain and the freezing temperature, and he did lunge right at me. I leaped to one side and as he shot by I shoved him as hard as I could using both hands, even with the broken arm scream-ing at me. He landed right at the lake's edge, so I hadn't been close enough, damn it. I'd wanted him to go into the chilly water. But he wasn't getting up, and I took off. All those years of running finally gave me a reward for good behavior.

I was in the trees and working my way around the lake toward the inhabited cabin, the one with lights, which—I was almost certain—was the Hamiltons'.

I thought I heard him a million times. I hid for ten min-utes, not moving, at least once; and maybe more than that. I was in too much pain to make sense, too cold to reason.

I still had the knife, and though I thought of dropping it, I was scared to be without it in case he caught up with me. When I remembered how it had felt when the knife went into him, I had to stop and throw up. This was a queasy case. I didn't remember ever getting the heaves over any case before. Probably, I thought, I could excuse myself for it over the knifing. But I'd gotten sick outside the barn, too. Maybe it was the torturing, not the knifing?

I knew I wasn't thinking clearly, but knowing that didn't seem to help. I actually shook my head, maybe in the hope that my brains would resettle in a more sensible configuration, but I was really sorry I did that after I got sick yet again. Something was wrong with me, something bad. I needed to go to the hospital! I giggled.

It sure must have been Tom that hit me with that shovel, I thought. *If it had been Barney, he would've killed me.*

I'd forgotten to move for a couple of minutes. I'd just been standing in the dark woods with my mind far, far away. I listened hard, but I couldn't hear anything. That didn't mean it wasn't happening. I didn't trust my senses anymore. But I made myself move, because I couldn't stay out in the cold. I had to reach shelter.

That was the hardest struggle of my life. But I could see the lights and they were getting closer. I was farther from the road, far enough that I could only see lights passing occasionally. And who could tell whose lights they were, anyway?

I finally approached the first cabin. The woods ended, not abruptly, but with a gradual shift from heavy brush and trees, to trees with no brush, to scattered trees, to lawn and cabin. I didn't know anything: where Barney was, if I was for sure at Pine Landing Lake, if Tolliver was even looking for me. How could he not be? But what if he thought I'd gone off voluntarily? We'd been a little irritated with each other. No, that would never happen. He'd never believe I'd leave him.

I was stalling because I was scared to step out into the open. I listened with all my ears and looked with all my eyes. My heart was thudding and my head began pounding in time with it. I was having to fight a terrible desire to lie down on the cold ground and rest there, just for a minute. I took a few deep breaths and braced myself. I stepped out into the darkening evening. The moon would be out and there would be a lot of visibility, but now it was still twilight, the deepest, darkest part.

One step out into the open. Another.

Nothing happened.

I began to move faster, crossing this lawn and going into the next. Saying "lawn" may give an impression of unbroken sweeps of trimmed grass, but that wasn't exactly accurate. These were summer cabins, or glorified fishing camps, and lawn care was not a big item in the time budget of people who spent weekends at the lake. The lots were not that large, and sometimes there was no division at all between one property and another. Sometimes there was a line of ragged bushes, probably something that flowered in the spring. The ground was often weedy, uneven, and always, it was wet. There were things strewn around: buckets, childrens' toys, boats covered in tarps, even a swing set. One careless cabin owner had left out his deck chairs. I know because I fell over one.

I'd never felt so alone in my life.

I got this feeling that this episode would never end. Forever, for always, I'd be stumbling in the dark through rough territory, with death waiting for me somewhere along the line.

I was actually surprised to find that I had reached the Cotton cabin, where we'd stayed. For the first time I was sure I was at Pine Landing Lake, and the next cabin, the one with lights, was the Hamiltons' place.

But I'd have to step into the bright light to knock on the Hamiltons' door. I might endanger them. Though it seemed to me that Barney Simpson must be heading toward Mexico or Canada in his SUV by now, I couldn't be certain.

I planned it in advance, real carefully. I would run from the shadows of the Cotton cabin, up the slight slope to the Hamiltons' driveway, up the steps to their little deck, across it to the door, *bam bam bam*. Ted would open the door, because it was night. He would let me in. He might not really want to, because I was such a mess and I was bringing trouble with me, but I thought he would.

I gathered myself. Just as I was about to take the step out of the shadows, a large dark shape passed between me and the cottage. It seemed more bear than human, but after a second I was sure I was seeing Barney Simpson—not the kindly hospital administrator, but the beast that had lived within him. He hardly walked like a man. His shoulders were slumped and his left leg was dragging. I was sorry I hadn't hurt him enough to stop him. I thought he was more dangerous now that he'd been wounded.

He stood almost directly outside the Hamiltons' side

door, down on the driveway; he didn't mount the steps to the deck. Their security light shone on the top of his head. Barney's hair was full of leaves and twigs. His suit was stained with blood and damp and dirt.

He had a big knife in his right hand. It was really more of a machete than a knife. I wondered if he'd gotten it out of his car, and if so, where it had been during our struggle. He'd been too cocky, then, apparently; he hadn't thought a weapon would be necessary, because he was big and strong.

Okay. I'd just wait until he left.

But Ted Hamilton was on the watch, as always. The door to the cottage opened, and the old man stepped out onto the little deck.

"Is it Mr. Simpson from the hospital?" he called. "Mr. Simpson, is that you?"

"Oh, Mr. Hamilton," said Barney. "Listen, I'm sorry to disturb you. But that young woman that was here to find the bodies, that Harper Connelly, she's having a mental episode and she's somewhere out here running loose."

"Oh, goodness," said Mr. Hamilton, and it was impossible to tell from his voice what his reaction was.

"I don't suppose you've seen her?" Barney asked, and I wondered if I was the only one who could hear the strain in his voice. Barney was having a hard time sounding and acting like a human.

"No, I haven't," Ted Hamilton said. "What do you plan to do when you find her?"

"Why, take her to the hospital," Barney said.

"Are you planning to cut off her head first? Because that sure is a big knife you've got there."

"No, Mr. Hamilton, watch out!" I jumped out of my hiding place, because I was so scared that Barney would attack the old man and his wife.

But Mr. Hamilton was pointing a gun at Barney. He was right on top of the situation, until I'd startled both of them by my sudden appearance.

With a roar, Barney came after me, and I turned to run back to the woods. But then the gun went off behind me.

And Barney wasn't running after me anymore.

Fifteen

I stopped and turned around. Barney Simpson was lying in the driveway, so newly cleaned of tree debris. Now he was getting it dirty again, because he was really bleeding from a hole in his shoulder.

Mr. Hamilton had come forward to the edge of the deck, and Nita was behind him. She was wearing another tracksuit, and her short hair looked just as neat in the overhead light as it had in the daytime.

"You think you need to shoot him again?" she asked her husband.

"I think he's done," Ted Hamilton said. "You scoot in there and call the police."

"I'm one step ahead of you, honey, I already did it when I heard his voice outside," she said. "Miss Connelly, you want to step around him, real careful, and come inside?"

"Thank you," I said, in a very shaky voice that didn't sound at all like my own. "I'd love to be inside. Inside anything."

"You poor girl, come on in."

I walked very carefully around Barney Simpson, who was clutching his shoulder and as white as a sheet, though the bright overhead light washed the color out of everything. I went up the stairs very carefully, since nothing in my body seemed to be working exactly right. I was careful not to jostle Ted or come between him and the downed man. I didn't want Barney to get any more like the Terminator than he already had.

When I was close to Nita Hamilton and she got a good look at me, she said, "We do need to get you inside. Ted, are you good out here?"

"Yes, honey, you take care of the young lady."

And just like that I was in a warm place. I could have predicted almost everything about the Hamiltons' cottage, from the maple furniture to the crocheted throws folded over the backs of their favorite chairs, from the framed baby pictures to the china rooster on an end table. Nita efficiently threw a towel over the wooden chair by the door, where they probably normally dumped their keys and coats. After I looked down at myself, I knew that was the only possible place for me to sit.

"You're bleeding," she said. "I'm going to get a rag and wipe you off. I know the EMTs will do it right, but you don't want to be sitting there dripping. I know I wouldn't."

And that was true enough, though I didn't really care that much just at the moment.

She was back with a clean rag and a white enamel basin of warm water in just a couple of minutes, and she began the tedious process of cleaning my face.

"Ted'll keep his distance, don't you worry," she said quietly, as if shooting men was an everyday occurrence at the lake cottage. "He won't get too close."

"When will the police be here?"

"Any moment. Your brother has been looking for you all over town," Mrs. Hamilton said, and my heart felt warm again. "He called out here and asked us to keep our eyes open, because he saw Barney Simpson's car parked at the other end of the lake. So we were prepared."

"I hope the police understand," I said.

"I'm sure they will. Nothing wrong with our sheriff. She's a good one."

I wasn't as sold on that idea as Nita, but then the sheriff wasn't answerable to me.

"How come your head's bleeding?" Nita asked, as if to make sure I was completely there with her mentally.

"He pulled me out of the car by the hair," I said, and she looked truly shocked. "He pulled some stitches out."

"Well, if Ted knew that, he'd shoot him again," she said, and that triggered a set of giggles that shook my body in an unpleasant way.

I thought, *Then I wish I'd told him,* but just then we heard an ominous sound outside. It was a deep groan, and it came from right outside the door. Ted Hamilton. Oh, shit.

Quick as a wink, Nita locked the front door, and just barely in time. The knob turned, and when the door wouldn't open to him, Barney threw himself against it.

"Come out," he bellowed, "come out here!"

"He's hurt Ted," Nita said. "That son of a bitch."

Even at that moment, I was shocked. But that was only the beginning. Nita opened a closet on the other side of the front door, pulled out a rifle, and aimed it at the door. "This is our varmint rifle," she told me, maybe because I was gaping at her. "He comes in here, he's dead. I might turn my own cheek, but I ain't offering up yours."

Barney threw himself against the door. Since I was still sitting to the right of the door, like a fool, I could hear the click in the quiet night. "Move!" I yelled. "Move, Nita!" And Barney fired Ted's pistol into the house.

The cabin had a good door, but the bullet came in and passed through the living room and into the kitchen beyond. Nita had moved to the side, and it missed her by a foot or more, but it was pretty shocking. For a moment I thought Nita would falter, that all her courage would drain away, but she raised the rifle and fired right back, and we heard a scream.

After a second of staring at each other, Nita said, "I have to see about my husband." Though I thought it was the worst idea in the world for her to open that door, I said "Of course you do" through stiff lips. I reached up my right hand and unlocked the door, and turned the knob as quietly as I could, though I'm not sure why I was trying to be so quiet at this late date.

The door swung open, and we saw Barney again down and bleeding, and Ted Hamilton crumpled on the deck in a corner, blood running from his shoulder. He was conscious, but only just. Nita said, "Oh," and it sounded like she was witnessing the end of the world.

Then she simply stepped over Barney to get to her man, and she knelt down by him, and she put pressure on his shoulder like the sensible woman she was, and I finally managed to subtract myself from the situation by fainting.

Sixteen

WHEN I was a little more aware of what was around me, things were better all around. I was being strapped to a gurney and I was willing to bet I was about to get a ride in an ambulance to the Doraville hospital.

"Doraville's not lucky for me," I said, or at least I thought I was saying that, but I guess I was just mumbling, because the EMT at my head, a plump young woman with an aggressive jaw, said, "You're gonna be okay, honey, don't you worry."

"Mr. Hamilton?"

"That's nice, your asking about him. We got the bleeding stopped. I think he's gonna be okay, too."

"Barney?"

"He ain't dead, but I bet he's gonna wish he was."

"Where's my—where's Tolliver?" *Had* to get out of the habit of calling him my brother.

"Tall, dark, skinny?"

"Mm-hm."

"Waiting for us to wheel you out."

And I smiled.

"That's sweet, she's happy to see him," the young woman said. Her partner, a man in his fifties, said, "Grace, let's just get her out of here," and she pouted as they got me down the deck steps.

Tolliver was by me, and he was beside himself. "He took you right out of the car," he said, as if I didn't know that. "I couldn't believe it when I came out and you were gone!"

"Well, you-all can talk all night if you want. Let us get this gal to the hospital," the older man said.

The ride back to the hospital took a while, and the young woman sat in back with me and chattered the whole time. She took my pulse and checked my temperature and did all kinds of things, including looking at the stitches in my scalp. From the slight face she made, I knew they weren't in good shape.

"Now, I understand you had a cracked ulna a few days ago?" she asked. "I think you've graduated to a broken arm, but we'll take us an X-ray to be sure."

"Okay," I said. We'd have to go into our savings to pay for my Doraville medical bills. That'd be that much longer until we could buy our house. But it was hard for me to worry about that right now, or much of anything else, being in this ambulance felt so blissful compared to my previous three hours of experience.

I felt so safe I actually fell asleep and had to blink my eyes open when we reached the hospital.

The whole hospital experience was déjà vu. I wasn't in

the same room—I think Ted Hamilton was in that one. I was down the hall and on the other side.

Sandra Rockwell was my most surprising visitor. After we'd done the "How are you"s and so forth, she said, "I want to apologize for something."

I waited.

"I knew whoever attacked you, I knew it had to be the killer. And there wasn't a trace of him. Or his vehicle. Turns out, Tom Almand says he parked over behind Hair Affair and cut across the back parking lots. Then he hid behind the Dumpster behind the motel. He was going to slash your tires, but then you came out, and he'd brought the shovel just on the off chance."

I tried to remember where Hair Affair was—two doors down from the motel, I thought. It hardly mattered now.

"How's he doing?" I asked.

"Tom?" She sounded surprised. "Talking his damn head off. But won't mention his son."

"Maybe Barney will," I said. Again, I felt as if I hardly cared. Chuck Almand was gone now, and no amount of confession or explanation would bring him back.

Tolliver came in just then. He'd been in the cafeteria getting coffee and breakfast. He'd gotten me some coffee, and though I wasn't sure if I was supposed to have it or not, I planned on drinking it. He bent over to kiss me, and I didn't care, either, what Sandra Rockwell thought about that.

Klavin and Stuart came in then. They both looked exhausted, but they were smiling.

"There's enough pathology between those two to keep the serial-killer writers busy for years," Klavin said. "As long as they're behind bars while they're being studied, that's fine with me."

"The writers are welcome to 'em," said Stuart. He smoothed his already smooth hair. "Those two are talking, and that's how we're filling in the cracks."

Tolliver took my hand.

I sighed.

They began asking me exactly what had happened the afternoon before, and I wasn't really ready to talk about it. But I'd had to do a lot of things I didn't want to do during my stay in Doraville, and this was simply another one of them.

"Did you suspect he was the one?" Stuart asked.

"Yes," I said, and they all seemed surprised . . . especially Tolliver. "Because when I was sitting there in the car, I was thinking about the hole under the barn, and I was thinking how strange it was that Barney Simpson knew there was a hole there. He said something about it when I was visiting Manfred here at the hospital. I might not even have thought about it, but when Doak Garland asked me a question about it, it was clear that Doak had no idea there was a pit under the stall. So it was not common knowledge. Yet Barney had known about it. And then I thought about the way so many of the boys had had a trip to the hospital. That would have been a good place for Barney to spot them and mark them for future attention. And he said something to me about that."

That was what they were anxious to hear, so I tried to remember the way Barney had talked about their methods, and explain about the pit and why it had been built, when the old house out of town was really more isolated.

"They would take turns," Stuart said. "Because it was hard to park two cars behind the old house. But sometimes, on weekends, they'd go together. Like double dating."

I felt sick, and put the coffee down on the rolling table. Tolliver patted me.

"Sometimes the boys would last four or five days, if they gave them food and water," Klavin said.

"Okay, enough," Tolliver said, and it was clear he was angry. "We know as much about this as we want to know."

"So, we're charging him with attempted homicide on you and Ted Hamilton," Klavin said, when he'd absorbed the rebuke. "But with the murders, we got enough to put him away forever. We'll just throw in other charges if there's any way at all he might get off. I mean, you can only give him life so many times."

"Some of the forensic evidence will tie both of them in, I hope. So it's not just their confessions."

"There was so much there, some of it's definitely going to come through. For one thing, there are hair matches already. And I'm sure we'll get some DNA matches."

I nodded. Though these men would eat, breathe, and sleep the case until it came to trial, to me it was at a close.

"How are you doing, by the way?" the sheriff asked. She just wanted to point out that Klavin and Stuart hadn't inquired. They both looked only a tad sheepish.

Tolliver said, "Her arm is broken all the way through. Her scalp stitches had to be redone and there are more of them now. The scalp wound is infected. She has multiple severe bruises and two loose teeth. You can see the black eye. And now she's got an upper respiratory infection, too."

Also, a torn fingernail, but he left that out.

Tolliver was glaring at them so indignantly that I expected they would break down and weep, but they just shuffled around uncomfortably until they thought of a good reason to leave. It didn't sound as though I'd have to come back to Doraville, maybe. At least, not anytime soon. That suited me just fine.

Manfred called, but I didn't talk to him. Tolliver did. I was too tired—too emotionally tired—to want to talk to him again.

The only guest I was glad to see was Twyla Cotton. She came in moving even more heavily, it seemed to me. Her face was so serious that it didn't seem she would ever smile again.

"Well," she said. She was standing right by my bed, and she couldn't meet my eyes. "They're caught, and my grandson's gone for good."

I nodded.

"I did the right thing bringing you here, and I'm glad I did. They had to stop what they were doing, even if it was too late for Jeff."

It had been too late for Jeff by months.

"They'll rot in hell," Twyla said with absolute conviction. "And I know Jeff is in heaven. But it's hard for us left here."

"Yes," I said, because that was something I knew about. "It's hard for those left behind."

"You're thinking of your sister who's missing?"

"Yes, Cameron."

"Kind of ironic, huh?"

"That I can find everyone else but her? Yes, you could put it that way."

"Then that's what I'll pray about for you. That you find your sister."

Looking at Twyla's stricken face, for the first time I wondered if I really wanted to find Cameron. If it would really give me peace. I switched my gaze over to Tolliver. He was looking at Twyla with an unpleasant face. He thought she was making me unhappy, and he didn't think I needed any more unhappiness.

"Thank you, Twyla," I said. "I hope . . . I hope your remaining grandson brings you joy."

She almost smiled. "He will. Ain't nothing can replace Jeff, but Carson is a good steady boy."

She left soon after, because we didn't have anything left to say.

Tolliver said, "Tomorrow, if you don't have a fever, we're leaving this place."

"Absolutely," I said. "Maybe by the time I get to Philadelphia I will have healed enough that I won't scare the clients."

"We can cancel and go to our apartment and just relax for a couple of weeks."

"No," I said. "Back in the saddle again." And then I made an effort to smile. "And when I'm a little better than that, we'll see about *really* getting back in the saddle." I tried to leer, but the result was so ludicrous that Tolliver had to choke back a laugh.

But I poked him in the ribs, and he let it out.

Back in the saddle again.